Returning to Taos

Returning to Taos

Lois Gilbert

Five Star • Waterville, Maine

First Edition, Second Printing.

Published in 2006 in conjunction with Tekno Books and Ed Gorman.

Set in 11 pt. Plantin by Christina S. Huff.

Printed in the United States on permanent paper.

Library of Congress Cataloging-in-Publication Data

Gilbert, Lois.
    Returning to Taos / by Lois Gilbert.—1st ed.
        p. cm.
    ISBN 1-59414-437-0 (hc : alk. paper)
    1. Taos (N.M.)—Fiction.   2. Sons—Death—Fiction.
3. Singers—Fiction.   4. Rich people—Fiction.   I. Title.
PS3557.I342235R48 2006
813'.6—dc22   2005028613

Acknowledgements

My thanks go to Wayne Oakes, John Thorndike, Mary Gilbert, Bob Jacobs, Claire Gilbert, Steve Gilbert, and all the members of the Speed Bump Writers Group, for their unflagging assistance, support and faith.

Chapter One

Tom steers with one hand and drapes the other over the seat, almost touching my shoulder. After a mile or two, he lifts the tangle of my hair and cups the back of my neck. His palm is warm, and the warmth makes me feel a little more real, a little less adrift. A few months ago it would have made the sparks fly between us, but now it's no more than a kindness.

Tom's eyes are as bruised as mine, and we're both pale, like ghosts. He wears his denim shirt open at the throat, and his faded khakis look old enough to be the same pair he wore when I was pregnant with Johnny. He was always a handsome man. Hair once black as a crow's wing glistens with new threads of white, and there's a more sorrowful cast to his face, a network of fine lines around his eyes and mouth. But even now, after everything that's happened, I'm still aware of his body next to mine, and those blue eyes, blue as a struck match. When I close my eyes I can smell the split-cedar scent of his skin, a smell that brings the past close.

A brown paper bag with string handles sits between us, and my heart beats faster whenever my elbow brushes against it.

What does Tom see when he looks at me, after ten years without me? A shadow? A husk? The sturdy Italian girl he fell in love with and married twenty years ago bears no resemblance to the stranger I see in the mirror every morning. Grief has sharpened every angle of my face and body, and my eyes have a stunned, shaken look. Anyone looking at me would probably think I was in the grip of a terminal illness.

The air coming through the window is still cool at six a.m., but the sun rises fast, burnishing the mesa with light. Tres Orejas Mountain lies sleek and low on the horizon, shadowed with piñon and juniper, the three ears a crisp line against the sky. The Colorado peaks hover on the far northern edge of Taos mesa, a curving blue ribbon in the distance.

Miles of sage stretch to the north, and when I sniff the rain-washed scrub, the smell is pungent as turpentine. A storm sweeps across the mesa to the west, maybe seventy-five miles away, a distant moving shadow, while the rising sun colors the sky over our heads. The landscape is stunning in its vastness, as incomprehensible as death, but it soothes me, all this dirt and sky, so far away from the concrete labyrinth of Manhattan. It makes me realize how homesick I've been for New Mexico. These are the colors I've tried to insert in every courtyard, every penthouse patio, every arboretum, park, and median I've been hired to fill: the burgundy-black of basalt, the subtle gray-green sage, the spark of orange lichen, the far-off blue of mountains. Looking at this is like seeing Tom again. This was my first love.

"Was Johnny happy here?" It's the first time all morning I've said his name out loud.

Tom keeps his gaze fixed on the road spooling out ahead of us. "I think so. He loved the business, and Jack and Maggie promoted the hell out of him. You can't turn on the radio these days without hearing his voice."

The silver knob of the radio in the dashboard gleams like a threat. It would be more than I could bear right now, to hear my son sing.

"Johnny's last CD is still flying off the shelves," Tom continues. "Half a million copies sold the first week it was out.

Plus all those copyrights—other artists are lining up for permission to use his songs. He was a star."

That's not enough, I think. Even though being a star was what he wanted, what he talked about, what he sacrificed everything to get, I can't believe it was enough. I stare out the window, reading road signs. Speed Limit, 55. Tres Piedras, 24. Tierra Amarilla, 67. I read them carefully, read every word, but the words don't cohere into meaning. Instead my thoughts fly to Johnny at fifteen, when he lived with me in Manhattan and crept out at night to sing at the Glass Onion, down in the Village. How long did it take me to figure out he was slipping down the fire escape at night? Two days? Two weeks? That was the beginning of our private war. The beginning of the end.

Tom rubs his chin and gives me a sideways glance. "I wish you'd change your mind about staying with Jack and Maggie. I have plenty of room, El."

"I'll be fine. Besides, they're expecting me. Maggie said the guesthouse is all ready."

"Think you're going to find something the police overlooked?"

"It's just a visit, Tom."

But it isn't. He knows it isn't. I'm going to Jack and Maggie's compound to live where Johnny lived, talk to the people he talked to, enter the last five years of his life and pull apart the puzzle of his death. Because there's just no reason for it, that I can see. No reason at all. And every maternal instinct I have insists on finding a reason, won't stop looking for a reason, something I can point to, something beyond my own shortcomings—and God knows there are too many of those. I need to know why it happened. I need to know who shot my son.

The road spins out like a silver ribbon ahead of us, and

after a minute or two I break the silence. My palms begin to sweat, as if I'm about to confess a crime. "Tom, do you ever feel Johnny around you?"

"His ghost, you mean? Nope. Can't say that I have." He says this lightly, as if he hopes I'm joking.

"I feel him, sometimes, late at night, or early in the morning. It's like he's standing in the corner of my bedroom, watching me. We talk, sometimes. It's nice. He's not . . ." Dead, I want to say, but I realize how it sounds. "I think he's worried about me. You don't feel that? You don't think he's worried about you too?"

A long silence ensues, while Tom keeps his eyes on the road ahead. It always grated on me, this stillness in him, this ability to detach, and it amazes me all over again how long it takes him to respond to a simple question. During the wait I count out the seconds in Italian, get as far as *venti-uno*.

Finally he takes in a deep breath and lets it out. "Do you think it might help to get some counseling, El? Just to get through the next few months? Because I don't think I could stand it if you went crazy right now."

Oh Tom, I think, and close my eyes. It only takes *venti-uno* seconds sitting next to him to bring me back to where I was ten years ago. "You know what you get from counseling, Tom? You get a kid in a suit who'll give you pills and tell you it's all right to cry. Trust me, I don't need any more of that. Besides, I like feeling Johnny near me. I like talking to him."

Tom removes his hand from my neck and puts it back on the wheel. "You just miss him, that's all. I miss him too." His voice starts to wobble, and I lean toward him and put my hand on his knee.

"What harm is there in thinking I can hear Johnny? It's not uncommon. I read somewhere that sixty percent of parents who lose a child have the experience of seeing them or talking to them after they die." I say this firmly, knowing statistics always used to impress him, although it could be forty or fifty percent, I don't really remember. "Don't you believe in an afterlife?"

"Not the kind of afterlife where we can sit down and have a chat with Johnny, no, I don't."

"So you're still an atheist?"

"Can't help it."

"And you're not having any trouble with it now?"

"It makes me face the loss. And that's been the hardest thing I've ever had to do."

"Would it change your mind if you saw him? If you heard him talk to you?"

"I don't think so."

I take my hand away from his knee, turn my face back to the window and try to smother the resentment that springs up in me. It was always easy for him to dismiss anything that smacked of spiritualism, or faith, but now his response seems so glib it borders on cruelty.

"Because my mind can manufacture just about anything out of longing," he continues, subdued now. "Right after you left Taos, I used to dream you were in bed with me. Even after I woke up, if I kept my eyes shut I could feel you lying next to me. But you weren't. It wasn't real."

Part of me vibrates like a tuning fork, hearing that. It's the first time in ten years that I've ever heard him admit that he missed me.

"I know Johnny's out there, Tom. He's not that far away."

"In heaven?" His voice aims for sarcasm, but doesn't quite make it.

"It's not like that." Even though I grew up in a big Catholic family, religion never really took root in me. All that doctrine about sin and hell seems ridiculous, especially now, when religion should be a comfort to me. What God would want to cause this much suffering? There's no lesson in this, nothing to be learned, and it hasn't made me a better person. It's just pain. Heart-ripping, absurd, pointless, impossible pain. The only gods I want now are tiny, no bigger than seeds, the kind of gods who might live in acorns or maple wings.

"Do you really think he's gone?" I ask. "I mean, completely gone? All that energy and talent and love just vanished?"

"No one's about to forget him. Look," Tom says, lifting his chin toward a dune of color against the sagebrush. As we draw closer I see a drift of roses, lilies, sunflowers, all kinds of flowers, still in their florist cellophane and green tissue paper, propped up next to candles, crosses, offerings. Ribbons are tied to the barbed wire fence, with notes attached to the bedraggled, wind-ripped satin bows.

We pull off the highway and get out to look. There are books in the ditch, photo albums, bits of clothing, handwritten letters and poems, ink bleeding across the pages, across envelopes, across hand-lettered posters declaring the love of strangers for my boy. "JW, you cracked the sky with your voice." "To the crown prince of rock!" "Johnny Waters, your songs will never die."

Every scrap is a nail in my heart, and I stagger a little, overwhelmed again by the fact of his death. There's no way I can look directly at it. It's like looking at the sun.

From the age of three he coaxed sound from the piano as if it were a living being he understood and talked to with his fingers. Nothing is more surreal than watching your five-year old son's fingers flying over a piano, pounding out a boogie-woogie beat and howling like a Mississippi bluesman, or navigating the complexity of Mozart with precision and authority. But more than anything, he loved to sing. When he was little he ran around the house singing into a hairbrush, a Popsicle, a Lincoln Log, anything that could pass for a microphone. And the voice that came out of him was as powerful as a river of clear, pure water.

"He was shot right here," Tom says, pointing to the heap of dead flowers. "The police think he was jogging to the bridge." He walks a little ways away from me, giving me room to feel this, and I watch him bend down to read a note someone's pinned to a bundle of iris.

The air in front of me takes on an electric brightness, and the sage seems more vivid, sharp-edged against the dun-colored landscape. The frayed collar on Tom's shirt appears perfectly visible from ten paces away, and when I look down, the roses on my black skirt seem to shimmer.

I know what's about to happen. I've felt it before, and I want it to happen again. Maybe Tom is right, maybe I'm crazy, but I don't care. I'm beyond shame; I'm beyond fear. I want this.

In spite of the sun my hands are freezing, and Tom's voice seems to come from the end of a long tunnel. "They say it was probably a gang initiation, some punks from who knows where, *Truchas, Espanola,* just another random shooting. They probably didn't even know who he was. The cops don't have a lead."

A sound like wind hissing through leaves fills my ears, although there are no trees, and no wind.

"Come on, Mom, cut the melodrama. I don't want you to think about how I died. I want you to remember me the way I was when I was loud and alive and you couldn't wait to get rid of me."

Tom's voice is muffled, distant. "No footprints, no clues. We had a hell of a rain that night, a real gully-washer."

"Johnny, this shouldn't have happened."

"Feeling bad about it won't change a thing. Besides, it didn't even happen here."

"You were shot somewhere else? Where?"

"What makes you think it's gonna do you any good to know where, or who, or why? None of that matters anymore—it's too late to change what happened. You know that. Look at all these flowers. Can you believe it? It blows me away. One girl left her diary. Her five-year diary, everything that happened to her since the second grade, with a note on the last page telling me she was going to marry me when she got to heaven."

"Oh. Well, that makes all the difference, doesn't it? Now you'll have something to look forward to."

A thin edge of light glows around Tom as he walks to the fence, smoothes out a long curled strip of paper tied there with a pink ribbon. He reads the contents and moves on to another note that's been blown against the barbed wire.

"Mom, I had a good life. Look at all this stuff. I made a difference to these people because I played my own music and sang my own songs. That's all I ever wanted. It was enough."

"You were only twenty-one! You never fell in love, never had kids—you didn't live long enough to know what a good life could be."

"You don't know what my life was like. There was love."

"You can't count some twelve year old who left her diary on a pile of dead flowers."

"I'm not talking about that. It was the real thing, Mom."

"Who was it?"

"I can't tell you that."

"Did your lover shoot you?"

"Leave it alone. I've told you all you need to know. There's no point in pursuing this. You'll only hurt yourself. Please, be careful."

"You never were."

"*It's not your time. Not yet. I know you told Dad you can hear me, but please don't tell anyone else. Bad things could happen.*"

"Tell me what happened," I say out loud, but the voice is gone.

Tom gives me a puzzled look. "That's all I know, Elena." He looks around at the wind-beaten tokens left by other mourners. "I wish I knew more."

Shaken, I stand and stare at the fading colors until Tom walks over and takes my hand in his. I'm frozen to the spot, unable to move.

"I don't like it here," he says, gently tugging me. "Come on. Let's go."

Back in the truck, listening to the tires spin on the pavement, I watch for the deep cut of the Rio Grande Gorge in the flat expanse of mesa ahead of us. Our first sight of it is the western edge, illuminated by the rising sun. The bridge that crosses the gorge is the third highest bridge in the United States, arching six hundred feet above the steep-walled crack of the Rio Grande Rift. The sun flashes on the steel, and my heart resists the walk we have to make across that void.

Tom parks the truck on the east side of the bridge. For a moment we sit there staring straight ahead, avoiding the inevitable, hardly daring to look at each other.

Finally I take the paper bag by its string handles and lift a weight that's hauntingly familiar, almost exactly the same as his weight at birth. I can't think about this. My body feels hollow, cold, my fingers numb as I cradle the bag in my arms and follow Tom. Together we take the long walk out to the middle of the span.

A semi shrieks past us without slowing, making the bridge vibrate. "Do you think we'll get caught?" I ask.

"Do you care?"

Tom is right. Nothing matters anymore. If I crawled over

the railing and pushed off into the abyss, I'd have no regrets at all about leaving life behind. Whatever keeps me from doing that is slender as a cobweb, too slight to be examined.

The early morning light on the gorge is almost unbearably beautiful. The rim is on fire while the lower depths wait in shadow. When I look down over the railing at the thread of the Rio Grande below us, an eerie, hollow vertigo passes through me, as if I were airborne.

When we finally reach the middle of the bridge, Tom's face turns pale as chalk, and a terrible silence fills the space between us. Don't cry, I think. I can't do this if you cry. Then, with visible effort, he straightens. My hands shake as I tear open the sturdy brown paper and sift through the ashes of my son's body. There are pebbles of charcoal, splinters of bone. I clutch a palmful of ash, hold it over the railing, then let it go. The dust of Johnny's body swirls in every direction, carried by an updraft above our heads. It blows back against us, into my face.

I never understood him. We were infinitely strange to each other. He was the loudest person I ever met, and loved every kind of noise the world could make. Where did it come from, that voice? Having Johnny was like giving birth to a different species altogether, a giraffe, or an angel, or some alien being with powers I could never hope to learn.

Tom and I scoop and let go, scoop and let go, until the bag is empty. Johnny's ashes fall and float and dance. A big wind snatches a cloud of ash and blows it up into the sky, where it sparkles in the air like a handful of glitter thrown up to the sun.

Chapter Two

On the way to police headquarters, I roll down the window to breathe in the high desert air of Taos—the perfume of sage, the rich, chlorophyll-laden scent of alfalfa, the clean fragrance of piñon—all the smells that bring back our marriage.

The first time Tom ever touched me I felt the caress in his handshake, a lingering as his palm slid away from mine and his fingertips cupped my fingertips, unwilling to let go. It was a touch that sent a sexual shiver right through me. A few hours later his mouth was pressed against the zipper of my jeans, warming the skin beneath with his breath, and the rest of the world disappeared when I felt that heat.

Back when we were dating I used to stand in front of my dorm in all weather, waiting for Tom's car to appear, a 1983 Camaro with wide seats. We'd go park somewhere and he'd let me out by the dorm hours later, my skirt on backward, lipstick kissed off, hair a mess. Johnny came out of one of those passionate nights, and it still makes me smile to remember how scared and secretly thrilled Tom and I were to have an excuse to get married right away. There was no white satin wedding for us, no ribboned-off pews or ushers in tuxedos. We went to a JP in Brooklyn, in a hurry to make it legal and move out west with Maggie and Jack, who were already looking for places to rent in Taos.

The year Johnny was born, Tom wrote a funny, breezy take on fatherhood called *So It Begins*, a hundred and fifty

17

pages that he tossed off as easily as a letter to a friend. Most of the chapter titles were taken from the old Ray Charles hit, *Makin' Whoopee*: "The Groom Is Nervous," "Picture A Little Love Nest," "He's Washin' Dishes, And Baby Clothes," and "The Boy's So Willin'." Three different publishers entered a small bidding war for the rights, and it sold for the astounding sum of ninety thousand dollars. We spent the whole advance on an ancient adobe house in a rural neighborhood bordering the Rio Pueblo, a mile west of downtown Taos. Eventually *So It Begins* sold a few hundred thousand copies, and the royalties trickled in steadily enough to support us as Tom tried to start over with another book. But the specter of his first success cast a long shadow between Tom and everything he tried to write after that, and over the next five or six years the royalties dwindled to nothing, while the cost of raising Johnny steadily increased.

We were happy, though. We owned our own home and we didn't need much cash to entertain ourselves. When Johnny was a toddler I used to let him run around naked in the back yard while I spaded in plants, pruned trees, and pulled weeds. Being outside meant he could roar at the top of his lungs and zoom off in all directions without driving us crazy, and we spent a lot of time out there. He was an astonishingly loud person for his size. Sometimes I had to wear earplugs when he and Tom started one of their long, shrieking romps indoors, games that shook the lampshades and toppled chairs and broke a light bulb at least once or twice a week.

Johnny was always a gorgeous kid, from babyhood to his teen years, hair lightened to platinum by the sun, his body lithe and quick, always in motion. There are no still shots in my memories—when I think of him, he's a blur. In stores I'd hustle down the aisles, slip around corners fast, and he'd zip right along behind me, making a game of it. Every time I caught a glimpse of his face disappearing around a bend, it squeezed my heart. Without question, he was the center of my life, and I loved him with a devotion greater than any I'd ever known.

And as he grew and moved along from one grade to the next, every one of his teachers announced to us in hushed tones that Johnny was gifted, *really* gifted, as if we might not have noticed. Right from the start, Johnny's passion for music was intense. Even when he was tiny, he'd listen to Bach or Thelonius Monk or Eddie Vedder for hours with his eyes closed, not stirring, absorbed, rapt with a kind of attention that sent a chill through me.

When he was six years old he used to sit under the piano and listen to me play. One day he was under there while I struggled through a technically complex piece from Boccherini that I'd been working on for weeks, and my fingering went slightly awry. Johnny crawled out from under the piano, reached for the keys and played the passage correctly. I stared at him, astonished. I'd always expected him to surpass me—I just didn't think it would happen when he was six.

Tom didn't really know how good Johnny was, and I couldn't make him understand. He thought we were both terrific musicians, and said so frequently, but he didn't realize there was a growing abyss between what I could do and what Johnny was capable of becoming. I was good enough to play in a lounge, or teach, but not nearly skilled enough to tour with an orchestra. The piano was a comfort to me, a meditation, a private activity, like yoga, or prayer. It was different for Johnny, and what he needed to learn was beyond me.

What Johnny's extraordinary ability meant to Tom was that Johnny was a lucky boy who would thrive anywhere. In our marriage Tom cultivated the belief that everything would turn out all right, no matter how much evidence there was to the contrary. When it came to the fact that Johnny was a prodigy, Tom was patient and serene and inclined to trust a method of child rearing that looked like neglect to me. I always buzzed around his complacency like a bee, ready to sting him into action, while he lectured me about being too impulsive, too hot-tempered, too greedy for things that cost too much.

But I knew Johnny needed the kind of teacher we'd never find in Taos, and I wanted him to grow up in a real city, a place large enough to give him the training he so clearly deserved. Desperate to leave, I nagged Tom to let us move back to New York so we could give Johnny the kind of upbringing I'd had, in a city big enough to nurture our boy's promise. But Tom refused to budge. The landscape, the air, the community of writers he found in Taos—that was enough for him. He didn't want to move. He liked walking into the Taos Community Auditorium for a play and knowing almost everybody onstage and in the audience. He liked the slow pace, the dusty roads, the stillness. He wanted to write, and this was the place where he was determined to do it.

The last time the three of us went east for Christmas, my father asked Johnny to play something on their upright grand. In his youth my father had been one of the best jazz trombonists of his day, accomplished, distinctive, creative, a musician's musician. He'd spent several years as a soloist with the Duke Ellington orchestra.

Johnny had been teaching himself Debussy's *Prelude à l'apres-midi d'un faune,* a complicated piece with lots of fast, fancy fingering, and I expected him to play that for my father, but instead he played a lovely, slow, classical piece that I couldn't identify.

While he caressed the keys my father's face remained fo-

cused, intent, alert in a way he'd never looked when he used
to listen to me.

When Johnny finished he said, "Did you write that, son?"
Johnny nodded, his ears pink. "I write lots of songs."

My father looked up at me and held my eyes for a long moment, then said *"Ha un talento."*

The pang I felt was so deep it seemed to have been put
there by nature, a mix of pride and envy and a slight undercurrent of fear, ominous as the sound of thunder on a bright
summer day.

"Would you like to stay here in New York and study
music, Johnny?" he asked.

Tom rose from his chair in the corner, dismay frozen on
his face. Johnny gave him a nervous glance, then turned back
to his grandfather. "Yes," he said.

After Johnny and I moved back to New York, Tom visited
us, but it was obvious he hated it. He was in a sour mood from
the moment the plane touched down to the moment we
kissed him goodbye. We went back to Taos to visit him, but
his writing wasn't going well and by then Tom and I had lost
the knack of fitting our lives together. Whenever Johnny practiced—and he wanted to practice, incessantly—Tom's face
tightened, as if it were no more than an interruption. We
fought about money, about where we should live, about the
future of our marriage. Ultimatums flew back and forth, until
finally the effort of pretending we weren't miserable overwhelmed us. A year after Johnny and I moved back to New
York, Tom sent me divorce papers, and I signed them.

Detective Gallegos works in an old municipal building
with the dimensions of a fortress, protected by thick adobe
walls, its high ceilings supported by vigas the size of stout tree

trunks. The building was probably a WPA project, constructed during the Depression years to create jobs for the locals, a monument to another era.

This will be my first meeting with Gallegos in person, and my stomach tightens with a mix of anticipation and dread as I walk up to the heavy wooden door, pull it open, and step into a large outer office. A receptionist looks up inquiringly, and I step up to her desk. She wears a crown of high hair, a fringe of bangs that rises three or four inches straight up above her forehead to create a stiffly lacquered, free-standing fence. Only the bangs stand up—the rest of her hair lies sleek against her scalp, brushed into a tight ponytail.

"Is Detective Gallegos in?"

"What's your name?" she asks, chewing her gum with caffeinated energy.

"Elena Waters."

She stops chewing momentarily. "Johnny's—?"

"Mother." I give her my most disarming smile, determined to make a good impression. Things will be different now that I'm here in person, because there's really no substitute for talking face to face. This time Detective Gallegos and I will connect.

The secretary leans over to press a button on the phone, then picks up the receiver. "*Está aquí la señora Waters. Sí, la madre de Johnny. Sí, ahora. Quisiera verle. No sé que quiere.* Okay."

She hangs up and speaks without looking at me. "Manny says you'll have to wait. It might be a while."

"Are you Consuelo?" I ask, radiating warmth and a willingness to communicate. "I think we've talked on the phone a few times."

"Mm," she says, eyes darting to her computer screen. "More than a few."

"If it's not too much trouble, would you mind giving me a copy of the autopsy report on my son? Detective Gallegos said he'd send it to me a couple of months ago, but I never received it."

"I don't know nothing about that," Consuelo says.

The smile remains fixed on my face, stiff as a coat of paint. "I guess I'll wait for Detective Gallegos, then."

"It might be a long time," she warns me. "He's really busy today."

I look around the empty office. No phones are ringing. No faxes coming in. No sound issues from the hallway, or the offices beyond. "I'll wait."

Deliberately I take the wooden chair against the wall that faces her desk, fold my hands in my lap and stare at the crest of her bangs as she picks up the phone and begins a long conversation in Spanish with a girl friend. Minutes tick by as I peruse the *latillas* in the ceiling and the heavy carved lintel above the door, half-listening as Consuelo giggles into the phone, telling her friend about the tamales she made over the weekend. After she finishes a lengthy discussion of recipe and technique, she hangs up, writes a notation on a Post-It and tacks it to the top of her computer. She opens a drawer, searches for a file and pulls it out. I watch her re-shuffle her papers, re-file her folders, close her drawers, and make another phone call. Whenever her eyes meet mine she stifles a sigh.

An hour crawls by like this, and my backside falls asleep on the hard wooden chair. Finally I get up and pace the office, massaging my tailbone back to prickling life while Consuelo watches me warily from her desk.

An old man in a cowboy hat walks in and pauses by Consuelo's desk. *"Quien es la gringa?"* he says, tilting his head toward me.

"La madre de Johnny Waters."

"Ah." He turns to look me over, then looks back at Consuelo. *"Manny aqui?"*

"Si."

He walks down the hall, opens a door, and I can hear Detective Gallegos greet him in Spanish. There's a burst of laughter, then the door closes.

I sit. I wait.

Thirty minutes later the old man walks out, giving me a friendly wave as he passes my chair.

The phone on Consuelo's desk buzzes, and she picks up the receiver, murmurs into it, then glances at me. "You can go in now."

Detective Gallegos stands in the doorway of his office, dressed in a turquoise chamois shirt tucked into Levis and scuffed cowboy boots that look like they've seen a lifetime of hard work on a ranch. He's older than I pictured him from his voice on the phone, with sad, tired eyes pouched in wrinkles, and hair that's mostly gray.

His eyes are shrewd, though, dark and bright as ice as he takes my hand between both his palms. "Ms. Waters, I'm sorry to have kept you waiting. Come in and have a seat." He walks back behind his desk, lowers himself into his large leather chair, and nods to the wooden chair opposite.

Books line the wall behind him, heavy, leather-bound volumes that look as old as the building. Two broad windows let in the morning light, but the three-foot windowsills and dark furniture swallow it up before it can illuminate much of the room. His desk is massive, made of dark cherry, scarred with use and layered with paperwork stacked neatly in piles.

I sit down obediently and fold my hands over my purse, determined to be polite and reasonable, so absolutely polite and reasonable that he'll have to listen to me. For the past two hours I've been telling myself I have a right to be here, but there are butterflies in my chest, and I have to remind my-self to take a deep breath before I begin.

"Thank you for seeing me without an appointment."

Detective Gallegos rests his eyes on me as he leans back in his chair and touches the index fingers of both hands lightly together. His fingertips tap against each other slowly, once, twice, clearly waiting for me to initiate the conversation.

I attempt a smile and blurt out the worst of all possible openers. "Have there been any developments on the case since we last spoke?"

The silence between us feels endless, an abyss that empha-sizes the separation of cultures, sexes, generations, a silence deep enough to make me aware of the earth turning on its axis while he makes me wait.

"Ms. Waters, you've called this department almost every day for the past three months, asking us for information about this investigation."

"Yes," I say, forcing myself to meet his gaze. "I know."

"Each time you called you got the same message from us: when we have something we can share with you, we'll call you. If that's all you came here to ask me, I'm afraid this visit of yours has been a waste of time."

His hostility flows through my body like electricity, and I stretch my cheeks in what I hope is a smile. "You're right, of course, and I apologize. The last thing I want to do is inter-fere."

"Then if there's nothing else . . . ?" He checks his watch, looks pointedly at the door.

"Well, there is something else, as a matter of fact. Johnny's father just took me out Route 64 this morning, to the place where you think our son was shot. And I know you'll think this sounds strange, but I'm certain he wasn't killed there."

"Why?"

I can't tell him the truth—*my dead son told me he wasn't killed there, officer.* No, the truth would ruin everything. Nervously I smooth the wrinkles in my skirt, then clutch the hard wooden arms of the chair. "I just have this feeling."

"You have this feeling." His eyebrows rise politely.

"Call it a hunch, or mother's intuition, or whatever you want, but I don't believe my son was killed by the highway. I think he was killed somewhere else."

He picks up a pencil and holds it delicately between his fingers while his mouth purses in a frown. "If Johnny were killed somewhere else, the forensics lab would have picked up evidence of that location on his clothing, or in the tracks surrounding his body. There was no evidence of anything like that, Ms. Waters."

"But it rained that night, didn't it? Maybe the evidence was destroyed by the rain. Isn't that possible?"

My words ricochet off him like a hand full of marbles flung at a wall. "Ma'am, I'm sorry for your loss, but you have to remember we know what we're doing. Believe me, progress is being made."

Before I can stop myself I laugh out loud. "What progress? As far as I can tell you're no closer to solving this than you were three months ago. You haven't made any arrests, have you? You don't even have any suspects, as far as I can tell."

He sets the pencil down on his desk, then realigns an already perfect edge of a stack of papers in front of him, with the slow deliberation of someone who wants you to know he's trying to be patient. "I'm sure you realize your son had several—how can I put this?—eccentric friends. It's taken longer than we expected to track these people down."

My grip tightens on the arms of the chair. Finally, I think. Now we're getting somewhere. Johnny was always drawn to outcasts, vagrants, homeless people, any self-exiled martyr.

When he was five he brought home a pregnant teenaged runaway who was hiding in a culvert at his school, and I found them at our kitchen table, scooping peanut butter out of the jar with their fingers.

"Can you give me a few names?" I ask. "Maybe I could help you track them down."

The detective leans back and smiles. "I'm sorry, ma'am, but I can't do that."

I stare out the window. A robin lands in the barberry bush outside, opens its beak and lets out a long, plaintive trill. Gallegos is obviously waiting for me to go, yet I linger, absurdly, desperate to salvage something from this meeting.

"I never received the copy of the autopsy you promised me," I say. "Could I have it now, please?"

A pained expression crosses his face. "Ms. Waters, you don't want to see it. You should let your husband handle this."

"We're divorced," I say.

Reluctantly he takes a manila folder from one of the piles on his desk and taps it with his fingers. "The autopsy's in here, along with our report and pictures of the crime scene."

I hold out my hand for the folder, and he slides it across the scarred surface of the desk. My pulse quickens when I open the cover, but all I see is an 8"x10" black and white photo of the highway and a gray drift of litter by the side of the road.

"What am I looking at here?" I ask.

"Your son," he says quietly. "He was lying there like that when we found him."

A small, dark lump in the photograph resolves itself into a sneaker sticking up from a sprawl of gray clothes. I move this photograph aside and look at the next picture. It's a close-up of Johnny's face and torso, seen from above. Lying on the gravel shoulder of the road, he's dressed in gray sweatpants and an unzipped, hooded sweatshirt that's flung open, revealing the spokes of his ribs under his bare skin. Eyes open, arms stretched wide, there's a sad, lost smile on his face, a smile that presses against my heart with a crushing weight. Hair matted, body spattered with mud. A dark flower of dried blood around the hole in the center of his chest.

The room begins to throb and I sag in the chair, suddenly close to passing out. "Thank you," I say, closing the folder. "I appreciate this."

Detective Gallegos nods. "Ms. Waters? Have you thought about seeing a counselor while you're visiting here? If you're interested in talking to someone, my secretary could give you some references."

Heat rises in my face, making my ears burn, and I straighten in my seat. "No, thank you."

He leans forward, consults a slip of paper lying on top of the pile on his desk. "I understand you were released from St. Andrews Hospital in late April."

Alarms go off inside me. Someone must have told him, someone I know. Tom? I can't believe Tom would have told the police.

He puts on a pair of bifocals and peers down at the paper, then back up at me. "It says here you were treated for an overdose shortly after you were notified of your son's murder."

"It was Tylenol," I say, and immediately regret it. Why am I defending myself? It's none of his business. "I took a little too much Tylenol, that's all. It was an accident."

He leans back in his chair, removes his glasses, breathes on the lenses and rubs them on his shirt, letting the silence develop like an accusation. "I'm not here to pass judgment. All I'm saying is maybe you'd be better off in Manhattan, close to your doctor, your friends, your family. Coming out here and stirring up speculation about your son's death—it's not helpful, Ms. Waters."

I smile, but it feels like an effort. "Are you telling me to get out of town?"

"Not at all. You do what you want." Underneath the casual tone, his preference is unmistakable. "All I'm trying to tell you is these hunches about your son's murder—well, it might be better if you let us do our job, that's all I'm saying. We both want the same thing."

I stare at him, unmoved. Clearly he thinks I should be on my knees in a church somewhere, weeping. Not here, infesting his territory, acting like a pushy *gringa* from New York with her own crazy ax to grind.

After a conspicuous pause, he stands behind the barricade of his desk. "Now, if that's all . . . ?"

I rise to my feet and clutch the folder to my chest. *Not on your life,* I think, and walk out the door.

Chapter Three

As I drive up to Jack and Maggie's gate, the barbered symmetry of the grounds announces the fact that nature is tamed here; the trees and shrubs elegantly, meticulously maintained, presumably by an army of gardeners who patrol the grounds with tweezers. The house itself is huge, a dazzling expanse of whitewashed walls, more square footage than I've ever seen contained in a single residence in New Mexico. Set against the green pines and granite cliffs of El Salto Mountain, it almost looks like a mirage. A security guard at the gate takes my name, and the tall wrought iron gates roll back silently to admit my rental car to the drive that winds through a grove of cypress.

After I park the car I look down and notice how wrinkled my skirt is, then wonder if I should put on lipstick. When I turn the rearview mirror up I take one look at my face in the unforgiving Taos light and freeze.

I look awful, I think.

My auburn hair is flat and dull and my cheekbones stick out like elbows. How could my skin look so old, so pale? Now I understand why Tom seemed so stricken when he first saw me step out of the car, why he was so sad and careful when he hugged me goodbye. I never thought I'd say it, but I'm too thin. Painfully thin. The extra fifteen pounds that have clung to me since I had Johnny have vanished, and I've lost another five or ten since then. How long has it been since I've eaten?

Yesterday. Peanuts on the plane, with apple juice. Before that, I can't remember.

Leaning back in the car seat, I close my eyes, knowing lipstick won't begin to disguise the damage. I don't even care—and Maggie certainly won't. More than anyone else, she'll understand what I'm going through, and I know she'll give me all the time I need to recover in my own way, in my own time. Even when we haven't seen each other in years, we always fall into an intimacy that goes beyond words. Our friendship has dwindled in the past five years to postcards and the occasional phone call, but Maggie was always the sister I never had.

Back in the old days, before marriage and motherhood, we were wild. My parents used to roll their eyes and shake their heads whenever Maggie showed up on the doorstep wearing her micro-miniskirts and safety-pin earrings. Even though I'd known her since kindergarten, our friendship took on momentum in high school, when the sound of Maggie's voice used to enter me like a shot of tequila, a promise of fun, a warm, glowing connection to an edgier, less boring version of myself. When I was with Maggie I lost the good-girl inhibitions of Catholic school, the crippling shyness and self-censorship that left me tongue-tied in most social situations, and I'd blurt out things that would send us both into explosions of laughter.

But we did a lot more than talk—we courted danger in ways that seem insane now, in the cold light of adulthood. Being with Maggie back then held the promise of illicit, forbidden activity, and after growing up in a family that said the rosary together every Friday night, I was ripe for corruption.

At sixteen Maggie was tall and bony and elegant, with masses of springy blonde curls that fell down her back, and she had a flair for wearing thrift store costumes in odd, striking combinations—cowboy boots with antique cocktail dresses, a man's tailored shirt and tie over a miniskirt, or overalls and ballet slippers. On Saturday nights Maggie used to twist my hair into a complicated chignon, paint my face and dress me up to look at least five years older, and we'd sneak out of her mother's apartment and head downtown. Any bar in the city would take our order for a glass of wine without carding us, and then Maggie would light a cigarette and exhale with a practiced air of cool detachment and sophistication I could only envy.

Maggie was always the bold one, the one with imagination and the daring to put it to use. She might walk up to a stranger on a subway platform—usually a good looking college kid, or a young man without a wedding ring—and offer to tell his fortune for a dollar. She'd close her eyes and hold his open palm in her hands, and her face would take on a blank, dreamy look as she murmured something too low for me to hear. Usually the man would laugh, but there was one who gave her a look of such hatred that it made the hair on the back of my neck stand on end.

In our junior year of high school Maggie taught me how to kiss by making me practice on a peach. Mouth slightly open, I would touch the tip of my tongue to the lightly furred skin, and then I'd close my lips, letting them press and linger. I still remember those drowsy summer afternoons I spent kissing a peach while Maggie watched. We were like two halves of one person, dark and light, yin and yang, melded together by years of small sins, petty crimes, and a lifetime of knowing each other.

I take a deep breath, get out of the car, walk up to the door and ring the bell.

The door swings open, revealing a young woman dressed in a black tank top and leather skirt, and it takes me a moment to realize it's Alison; it has to be, though it's hard to believe this is the same scabby-kneed child I held on my lap ten years ago. Alison must be twenty now, I think. And what a dark beauty, with Maggie's pointed chin and heart-shaped face, and Jack's thick chestnut hair. My eyes take in Alison's new figure, the high breasts and coltishly long legs. Johnny must have noticed those legs, I think. When my gaze moves back to Alison's face I can see her eyes look puffy, as if she's been crying. All this runs through my head in the time it takes to smile.

"Alison, it's been too long." I drop my suitcase to hug her.

"Elena." The young woman gives me a timid smile and a quick, soft embrace, then steps back. "Come on in."

Inside the house, water splashes over granite boulders into a lagoon filled with floating lilies, and a stained-glass skylight allows light to filter down through successive layers of palms, vines, and ferns. A curving staircase to the left of the waterfall leads my eye upward, toward the vast, cathedral ceiling and balconies of the second and third stories. The humidity feels wonderful, after the dusty heat outside.

I turn back to the young woman and feel an unexpected surge of affection at the sight of her grown-up face. "You look great, Allie. Or do they call you that anymore?"

She grins at me. "You can call me anything you want, but it's Alison in front of Mom and Dad. It took me five years to train them to make the switch."

She's still so young, I think, marveling at the way she moved, her limbs supple, her hair glossy as a puppy's. It's hard to believe Maggie and I were already married at her age. "Did you come home from Stanford for the summer?"

"No, I'm home for good—I dropped out a couple of months ago. I work for my dad now, as a production assistant."

"Why?" I ask, surprised. Alison was always a great student, bright, hardworking, at the top of her class. "Weren't you about to graduate?"

She lifts one perfectly tanned shoulder, lets it fall. "Things change."

"I see." A needle of worry pricks me as I register the shadows under her eyes, the tension in her shoulders. Something about the set of her face reminds me of my own, a mask of effort over pain.

We stand there smiling at each other like strangers, caught in the silence of good intentions and fear of saying the wrong thing, until Alison turns to the intercom by the door, presses a button and murmurs into it. And then back to me with the same sweet, restrained smile, a token to get us through the rest of this conversation.

"Mom said you're hiking up Santa Barbara Canyon next week?" she asks.

"I wouldn't miss it." Twenty years ago the Santa Barbara was our first jaunt into the wilderness, back in the days when Maggie and Jack and Tom and I did everything together. In the past few years it's been Jack's birthday ritual to make the trek up there with a few chosen friends and family members. According to Maggie, Johnny went up there with them last year, and he'd been planning to go this year, so I'm determined to make the trip. I know there's no logic to this decision. In my mind it's a way of touching him, a way of holding onto who he was by walking in his footsteps, and maybe they'll lead me to a place I can't get to any other way.

"What's the forecast?" I ask.

"Clear. It shouldn't be anything like the storm we went through last time."

"I brought my rain gear, just in case. Are you coming with us?"

"That's what they tell me."

A door clicks shut and I turn to see Maggie striding across the floor, wearing red silk pajamas and a kimono that flares out behind her. She's a little heavier than the last time I saw her, a big-shouldered, handsome woman, with the same unruly halo of blonde curls.

"Elena!" she says, and gives me a tight warm hug. "I'm so glad you're here. How was the trip?"

"Maggie, you look terrific." We hold each other silently for a moment, rocking, and her warm, substantial body feels so good next to mine it's hard to let go.

Finally Maggie holds me at arm's length, cocks her head and gives me the same searching, interrogative smile I received from most of my friends these days, her eyes traveling slowly over my thin face, tangled hair, unvarnished nails and lack of makeup. Next to Maggie, I feel like a refugee.

"When did you get into town?" Her voice is tender.

"Yesterday. I spent the night at the Kachina Lodge."

"You could have come here, honey."

"It was late."

"We never get to bed before three. Can you tell? Here I am, still in my bathrobe at one in the afternoon." Her face becomes solemn as she takes both my hands in hers. "I've been thinking about you every minute since it happened. Johnny was a great kid, honey. I was crazy about him. We all were." Her eyes become glassy with tears, and my throat closes as I teeter on the brink of an abyss I can't afford to feel. Not now, I think. Not yet.

Maggie's face changes as she realizes this, and she gives me an apologetic smile and tugs my arm. "Come on, let me show you the guest cottage. We need to get you settled."

We walk outside toward a large pool that occupies the center of a courtyard, with an emerald lawn beyond that's scattered with clumps of aspen and several smaller buildings. The courtyard is utterly still, filled with the kind of silence money can buy. A trim white adobe guesthouse sits on the far side of the lawn, tucked behind a bank of wisteria in full bloom. Maggie sets a brisk pace as we walk toward it, then slows as we approach the door.

"Johnny lived here." She gives me an anxious look. "His things are all still inside—the police were great about getting in and out of here without disrupting us too much, and we haven't touched anything. But if you feel uncomfortable staying here, just say so. There's plenty of room at the main house—we wouldn't even know you were around."

"Thanks, Maggie. This is where I want to be."

When she opens the door, I catch the faint scent of Johnny, the light, unmistakable odor of his clothes, and tears spring to my eyes before I can fight them back. I blink hard as I look around.

It's a sunny, pleasant room, without any of the familiar rubble of Johnny's childhood—no brightly colored sports equipment, no video games, no Mac computer. A grand piano takes up most of the room, facing a picture window that frames Taos Mountain and the broad sweep of mesa to the west. Tall bookshelves line the walls, containing hundreds of books and thousands of CDs. Three enlarged, framed reproductions of his CD covers line the wall leading to the kitchen.

"This is beautiful," I say, swallowing the lump in my throat, looking out at the silhouette of the mountain.

"Thanks." Maggie smiles at me, and I smile back at this very blonde, sunny, made-up woman, with the same caliber of energy and charm I remember from kindergarten.

"It feels like old times," Maggie says shyly. "Seeing you here. I've missed you."

It's true. In spite of the plush surroundings, it does feel

like old times, and I've missed her too. "I knew you and Jack were doing well," I say, looking out at the big house across the lawn. "But this place is incredible."

An embarrassed look flickers across Maggie's face as she laughs. "I guess it's strange seeing it all at once, but it seems like it took forever for us to finish it. After we left Destiny, we figured we could afford to build the house we always wanted. It's ridiculous, I know, and you wouldn't believe our utility bills. But we like it."

Before Tom and I split up, Jack and Maggie had been working in A&D for Destiny Records, cruising every small club in the west for breakout talent. They used to drag us out to bars in Red River, Espanola, Raton; dirty, dark places that smelled like stale beer and urine, and we'd sit through every set until the lights came up at one or two in the morning. Then they'd go to work. It was illuminating to see how the two of them would approach the band—Maggie fawning and gushing, telling them how great they were, while Jack held himself slightly apart, as though he was more impressed by their potential than their skill. Within minutes Maggie had them in the palm of her hand, drunk on her flattery and optimism, and the kids were willing to do whatever it took to get Jack's approval. Musicians trusted them. Even back then, Jack and Maggie emanated power like heat.

Within five years, they had the rights to some second-level Albuquerque bands who scored a few hits, then worked their way up the ladder at Destiny and produced a dozen Top Ten pop CDs and twenty R&B hits. They walked away from Destiny to start an independent production company of their own, and apparently the money has been pouring in ever since.

"I've already planned a getaway for the two of us," Maggie says, smiling. "Tomorrow morning we'll go down to Ten

Thousand Waves in Santa Fe. Private hot tub, sauna, steam, and a ninety-minute Master's Massage. Then we'll go out on the town and have some champagne and a big meal. Pour ourselves into the limo and snooze all the way back. Doesn't that sound good? Come on, you'll love it. You look like you could use some pampering."

God preserve me from those who love me, I think, tracing the contour of a large piece of carved jade on a pedestal by the door. Now that I'm finally here, I have no intention of letting Maggie drag me ninety miles away, but I can't say that. The last thing I want to do is hurt her feelings.

"Alison looks so different." I search her face. "I can't believe she's the same girl. Why did she drop out of Stanford? She only had one semester left, didn't she?"

Maggie leans against the wall and twists a curl around her finger, a gesture she used whenever she was nervous. "Alison was unhappy there." She lifts her shoulder in an unconscious echo of her daughter's response to the same question. "She wanted to come home."

"Didn't you try to talk her into going back?"

Maggie bites her lip, and when she speaks her voice is so low I can barely hear her. "I guess I missed her too."

I know it's crazy, to feel this blood-racing frenzy of—what, exactly? Resentment? Crazy or not, I felt it. There's a small pain at my throat, like the pressure of a knife-point, and a rush of jealousy fills my veins. All this wealth, these things, the garden, the house—it means nothing to me. But the fact that Maggie still has Alison, has her living close, and can see her whenever she wants—it fills me with a bitterness that shocks me.

Maggie gives me a worried look. "Are you okay, honey? I mean, I know you can't be, not really—I don't know what I'd do if I lost Alison. And then when you had to go to the hospital, we were all terrified of losing you too. But—how are you doing?"

I hold out my hand at waist level, tip it this way and that. "Still rocky."

"You poor baby. You never deserved any of this."

"How's Jack?" I ask.

There's a long pause, and Maggie averts her eyes. "I'm not really sure."

"Don't you two talk?"

"Almost never," she says, and lets out a strained laugh. Every muscle in her face seems to sag, the incipient lines to deepen. Her voice isn't much more than a whisper, and the pain in her face squeezes my heart with a quick shot of guilt. *This is what you wanted, isn't it? Now you're not the only one who's suffering.*

I walk over to her and put my hand on her back. "I'm so sorry. I had no idea you two were in trouble. How bad is it?"

She's quiet for a moment. "It's bad, but there won't be a divorce. I'm not letting him off that easy."

"Is he having an affair?"

"No. Not now, anyway."

The meaning of those last three words sifts into me, but one look at her face tells me this isn't the time to ask for details. We give each other a look, acknowledging mutual heartache. She's so warm, so familiar. I've loved this woman for almost forty years, and no one knows me as well as Maggie does. Being with her makes me feel anchored, grounding me to the past we share.

Maggie walks across the room and opens the refrigerator, revealing fully stocked shelves of fruit, cheese, bread, paté, cold meats, and deli salads. "Looks like you have the basics, at least. Anything else you think you might want? Beer? Wine? Scotch?"

I shake my head. "This is a lot more than I was expecting."

Maggie crosses the room and gives me a brisk pat on the shoulder. "If you need anything else, there's an intercom by the door. And before I forget, we're having a party tonight for the governor. Around eight, out by the pool, very casual. You should probably get some rest."

"Come on," I say, and take her hand. "Sit with me."

We walk over to a loveseat by the window, sink into the cushions and look out at the mountain. Maggie gives me a sideways glance, then squeezes my hand. "I meant what I said, honey. It's really good to see you again."

I take a deep breath and let it go. It feels good to me too, to sit in a sunny living room with her warm, plump hand over mine, an oasis of calm in the middle of a rough day. "Tom and I spread Johnny's ashes this morning," I say quietly.

Leaning back, I let my head fall against the couch as my body relaxes into the cushions. After a few seconds of silence I come to a decision, although my heart skips like a stone on water when I open my mouth. "Can I tell you a secret?"

Maggie's gaze settles on me. "You have my full attention."

"I talk to Johnny," I say, as lightly as I can. "And he talks to me."

She examines me for a long moment. "You're serious."

"He comes to me, and I hear him." I smile helplessly. "I know it sounds crazy, but we talk. There's no other word for it."

Maggie's eyes widen. "What does he say?"

"When Tom and I stopped at the shrine by the bridge, he told me he wasn't shot out there. He said it happened somewhere else." Abruptly I stop speaking, aware of the deepening frown on Maggie's face.

"You're scaring me, Elena."

40

"Why should it scare you?" I try to laugh. "I read some-where that fifty or sixty percent of bereaved parents talk to their dead children. Think of it as a coping strategy. I've become an expert on coping strategies in the last few weeks."

"But we know he was shot out by the bridge. I'm sorry, but this can't be healthy if he's telling you things that aren't true. Have you told anyone else about this?"

"Tom. He wasn't too happy about it either. Then I went down to the station and talked to Detective Gallegos." I don't mention the fact that Gallegos made me wait for two hours before he let me into his office, and checked his watch rather pointedly the whole time I was there. "I thought it might give them a lead, a clue, something."

Maggie stares at me, opens her mouth as if she's about to say something, then closes it.

"What?"

"Why don't you let the police handle it, Elena? The case is still open."

"But not active."

"Give them a chance. Something will come up."

A few seconds ticked past as I sat there, flooded with bone-crushing disappointment, suddenly conscious that I lived in a world that was foreign to Maggie, a world of con-stant, bitter awareness of what I'd lost. "You know what hap-pens when you lose a child, Maggie? You both die. Nothing's the same after that. You ask yourself over and over, why did it happen? Why couldn't I have saved him?"

"The police will take care of it," she said gently. "You have to be patient."

"The police keep telling me it was a random shooting, a freak killing—as if he were hit by lightning, or crushed in an earthquake. That's not good enough. I want to know why he was shot. I want to know who killed him."

Abruptly Maggie removed her hand from mine, stood and moved over to the window. "Why doesn't Johnny tell you?"

"I don't know. Maybe he will, eventually. Right now I think he's trying to protect me."

"Elena, this sounds so morbid. Don't you see that? You can't let yourself fall into this new-age mystic crap so you can hang onto some part of him. You have to let go."

My face trembles, as if I've been stung, and I fold my arms tightly across my chest. "Easy for you to say."

"Honey, if you need help, I know a doctor. In fact he could probably see you today, if you want—all I have to do is make a phone call."

"I don't want a shrink, Maggie! I want to find out who killed my son. Why is that such a terrible thing?"

Maggie's voice is suddenly angry. "Did it ever occur to you that finding Johnny's killer won't change a thing? Johnny's dead, Elena. He's gone. You might dig up all kinds of shit about his life, but he's *dead*."

I look away. "I know that."

"Then why are you trying to punish yourself?"

I flinch. This is too close to the truth. I get up, walk to the window and lean against it, my forehead touching the glass.

"When was the last time you talked to Johnny? I mean, really talked, before he died?" Maggie asks. "When was the last time you called him?"

"Thanksgiving," I whisper.

"Thanksgiving. And he was killed close to the end of March. Five months is a long time to go without talking to your son, isn't it? And how long has it been since you actually saw him? Three years? Four?"

Her words flick against me like a whip. It isn't my fault, I want to say. But it is. Five years, I think. How could I have let my anger keep us apart for five years? What a waste! Why did

I think the force of my fury would finally convince him to come home and go back to school, to become the child he never was, the child I wanted him to be? By the time that hope faded, he'd already withdrawn behind the armor of his fame. After his first CD was released, the critics began to label him "the next big thing," and an army of publicists, assistants, consultants, trainers, and a hectic schedule formed a barricade between us. Whatever clout I had as his mother wasn't enough to penetrate that wall, not when he didn't want to see me. And yes, damn it, it made me mad. It made me stop trying.

I laugh softly, but there's no humor in it. "Don't you think you might have had something to do with that, Maggie? You took him in and he didn't need me anymore. You made sure of that."

Maggie's face goes white. "We did you a favor, Elena. Or did you want him to hitch all the way out to L.A. and try his luck with the sharks out there? Maybe you wanted him to sleep under a freeway while he waited for his big break."

"Maybe he would have come back to me. Maybe he'd still be alive."

"And maybe he would have died a lot sooner! We helped him become a success, to do the work he loved. Doesn't that count for something? We didn't do it to shut you out. I begged him to call you. I begged him to write you, to let you know what he was doing." Her big eyes swim at me, yearning for pity. "I did my best, Elena."

All the air goes out of me, and exhaustion seeps in. "I know. I'm jealous, that's all. You had the last five years with him, and I didn't."

Maggie takes me by the shoulders and gives me a shake. "Come on, honey. You know he loved you."

"That's what he tells me."

Her eyes remain fixed on my face. "You barely spoke to him after he moved back here, and now that he's dead you really believe you can talk to him?"

"I know how it sounds, but he's still with me."

"Elena, please, having long fantasy conversations with your dead son . . . it's just not right. Don't you see how dangerous this could be? There are asylums filled with people who hear voices other people can't hear. I don't want you to get caught in that place where you hear Johnny and none of us can." Her voice begins to wobble. "I don't want to lose you, too."

The tremor in her voice makes me see the depth of what she's lost, and I soften, finally, and fold her into my arms. She was Johnny's godmother, after all, and he spent the last five years of his life living here, with her. If anyone on earth knows how I feel, it's Maggie.

And yet, while I hug her and cling to her deeply comforting bulk, I think, take her, God, and bring Johnny back. I'll trade you. She can die, if you'll let Johnny live.

Chapter Four

My eyes are closed. No longer asleep, but postponing waking up, I wait for Johnny. Dream-like, he walks toward me with the same loose-limbed grace, and his face is older, older than he ever was in life, maybe twenty-five or thirty. He needs a haircut. Shaggy blond waves fall over his face as we walk, and he's taller, a little over six feet, as tall as his father. We're on the dirt road behind our house in Taos, and it must be autumn because the rabbitbrush is fat with yellow blooms.

He gives me the same irresistible smile that bailed him out of trouble for all the years we lived together, sunny and guileless as a six-year old.

"I love you," I say.

"I know," he says. "You're my mom. It's part of the deal."

"Was it worth it, running away from me?"

"I'm still here, aren't I?"

"Barely," I say. "Tom and Maggie think this is all in my head."

"That's the only place that counts."

"I'd do anything to bring you back."

"You'd let Maggie die? You think you could live with that?" He says this in an oddly disinterested, curious tone.

"Yes."

"What if you had to kill her yourself?"

I barely hesitate. "I could do that."

"And Dad? Would you kill him to give me my life back?"

There's a sickening lurch in my belly. "Yes."
"Would you kill yourself?"
"To save you? Of course." His questions are painting me into a
corner I don't like, demonstrating an intelligence I'm not used to.
"Now tell me why you died."
"What happened to me wasn't so different. It was all about
love. Love can make you crazy."
"Someone shot you because they loved you?"
"Mom, it's too late to change what happened to me. If you
don't quit poking around they'll come after you."
"Who were you in love with, Johnny?"
He takes my hand and pulls me to a halt in the middle of the
road, and when I look at him, his eyes are lit with a strange fire.
"I'm serious about this. They're gonna kill you if you don't leave it
alone."

It's almost dark. The pool is lit with candles flickering
inside glass globes, there must be a hundred of them, and
the air is full of the smell of barbecued meat. My head feels
thick, and it takes me a minute to get my bearings as I look
out the bedroom window and see at least twenty-five
people scattered around the lawn. They're all under thirty.
Half of them are variations on blonde, on tan, on figures
drawn to perfection, and the other half have shaved heads,
tattoos, and ragged clothes. Two beautifully turned-out
teenaged girls float past my window, manicured, coiffed,
decked out in Versace. The clink of silver, crystal, and
china floats on the soft summer air as caterers unload ham-
pers of food.

Throwing on Johnny's robe, I walk to his bathroom, pee in
his toilet, wash my hands in his sink, then study my reflection
in his bathroom mirror. For a second I can see his ghost in the
planes and angles of my jaw, cheek, and brow. The image of

his face in the dream drifts through me, the eerie, tantalizing glimpse of the man he would have become.

His medicine cabinet is packed with the usual cough and cold remedies, menthol throat lozenges, Band-Aids, nearly empty bottles of antibiotics, jars of aspirin, and several boxes of condoms. There are no gaps in the shelves, no evidence that anything was taken away by the police. I take everything out, open every bottle and box, searching for something they might have missed, but nothing unusual appears.

The desk in the corner of the living room draws me like a magnet. The deep drawers hold orderly stacks of fan mail, clippings and posters from Johnny's tour, and I paw through these, searching for a checkbook, or any sort of banking receipt. Nothing. No sign of what Johnny earned or spent. Did Jack cover all his expenses? Was he given an allowance? Or have the police removed every financial vestige of his life?

Back in the bedroom, I turn on the switch next to the walk-in closet, and the ceiling inside it glows with soft, flattering light. There's a full-length mirror at the back, with a rack of suits against one wall, and more casual clothes on the other side, along with shelves for sweaters and scarves and shoes. When I open one recessed cabinet door I see a long, intricately beaded coat made from blond doeskin, and a black leather Harley Davidson jacket with matching pants, loaded with zippers and buckles.

One by one I remove the suits from their wooden hangers, dipping my fingers into every pocket. The suits surprise me with their rich, lovely texture in wool or silk or linen, fabrics that whisper *money* as they flow through my hands.

When did this kid learn how to buy good clothes? Johnny bought me a bathrobe for Mother's Day when he was eleven, a scratchy polyester blend from Wal-Mart in a vivid purple not found anywhere in nature, a robe that's in my suitcase right now, a robe I'll keep until I die. But damn, I think, fingering the suits. I wish he'd given me a robe after he learned to buy clothes like this.

A brisk knock comes from the living room, and a deep male voice calls out as the door swings open. "Elena? Are you awake?"

Jack appears in the doorway to the bedroom, a tired smile on his face. He walks toward me with his arms spread wide, then crushes me to his chest and holds me tightly for a moment in silence.

"Maggie set you up all right?" he murmurs into my hair.

I pull away. "Yes. Thanks, Jack. This place is gorgeous."

We smile at each other. He looks just the same. Older, of course, the hair in his sideburns laced with white, but still ruggedly handsome. His clothes are understated, a black T-shirt and soft-looking gray slacks that have no crease.

Suddenly I remember something I'd almost forgotten. A bar. The four of us went there one night, back when we were in college. Mid-week, the place was dark, practically deserted. A grand piano occupied a corner of the stage. This was only the second or third time Maggie had been out with Jack, and he kept eyeing the door as if he were looking for someone else.

"Too bad the blues player isn't here," he said. "I heard he was worth listening to."

"Elena's musical," Maggie said. "Her father played trombone in Duke Ellington's orchestra."

"Is that right?" Jack said, perking up.

"She took piano lessons for nine years. Isn't that right, El? Go on, show him."

I didn't want to. I didn't want to stop holding Tom's hand. But Maggie sounded nervous, and she was rarely nervous about anything, so I rose from the table, walked over to the piano and sat down on the bench.

The piano had been tuned recently, and it had a surprisingly rich tone, mellow and light, with a smooth action that made it easy to play. I began with Liszt's Sonata in B Minor, just to make a splash. By then I'd given up all thought of performing professionally—I didn't have the temperament for it, the obsessive focus my father had, or his need for applause—but I could still put on a show, and that night I let myself lean into the keys and plunge into the music.

Tom had heard me play before, and by now I knew it was all noise to him, something he knew he was expected to like, but secretly only tolerated. But Jack was different. His face lit up. He was clearly excited by the music, and the more carefully he listened the better I played. And as I played I noticed he was really quite good-looking, with that lick of sandy hair falling across his forehead and those hazel eyes rimmed in dark lashes. Jack's face glowed with a flattering attention that was all flowing my way.

"How about something a little quieter, so we can talk?" Maggie called out.

But Jack didn't want to talk. "Don't stop," he said, raising his glass. "It's wonderful."

So I continued. Maggie went off to the ladies' room, and when she came back Jack turned to her, his face flushed with the music. He said, "You should have told me she was really good." She looked measuringly at Jack, a long look. Tom caught my eye and raised an eyebrow, and I stopped playing.

"It's great to see you again, El," Jack says. "It's been, what, six, seven years?"

"Ten," I say.

"Ten? Impossible. You don't look a day older."

"Am I supposed to lie to you too?"

"Absolutely."

"You look terrific, Jack. And that's no lie."

He shrugs, obviously pleased, and lets out a low laugh. "Next week I turn forty-two. Can you believe that? Forty-two. Jesus."

He looks older than forty-two, I think, studying the shadows under his eyes, and the new gray in his hair. It's taken a toll on him, being a starmaker.

He comes closer and leans against the doorframe of the closet. "Is there a reason we're standing in here?"

"I was just looking through some of Johnny's things."

He nods slowly, thoughtfully, then tilts his head, studying me. "There's food out there, if you want anything."

"Thanks. I'm not really hungry."

"I heard about the hospital," he says. "That must have been rough, on top of everything else."

I lift another coat from the rack, slip my hand in the pocket and take out a dry cleaning stub.

He shifts his weight uncertainly. "How's the partnership?"

"I'm not going back to New York," I say, hanging the coat with the others.

"You mean it? You left the firm?"

"I tried to give them my resignation, but they wouldn't accept it. They're calling this a leave of absence. They think I'm coming back."

His eyes are warm, his gaze affectionate. "Maybe you will."

"I don't think so, Jack. I don't think I'll even miss it." Turning to a pile of sweaters on the shelf, I shake one out and study both sides. A thick cashmere in a soft moss green. Carefully I refold it, put it back on the shelf and pick up another in ivory. "My last project was a parking lot for a sewage treatment plant. Before that, I designed exterior pedestrian areas for a strip mall in Jersey. Believe me, the thrill is gone."

"That's too bad," he says. "You worked hard to get there."

I pause, stroking the sweater in my hand. "Yes. I did."

"Going back to school, getting your degree . . ."

"Five years of night school," I say. "It can really force you to explore the side effects of sleep deprivation."

"But you did it. And then interning for Pritchard & Bliss, working your way up the ladder there—Johnny always said they were the best."

"Did he?"

"He was proud of you, El."

I never knew what Johnny thought about my rise through the company. Mostly it happened after he moved out. Now I wonder if he saw the write-up in *Architectural Digest* about the Japanese garden I designed for the couple on Martha's Vineyard, or the small park in Queens that was featured in *Landscape Architect*.

"You could open your own greenhouse with the money Johnny left you," Jack says. "He made a fortune."

Irritated by Jack's idea of consolation, I mutter, "I'd spend every cent of that money to find whoever killed him." I look around at the shelves. By now I've gone through everything except his shoes. Brushing past Jack, I walk toward the bed.

One by one I toss the pillows on the floor, then peel off the bedspread. The sheets come off next, and I tug one corner of the enormous king-sized pillowtop mattress. It's heavy, too heavy for me to budge more than a foot.

"Help me with this, will you?"

After a moment's hesitation, Jack lifts one side and we flip

51

it over. It grazes the stained glass lamp on the nightstand and nearly sends it crashing to the floor. The mattress lands with a thud, half on the floor, half on the box springs.

"Are you looking for something in particular?" he asks. "Or is this just therapy?"

"Give me a hand here," I say, not really caring what he thinks, and push the mattress all the way off the box springs. This need to search the house feels a lot like the cleaning frenzy that seized me the week before Johnny was born. Everything had to be spotless, then. Now I want everything to be revealed.

Jack helps me remove the bedskirt from the base of the bed, and I bunch it up and throw it over a chair. Lifting one side of the box springs, I nod to the other corner, and he rolls his eyes and lifts it with me until it's completely turned over, exposing the lattice of wooden supports and springs underneath. There's nothing hidden there. No notes, no letters, no diaries, no pictures.

I look up at Jack. "There was a lot of fan mail in the desk—why didn't the police take it?"

He licks his lips, hesitating. "To tell you the truth the police didn't spend much time searching in here. They took almost nothing."

The shock must be visible on my face, because he looks nervous as he runs one hand over his close-cropped head. "Our lawyer told us about a local celebrity whose house was ransacked by the state police during an investigation, and then most of the stuff showed up later on eBay. So we had a few lawyers here when the police searched the house."

There's a loud splash outside as somebody falls in the pool, followed by squeals of delight and scattered applause. Neither of us moves. We stand there, staring at each other until he speaks, his voice low, soft, consoling. "Sooner or later somebody will come forward, Elena. Somebody must have seen something, or heard something. Give it time."

Why does this make me even more angry? It sounds so reasonable. But it's facile, and easy, and it reminds me that Jack lost a singer, while I lost a son. I struggle to make my voice even. "It's been three months, Jack. Most homicides go unsolved if the investigation is more than a month old."

He lowers his head. "You're right. I know you're right. What can I do to help?"

"Who do I talk to set up a reward?"

"A reward for—?"

"Anyone who can give the police information leading to the arrest and conviction of the killer."

"How much are you willing to spend?"

"A million dollars. His estate will cover that, won't it?"

"Have you talked to Tom about this?"

"Not yet. But I will. I want to hire a detective, too."

"We use an agency in Albuquerque that's pretty good."

"Thanks, but I was thinking about using someone from New York."

"Okay," he says, holding up his hands, palms out, a gesture of surrender. "I'll call the local networks tomorrow, see if we can set it up and publicize the reward."

I pass my hand over my face and force myself to take a deep breath. "I don't mean to sound ungrateful, Jack. I know you did a lot for Johnny. He wouldn't have made it in the business without you."

Jack steps away from the wreckage of the bed, looks out the window and slides his hands in his pockets. "Can you ever forgive me for that?"

There's no answer to that question, and the silence builds between us.

"It's a hell of a business, El," he says. "You couldn't hate it more than I do."

This makes no sense at all. Music is Jack's life. I've seen him quiver like a pointer in clubs where unsigned artists howled into a microphone, his radar alert to something that everyone else missed. He could find the sullen teen punks with voices like gravel thrown in a blender, the ones too young to be taken seriously by other producers. Maggie knew how to cultivate them, nourish their egos, cajole, threaten, and groom them for the big time, but it was Jack who discovered them. A few years later some of these kids were stars, fixtures on VH-1 and MTV, booked on aggressive tours that went on for years and pumped their product into mainstream America.

"Now it's all corporate rock," Jack mutters, staring moodily out the window toward the shimmering lights reflected in the pool. "Corporate crap, written by corporate songwriters who've found a formula and stick to it. The outfits, the videos, the choreography, the image—that's what's important. Not the music. All these mergers have made record execs paranoid, and the demand for quarterly profits doesn't give anyone time to develop a career. The kids on the scene now just sing whatever their owners tell them to sing, so they can turn them into profitable corporations."

"Didn't you do the same thing with Johnny?" I ask.

There's a hush between us, and he turns back to face me, his eyes haunted. "Johnny was different. That kid was on fire. He did it all . . . composing, arranging, singing, playing—he was a genius, El."

A dead genius, I think. The first time I heard Johnny sing at one of the clubs in Manhattan, I blushed to my toenails. He exuded sex. He had the fearlessness of Elvis, along with the stamina, drive, and hunger to be a star. I could see the danger, even then, when he was fifteen years old. His voice was unforgettable: bright, open, with a nice metallic ping up top that warmed into an even, burnished luster in mid-range. He'd been in a program for gifted young adults at Juilliard since seventh grade, and tossed off high C's with abandon even after his voice changed. He could negotiate delicate diminuendo effects and attack key phrases with heart-stopping accuracy. He could have become a legendary tenor, but he wanted to be a rock star. And by the time he was seventeen, Jack had signed him to a five-year, seven-figure recording contract.

"Hello? Anybody home?" Maggie's voice comes from the living room, and a moment later she sails through the doorway to the bedroom, looking tall and regal in a deep blue dress that skims her curves. She takes in the overturned bed, and her eyes dart from Jack's face to mine. "What's going on?"

"Nothing, Maggie," Jack says. "We were just talking."

From across the room I can smell her perfume, something citrusy and expensive I know I can't buy in a store. Alert to the undercurrents between us, she flashes a look at me, then Jack. "The governor just walked in. He's looking for you." Then, turning to me, she says, "Did you eat yet, El? We have an amazing buffet—Mike flew in some fresh seafood for us from Sebastian's in Denver."

"Mike's back?" There's an edge in Jack's voice.

"Your brother Mike?" I ask. Mike was always the black sheep in Jack's family, a reckless adventurer who'd gone bankrupt twice before he was forty. Every time our paths crossed he'd brush up against me in a big hug and let his hand trail over my backside. There were times when Mike's clumsy flirting was merely irritating, like a dog licking the back of your leg, and other times when it cheered me up tremendously. "Is he still with the state police?"

"They canned him a year ago," Maggie says. "Then he got a job working as a security guard for the MGM Grand in Vegas."

"Unfortunately they had a big robbery there," Jack says. "It had nothing to do with him, but they let most of the guards go."

"So you took him in?" I look at Maggie.

Her eyebrows go up and down as she glances at me, and in the shorthand of our friendship I know this means her patience with Mike is wearing thin. "It's been, what, four months now, Jack?"

Jack shrugs, gives me a look. "He's my brother."

"Anybody home?" a voice calls out from the living room.

"Speak of the devil," Maggie mutters as a man appears at her elbow, swirling ice in a glass of whiskey.

Mike is a slender, wiry man with compact, muscular arms packed into a tight blue cowboy shirt with snap-button pockets, and a heavy gold chain around his neck. His face is deeply tanned and looks cheerful and thickheaded, unlined by the anxiety and shrewd intelligence that makes Jack's face come alive. Mike's eyes brighten as his gaze takes me in from head to toe, and he sweeps me into his arms.

"Elena! How you doin'?" he asks, smacking my cheek with a moist kiss, lifting me several inches off the floor with just one arm snaked around my waist. "When did you get into town?"

Smiling, I pull away and tighten the sash on my robe. "Just got here, Mike."

He points his index finger at me, cocks his thumb down. "You look good enough to eat, sugar." Flattered and shaken, I brush the hair back from my forehead, feeling like I've been tossed across a bed. He gives me a wink and turns to his brother. "You busy, Jack? We need to talk, but I can come back later."

Jack is silent long enough to make me think he might not answer. "I didn't expect you to make it, Mike. How was the flight?"

"Got here by the skin of my teeth." He takes a quick, deep gulp of whiskey. "There was a storm south of Denver that knocked me all over the cockpit."

"We'd better get back to the party, Jack," Maggie says.

"What the hell happened in here?" Mike asks, looking around the room.

"Nothing that concerns you." Jack's voice hardly rises, but the chill is unmistakable.

"Relax, bro. I'm just asking, that's all." He takes another sip of whiskey, gazing evenly at his brother while Jack glares at him.

"Jack," Maggie says. "The governor's waiting."

Jack turns to me. "Come on, El. Let's join the party."

"Maybe later, Jack—I'd like to finish this." After giving them an apologetic smile, I turn my back on all of them, open the nightstand drawer and rifle through the contents.

Maggie shoos the two men out the bedroom door, then turns to me as she pauses on the threshold. "Want me to have the caterer send in a plate?"

I look up. "I'll grab a bite later."

"You know you have to eat, honey."

"I will. I promise. Go on, now." I turn back to the drawer and hear Maggie walk out the front door, then click it shut behind her.

The contents of the nightstand drawer reveal only notepads, pens, pencils, paper clips, Kleenex, a travel alarm, and loose change. Nothing else. No phone numbers, no day-planners, no invitations, no notebooks.

The drawers in the bureau are full of socks, underwear, T-shirts, sweaters, jeans, shorts, and bathing suits. I pick up a shirt, press it to my face and inhale the faint scent of his body, and with the smell of him so close, so real, my knees start to weaken, and a terrible lethargy steals over my limbs.

Bringing the shirt with me to the living room, I sag on the couch and stare at the lights of the party outside the window. The room is dark, and the darkness soothes me as I stroke the shirt in my lap. It seems like I've spent most of the last three months sitting in a chair like this, motionless, blank, looking out a window, listening to street noises or the ticking of my watch.

The knock is no more than a polite tap, scarcely audible.

"It's open," I call out, not bothering to get up, half-expecting Maggie to walk in with a plate of food I don't want. I swivel to see Alison's head poking around the door, looking uncertain, and my heart lifts at the sight of her.

"Are you busy?" she asks. "I don't want to disturb you."

"Not at all. Come on in."

Dressed in high heels, a sparkly black miniskirt, and a silky top, she's a dazzling girl, blessed with youth and privilege. Yet she still seems to project the unaffected, awkward honesty I remember from ten years ago.

"Had enough of the party?" I ask.

"It's my parents' scene. The governor's a fascist, in my opinion," she says, leaning against the door. Almost absent-mindedly, she reaches out to flick a switch, and recessed lights come on, illuminating the artwork.

"When did they start entertaining Republicans? Maggie and Jack used to be die-hard Democrats."

Alison wanders through the room, picks up a copy of *Bill-board* magazine from the coffee table, leafs through it, then puts it back. "They started handing out big bucks to both parties when my mom figured the state taxes were killing us. These parties are all a business write-off, anyway, no matter who comes."

A wisp of nostalgia floats through me at the sound of her voice, which carries the same sturdy huskiness that I remember from ten years ago. Seeing her move around the room with elastic, effortless grace fills a hunger in me I didn't know was there. I've missed her.

When Alison was only a month old, she stayed with us for two weeks while Maggie and Jack went on tour with a band they'd been cultivating for a year. One night Alison started whimpering in her crib and I took her into our bed so she wouldn't wake Johnny. It was a warm night. She was so tiny, naked except for her diaper, and I was bareskinned, aware of her creamy, delicate baby skin as she lay on my chest. I smelled her freshly shampooed head and something passed into me then and flowed out toward her, some deep, indefinable, indestructible sense of belonging. *I will protect you,* I thought. *I'll always do my best to take care of you and make sure you're safe.* Her body became quiet, as if she was listening, and then she settled into me as if she understood.

When Maggie finally returned from the tour she was exhausted and frazzled and confessed to me that she'd never felt that mother-child bond everyone talked about, the maternal connection she thought she was supposed to feel. I didn't say a word, but my heart lurched with guilt, and I wondered if I'd stolen it from her that night. Maybe there's only one moment in a child's life when she's imprinted by a mother's love, and I'd snatched it away from her.

Of course things changed. Kids forget. They move on. And I left Taos, and Tom, and Maggie, and Alison. Even though I wrote Alison and called her and begged Maggie to let her visit us in New York, it never worked out. Alison had a new pony she couldn't bear to leave, or a ski club trip, or they were all going to Barbados for a few weeks of snorkeling. After a while I stopped trying, and the silence between us grew into an abyss neither one of us tried to cross.

Alison completes her circuit of the room and sits beside me on the couch. Tentatively I reach out and smooth the tangled hair back from her forehead, then put my hand on her bare arm and give her a squeeze. Her skin is cool. She looks so grown up now, almost formidable in her adulthood, yet oddly vulnerable, too, exactly like the little girl I remember.

"So how do you like working for your dad?" I ask.

She lets out a dry laugh. "You know what they call me around here? The Eliminator."

"Why?"

"We get about three hundred demo tapes a week from musicians who are trying to break into the business. I spend most of my time listening to them and sending out rejection letters. I'm the one who tells them they're not good enough, not commercial enough, not original enough. And when I'm not rubbing salt in their wounds, I'm pampering egos the size of Mount Rushmore. Some of the people we have on contract think nothing of calling me at three a.m. to bitch about their tour dates."

"What would you do if you weren't doing this?"

Her face softens, and she heaves a big sigh as she flops against the cushions. "I don't know. Travel, probably."

"Where would you go?"

A smile tweaks the corners of her lips. "Places that never heard of MTV. Borneo. The Trobriand Islands. Zimbabwe. I'd like to see places where everybody sings, you know? Where singing is just another part of life, and everybody's included."

"You'd make a good anthropologist."

She lifts an eyebrow. "Not a likely scenario. Not with these parents. Not with the business they've built."

"They want you to be happy, don't they?"

Her face changes as she looks down and starts picking at a loose thread on her skirt. "I guess you know my mom and dad have been having problems?"

"They told me." All I can do is stroke her hair. "I'm sorry, honey. I know this isn't easy for you."

Alison looks away, distressed. "Dad says he wants a divorce. I don't think my mom can handle it. It's like they're two halves of one person, one partnership. Her whole life revolves around him and the business." She leans her head against my shoulder, a warm and welcome weight.

"Maybe she and Jack can go on as partners."

"That won't happen. He says he wants to walk away from all of it. The musicians are all in shock—they can see the writing on the wall, and for my dad to abandon them is almost as big a deal as abandoning her. Some of them bought houses here because of him. They trusted him to stick around."

In the dim light of the room her dark hair frames the pale oval of her face, and her eyelashes cast shadows on her cheeks as she looks down at her hands.

"Maybe you should go back to school in the fall, Alison. Give your parents some room to work it out for themselves."

She blinks and looks away, and when she speaks again her voice is unsteady. "I know it sounds stupid, but I can't shake the feeling that something bad will happen to them if I go away. I keep thinking they're going to die."

Automatically I reach out to wrap my arms around her shoulders and gather her in. Alison feels so little, so thin when I hug her, it's almost like hugging the bony child she used to be. I want to spread my mother hen wings over her, reassure her, protect her, and tell her everything will be all right. But even if I did, this is a grown-up I'm dealing with, and she probably wouldn't believe a word of it.

When I finally release her, she leans back and looks at me. "You're wearing his robe," she says softly.

It's not a question. I pull away and stroke the heavy silk as my mind catches up with the implications. "Were you and Johnny . . . did you two ever go out together?"

She looks up guiltily. "A few times." Twin flames of color appear in her cheeks, turning her tan to rose. "It wasn't serious."

"But you were good friends?"

Alison nods.

"I'm glad he had you," I say, stumbling over the words. "I mean—it must have been hard for him, leaving everything behind, adjusting to this new life."

The silence expands between us, and I wait, willing her to go on.

Finally she speaks. "We were friends, but he was always a one man show, you know? When Johnny was onstage, or in a car, or out shopping, he was surrounded by security. No one could get close to him. Even though millions of people knew his name, he was alone. During his concerts he was onstage by himself, just him and the piano in the spotlight. The backup singers and the other musicians were all offstage, out of sight. And that was what his life was like. There were about fifty production assistants who traveled with him, and he had nine personal assistants. But I think he was lonely most of the time."

"Did you ever see him give a concert?" I ask.

"Sure. Lots of times."

My heart contracts, imagining it. Why didn't I ever go? Why did I have to be so proud, so foolish? With a child you never imagine you'll run out of second chances. "Was he good?"

"He was the best." She says this quietly, with absolute assurance. "As a performer he was amazing. I've seen thousands of performers, and he was unbelievable. He couldn't wait to get out there. He really loved it."

"He told me he was in love," I say softly.

Alison stands abruptly and moves to the window, her back toward me. The decibel level of the party increases as the music goes up in volume and tempo. People are shouting to be heard over the noise.

I watch her back. It fits, in so many ways. They were almost the same age, and knew each other all their lives. They were practically living together here in this compound, which must have felt like their own private Eden. And Alison is a gorgeous girl. But if she loved him, why would she try to hide it now?

"It's a warped life," she says. "You sing your heart out in front of fifty thousand people in a coliseum and hear them roar back at you, that's a big wave, and you ride it or die. Coming down from that wave . . ." She shakes her head. "It's hard. You can make stupid choices."

My pulse kicks up a notch. "Did Johnny make stupid choices?"

"Sure." She turns toward me, and her eyes are flat and hard, holding a grudge. "He was an idiot, sometimes."

"About—?"

"Everything." Something flares behind her eyes, half warning, half hurt. "He was a snob, too," she says, a challenge in her gaze. "He had to be. He had to hold himself a little bit above us, a little bit apart. It was part of the mystique." She says this with a sour familiarity, as if she's come to this conclusion more than once.

"Was anyone jealous of him? Jealous of his success?"

She gives me a brief, taut smile. "You bet."

"Who?"

"Just about everybody in the business. Johnny was a lucky man."

I look back at her until she gets it, and then she flushes. "Well, he was lucky for a long time, anyway."

She stares out at the lights of the party for a moment, then turns back to me with a smile of apology, holds her fingers out and waggles them invitingly. "Come on. You need a sandwich." She nods in an exaggerated up and down motion that reminds me how I used to nod in exactly that way when I wanted her to agree with me. I roll my eyes and let her lead me to the kitchen.

Alison pulls bread and mayonnaise from the refrigerator as my eyes wander to the cupboards, and something about the closed cabinet doors fills me with the urge to fling them open. She keeps an eye on me as I move toward them and start pulling out cans, jars, and boxes.

"Sometimes I feel like I'm losing my mind," I say, taking a bag of chips off the shelf and tossing it on the counter. "All the normal things I used to do every day without thinking—eating, or taking a shower, or getting dressed—now it all seems like so much trouble, so much *effort*. Most of the time I'm so tired I don't want to get out of bed, but then I get these bursts of adrenaline and feel so wired I think I'll explode if I don't keep moving."

I drag a chair over to the counter and step up on it to paw through the contents of the cupboards. Cans of Chef-Boy-Ardee, baked beans, sardines, smoked oysters, peanut butter and jelly. Boy food.

Alison spreads mayonnaise on the bread, then brings out a block of Swiss cheese and a ripe tomato from the refrigerator.

"Everyone says 'Give it time.'" I bite the words off impatiently as I slap the cans down on the counter. "If I hear that phrase one more time I think I'll hit somebody."

She raises an eyebrow, keeping her eyes on the bread. "Good to know." Calmly she slices the tomato and cheese, then arranges them on one slice of bread and puts the other slice of bread on top.

There's a case of Slim Fast in the cupboard, and ten bags of tortilla chips. Candy by the bushel. His poor teeth, I think, before I can stop myself.

"You should eat this," Alison says, handing the sandwich out to me.

Not wanting to hurt her feelings, I climb down from the counter, take a bite and chew. Nothing tastes the same anymore. Holding the sandwich in one hand, I open a drawer and stare at the silverware, then close it.

"I want to take all the books down from the bookshelves," I say, swallowing the lump of bread in my throat. "Maybe there's something he left in one of them, some clue, some reason . . ." My voice starts to wobble, and I put the sandwich down.

"I'll help you," she says quickly, and we go back to the living room.

Alison takes an armful of books from the shelf and lowers them to the floor, while I do the same, and together we spend the next hour going through every book in the room. It's an odd, eclectic collection, hundreds of titles covering everything from growing your own bonsai to what looks like the complete works of Clive Cussler. Tom would die, I think, looking at the row of fat bestsellers. There are some titles he'd approve of, though: *Moby Dick. The Heart of Darkness.* A tattered paperback copy of *Shoes of the Fisherman.*

"Shoes," I mutter. "I forgot to look in his shoes."

Alison looks up as I rise and head for the bedroom, and I feel her follow me past the overturned bed to the softly illuminated closet. Below the rods where the suits are hanging, there are racks of cowboy boots, dress shoes, athletic shoes, hiking boots, even golf shoes.

I sit down with my legs tucked under me, pick up the golf shoes and stare at them in disbelief. "Golf. Now there's a sport he used to despise."

Alison hides a smile. "He wasn't very good at it. I think he just liked walking on grass. After the first few holes, he'd take these off and play in his bare feet."

"Did you know the police think Johnny was jogging to the bridge the night he was shot?"

She gives me a look, as if to say *so what?*

"He hated running, or at least he used to. Whenever we walked in Central Park he always made fun of the joggers."

She picks up a sheepskin slipper and strokes the fleece. "Johnny had to stay in shape for touring. Singing for hours at the top of your lungs—it's hard work, you know? His personal trainer was really tough on him, and Johnny used to bitch about how many sit-ups he had to do every day, but his solar plexus was hard as a brick. He could have changed his mind about jogging."

"Maybe." I put the golf shoes down and pick up a pair of knee-high beaded doeskin boots. "These are nice, aren't they? I think they match a coat somewhere in here." As I rise to search for the coat, the boot in my hand turns upside down and a folded piece of paper falls to the floor.

Alison gives me a look, her eyes wide as I reach out and pick it up. Crumpled and faded, the paper has torn edges and measures no more than five by seven inches when I unfold it. Smoothing it flat on my knee, I see a hand-drawn diagram in black ink, showing the road south of Taos, leading down to the villages in the canyon by the Rio Grande. The place names are written in neat block letters: Pilar, Apodaca, and Embudo. There's a small X by the road near Embudo, where a footbridge crosses the Rio Grande, a bridge I've walked across many times, back in the days when Tom and I used to skinny-dip in the river.

And then, at the bottom of the map, in the same unfamiliar printing:

8 p.m., September 21
9 p.m., December 17
8 p.m., March 1
10 p.m., June 21
I'll meet you on the footbridge. See you there—Sally

Alison leans over my shoulder, reading along with me, and when she finishes she sits back on her heels.

Suddenly my heart is banging in my chest. "Do you know who Sally is?"

"No, but tonight's the twenty-first," she says, meeting my eyes. "And it's only nine o'clock."

A ripple of goosebumps travels up my arm, knowing Johnny touched this paper, folded it and placed it in this boot. Why? Why would he put it here, and who is Sally?

Chapter Five

"Let's take my car," Alison says.

I hesitate, then think, why not? It might be useful to have another pair of eyes, another pair of ears. And something about the determination on her face is so familiar it's like looking in a mirror. "Let me get dressed, and I'll be ready to go."

"Me too," she says, glancing down at her skirt and high heels. "I'll meet you in the driveway out front in two minutes."

In the bedroom I change into a long-sleeved shirt, jeans, and sneakers, pull my hair into a ponytail and snap an elastic band around it. Slinging my purse over my shoulder, I head out to the living room, switch off the lights and walk out the door.

A few minutes later we're in her black BMW, speeding down El Salto Road, past Arroyo Seco, onto Paseo del Pueblo Sur, pressing south through Taos. The moon is bright, almost full, and as it rises over the dark silhouette of the mountains, it paints the road silver.

"Why would anyone want to meet in Embudo?" I ask. My memories of the place are of a tiny village, no more than a sprinkling of homes thirty miles south of here, on the banks of the Rio Grande.

"I have no idea," Alison says. Dressed in black jeans, sandals, and a long white shirt worn loose over a black halter-top, her face glows with purpose as she negotiates the curves. "At ten o'clock in Embudo, nothing's happening unless the coyotes are singing."

"And why would Sally even be there? She must know Johnny's dead—the whole world knows he's dead."

"But something's going on down there. Some kind of party, maybe? Or a jam session? It shouldn't take more than an hour to check it out, even if nobody shows up."

The mesa is beautiful at this hour, a sea of sage that looks blue in the moonlight, and we ride for a few minutes in silence until I break it. "Alison, I don't want to pry . . ." But I do, I think wryly. "Could you tell me what happened, exactly, between you and Johnny?"

There's a pause, and I can feel her choosing her words. "We went to a few parties together. There were lots of low-level promoters involved in his career. DJ's, journalists, fan clubs, people like that. People who wanted face time with him, but weren't important enough to schedule interviews. So Dad would invite them to a banquet hall with an open bar and Johnny would make an appearance. We went to a few of those."

"Doesn't sound like much fun."

"We'd talk, after." Her voice softens. "He'd ask me all about college. What I was studying, what Stanford was like. We'd talk about everything, politics, music, people we knew, the business. He was really smart. But God, he was always so opinionated, you know? When we were arguing about something I'd start saying things I didn't even know I felt, things my parents were never interested in knowing about me. I've never had conversations like that."

My throat aches at the thought of Johnny sitting here in this seat, talking to the girl beside me.

"He was always asking me 'What do you want?' " She

laughs. "He was a lot like you, El. He wanted to talk about the big stuff. What I wanted in life, why I wanted it, how I planned to get it—that kind of thing."

"Why did you break up?"

Alison stiffens, and the tension returns to her voice. "It wasn't like that." Her hand touches the wheel lightly as the car purrs around the horseshoe curve, up to the lookout point and down again into the twisting canyon that leads to Pilar and the river.

She glances at the rearview mirror. "Someone's keeping us company."

Twisting in my seat, I see the headlights of another car behind us. "Do you know who it is?"

"I can't tell," she mutters.

Abruptly she floors it, and I press one hand to the dashboard and jam my foot down on an imaginary brake as the speedometer needle rises and quivers around ninety. The car flows around turns until the headlights behind us disappear, and then Alison guns it down the straightaway toward Pilar.

With a sharp jerk she hits the brakes and twists the wheel, making a hairpin turn that sends us down a steep, bumpy dirt road. Alison flicks off the lights, and we wait until the car behind us streaks past the turnoff.

The canyon is silent except for the susurrus of the Rio Grande and the ticking of the engine as it cools, but my heart drums against my ribs as if we were still being chased. "What was that about?"

Alison shakes her head. "I'm not sure, but that car was behind us ever since we left El Salto. Wouldn't pass me when I slowed down, then speeded up when I did."

My body goes cold at the thought of being followed, but a nagging sense of doubt remains. She never mentioned the car until I asked her why she broke up with Johnny. I never even noticed the car until she pointed it out, and then she lost it easily enough.

"It's already ten o'clock," Alison says, checking her watch. "If we want to catch Sally we need to hurry."

"Let's go," I say, and open the door.

An old chile stand marks the trail to the footbridge, which was built at least thirty years ago by locals who wanted to avoid the long trek to the Embudo station bridge. When we ascend the ramp and step on the planking, the bridge creaks and sways under our weight, and we exchange a look and retreat to the solid bank of the river.

I look at my watch, and Alison does the same. It's five past ten. "Do you think we're too late?" I ask.

"Maybe," she says, and I feel an odd relief.

Another car whizzes past on the highway above us, and then silence reasserts itself in the canyon. As the minutes tick past I feel a prick of anticipation, as if something is about to happen. But nothing happens. I watch the water moving under the bridge and think about the last time I was here with Tom and Johnny and Alison, when we lay in the hot sun of August and let the heat bake our bones.

"Do you remember when we were here before?" I ask.

"With you? No."

"You were little. Not more than five, I think. Tom and I took both you kids down here for the day."

"I don't remember that."

The day is still vivid in my memory, clear as a photograph. Johnny's hair was light as milkweed, his body deeply tanned. Alison's dark, lovely face was open, happy to be with us. On the beach she waved a willow switch for a sword, while Johnny made claws with his hands and roared. They played monster, racing around in and out of the water, making up dialogue and sound effects. The glow of their skin, the curve of their foreheads, the expressiveness of those small shoulders—I never tired of watching them, or the way Johnny's head would tilt as he stopped to listen to the world. Traffic, birds, the rustle of water, or leaves in the wind—he listened to all of it with his eyes closed, his face intent, attentive, rapt.

When the two kids finally had enough water and sun they came over to where Tom and I were stretched out on a blanket in the shade, and flopped down between us. So familiar, I drank them in, and kissed their cheeks, like warm silk against my lips. Tom and I shifted until they were both snuggled against us, and then I pulled Johnny close. Every nerve ending in my body stretched toward my son, more in love with him then than I'd ever been in my life. His skinny arms and legs sprawled carelessly against me, and he tilted himself away so I could scratch his back, idly, slowly, the way he loved to be scratched, almost tickling but not quite. The spasm of feeling that traveled through me then is still vivid in my memory, a kind of love coupled with terror, the same awareness that came with his birth, knowing my heart would never be safe again.

A sound like a pistol shot cracks the air, and I freeze. It comes from underneath the bridge.

"Relax," a woman's voice calls out from the trail along the bank. "It's a beaver. He slapped the water with his tail. Did you see him? He was over there, swimming upstream."

The woman walking toward us is at least sixty-five years old, with smooth, slightly flattened features. "I'm Sally Wounded Head," she says, in a soft, clipped Indian accent. "Are you here to sweat with us?"

Dressed in a man's red flannel shirt over dark jeans, with a canvas bag clutched in her fist, her figure resembles an apple on toothpicks. Alison's face blooms with relief at the sight of her, and I finally understand why she wanted to meet the mystery woman. If Johnny couldn't give his heart to Alison, at least Sally wasn't the reason why.

"I'm Elena Waters. I believe you knew my son, Johnny."

Sally looks me up and down, an amazed smile tightening the wrinkles in her brown cheeks. "You're Johnny's mom? Sure, he was a regular." And then her face changes. "It was a terrible shock for us, him dying like that, so young."

"This is Alison Dalton," I say.

Sally smiles at Alison, then brushes past us to waddle up the ramp to the bridge, apparently taking it for granted that we'll follow her across. "So how did you hear about us?"

Alison hesitates, but I walk up the ramp after Sally. "There was a map of this place in his house, with today's date on it." I turn around and beckon to Alison as Sally's heavy steps make the plywood shake beneath my feet. Tentatively Alison ascends the ramp, and we follow Sally across the bridge.

"We took a chance coming here," I call ahead to Sally. "We didn't know what the map was for."

Sally nods vigorously as she descends the ramp on the other side. "I made it for him. He used to come and sweat with us. You ever been in a sweat lodge before?"

"I've heard of them, but I never—"

Sally interrupts. "Look, there's Selo. That crazy man, his fire's too high. It's going to be a hot one tonight." She says this with relish, as if it couldn't be too hot for her.

The three of us climb over a broken fence and continue up the other side of the river, toward the smell of smoke and a wide pebbled beach. Four men with long graying hair are gathered around a fire, and all of them are barechested, dressed only in swim trunks. In the moonlight their faces look like an illustration out of a book by James Fenimore Cooper, faces from another time, another world.

An old man with long silver hair emerges from a hut made of tarps flung over a framework of branches. "Sally, good to see you," he says, smiling at our companion. Then he looks me over. "Who's your friend?"

"This is Elena," Sally says. "Johnny's mom."

"Johnny Waters?" For a moment his gaze locks on mine. His eyes are fathomless, dark, and a warmth passes through me, an odd sense of comfort as he smiles a wide, welcoming smile. "Good to meet you, Elena. And your friend—?"

"I'm Alison," she says.

"I'm Russell Black Crow. Over there is Selo Crazy Bull, Phil Ruiz, James Bad Cobb, Bob Jacobs, and you already met Sally." His accent is like Sally's, a breathy, clipped singsong. The other men stand and nod.

"So you're going to sweat with us tonight?" Russell asks, beaming at me as if I'm a long-awaited guest.

I hesitate and look at Alison, who moves her chin minutely to the right, then left. "We didn't bring the right clothes," I say apologetically. "We don't even have a towel."

"Spirit led you here, didn't it?" Sally says. "I wasn't sure which dress I wanted to wear tonight, so I brought all three. We can change behind that clump of junipers."

"I have towels over there," Russell says, and turns as if it's all settled, while Sally walks off as if there's no doubt in her mind we're going with her.

And I realize she's right. Before Johnny's death I would have backed away, but not now. Johnny was here with these people, just a few months ago, and he did whatever they do in a sweat lodge. Right now, that's all the incentive I need.

"I can't go," Alison says, hanging back.

I look at her. "It's okay, honey. They won't hurt us."

"I mean it," she whispers. "I'm not going to sweat with them."

"Why not?" I say.

Her face hardens into a stubborn look. "I don't want to, that's why. I was in one of these things once and it lasted forever and I thought I'd die. It's not like a steam bath at a spa. It's hot as hell in there."

I glance at Sally's broad back as she picks her way toward the trees. "These people knew him, Alison. Maybe they know why he was killed. I have to stay."

"I have a really bad feeling about this, Elena."

I lift my palms. "I'm sorry."

Her face is a mask, but I can hear the displeasure in her voice. "I'll wait for you in the car, then."

"Don't be silly. It might take hours."

"How are you going to get back to Taos, if I leave?"

"Why can't you just try it, Alison?" I say. "If it gets too hot, you can step out for a while."

"Forget it. I'm not doing it, and if you had any sense you wouldn't either."

I stare at her, bewildered by her resistance after coming this far. She looks angry, and a rising impatience fills me as she crosses her arms tightly and refuses to look at me.

Russell ambles over to us with an armload of towels. Although we've hardly spoken above a whisper, he's clearly aware of the tension between us. "You need a ride back to Taos, Elena? Sally lives up there. You can hitch a ride with her."

Alison gives me one last imploring look. "I don't want to leave you here."

"Then stay."

She shakes her head, visibly upset. "I guess I'll see you in Taos."

I reach out to hug her goodbye, but her body feels rigid,

unyielding, and she pulls away and walks off, her back stiff with resentment.

For a moment I stand there staring after her, caught in the uncomfortable feeling that I've let her down, but why? After driving all this way, why wouldn't she risk staying while I talk to these people? One of the men bends to stir the fire, releasing a shower of sparks. For a moment I wonder, is this crazy? Should I leave too?

Russell walks over to me and touches my arm, then gestures with his chin toward Sally, who stands by the clump of junipers, waiting for me. "Go on," he says. "You made the right choice."

Still uneasy, I walk toward the trees, where Sally's face remains smooth and unperturbed as she waits for me in the moonlight. She nods when I reach her, and silently holds out a long, loose dress made of thin white cotton, with flowers embroidered around the neckline.

"Why do you wear a dress in the sweat lodge?" I ask, taking it and following her behind the screen of trees.

Grunting softly as she bends down to untie the laces of her black tennis shoes, she says, "It keeps you covered, but lets your skin breathe. Much more comfortable than a bathing suit. Course, next time, you can wear anything you want. Nobody minds."

I toe off a sneaker, then stand on one leg to pull off my sock. "I didn't know women were allowed in a sweat lodge with the men."

"Times have changed. If you go back to the rez, now, back in South Dakota, you'll still find some old grandpas who don't want women in their sweats, but the medicine men 'round here know better than to keep me out."

"You said Johnny was a regular?" I ask, pulling off the other sneaker.

"He came every couple months, since last year. He was interested in the Lakota way, Lakota beliefs. He liked to sing with us."

"You're Lakota? Not Taos Pueblo Indians?"

Sally takes off her flannel shirt, exposing a brassiere that's gray with age, and when she steps out of her jeans, her legs poke out from the biggest pair of underpants I've ever seen. "Pueblo Indians don't sweat. There's a community of Lakota people here, in Taos, Pilar, Embudo, all down along the river. We get together and sweat, keep the old ways alive. The sweat is a purification ceremony."

I pull off my shirt and step out of my jeans as Sally glances at my pale legs and smiles to herself.

"You think Johnny needed to be purified?" I ask.

She shrugs as she unsnaps her bra and folds it carefully. "We didn't ask about that. He used to pray for strength, though. It sounded like he was about to do something that scared him, something dangerous. He always asked the Creator for strength." Lifting the blue dress over her head, Sally's head disappears, then pops out again as the material settles over her.

Mulling over her words, I pick up the dress she's brought for me and pull it over my head. "Do you think he was scared about performing?"

"This was something different, I think. Something private. Something that could bring trouble to him."

When we're both ready, I leave my clothes folded over my purse, then follow her back to the fire. There's a thick braid of grass in Russell Black Crow's hand, and he touches the braid to the fire, then blows on the tip until it glows like a firefly in the darkness. The smoke curls up as he wafts it up and down in front of Sally, who turns obediently to let him do the other side.

"Stand here and I'll smudge you next," he says when he's finished with Sally. The smoke is sweet, and he waves it along my arms and legs, front and back. This is how Johnny must have stood, I think, and this must be what he saw, what he smelled, what he felt. An unexpected reverence wells up inside me, the kind of reverence I used to feel in church when I was little. When I lift my head I hear the soothing rush of the river, and the stars are pale next to the brightness of the moon.

Russell whispers in my ear. "When we're ready to enter the lodge, follow Phil clockwise around the fire."

At a nod from Russell, we move silently in a circle around the fire, enter the hut and sit on a blanket next to an open pit in the center. It's dark, and so crowded my thighs press against Sally and Phil. The curved canvas walls and huddled closeness of half-naked old men gives me a whiff of claustrophobia, and I take a deep breath to still the anxiety in my chest.

Selo Crazy Bull brings in seven melon-sized rocks, one at a time, each precariously balanced on a pitchfork until he drops them into the pit, where they glow with heat in the blackness.

Russell anoints the rocks with cedar and sage. "*Mitakuyeoyasin.* To all my relations," he says in a low voice, as the scented smoke fills the sweat lodge. The men shift and mutter as the heat grows in the close, sweet-smelling dark.

With each addition to the pile of red-hot basalt in front of us, Russell greets the four directions, as well as the earth, the sky, and the center of our circle. A bucket of water sits by his side and when he throws a dipperful on the rocks, the steam assaults us, wraps itself around the circle and squeezes the breath from my lungs. Suddenly this is far hotter than an ordinary sauna, and the sweat jumps out of every pore on my body. I'm afraid to open my mouth, and shield my nose against the burning air.

The others shout "Ho!" as the heat presses against us, and I hear myself shouting with them. It's a relief to shout. Next to me Phil's deep bass voice is as close as my shoulder, but the hut is so dark I can't see a thing. The atmosphere is full of labored breath, and soft, approving grunts.

And then Russell Black Crow begins to speak. "*Tunkasila,* Grandfather, we're here tonight to ask a blessing for our guest, Elena, the mother of our friend, Johnny. We pray that our Johnny is happy walking the spirit path, and we want to sing him into the next life that waits for him."

Immediately the men around me belt out a chant in words I don't understand. The hut fills with sound, and Sally bellows next to me. Within minutes the sweat rolls off me in sheets, as if every inch of my skin is weeping. Darkness and heat enter me, blurring the edges of reality, of consciousness. The song ends abruptly, and Russell flings back the tarp to let in cold air. Gratefully, I suck it into my lungs.

When the flap goes down we're in the dark again with the smothering heat. The close, smoky atmosphere makes me dizzy, and I dig my nails into my knees to keep myself from fainting.

Russell speaks. "And now, *Wakan Tanka, Tunkasila,* Grandfather, we want to send up our prayers for our friend Johnny, and for his mother Elena. There is a darkness over all of us who loved him, Grandfather. We want Elena to know that we are with her in our hearts."

"*Ho,*" several of the men say when Russell pauses. My heart pounds against my ribs.

"Grandfather, please give Elena peace in her time of trouble, and let her receive whatever message Johnny's spirit may have for her."

79

There's a silence I can feel in the pit of my stomach, and then the air in front of me begins to sparkle. In spite of the heat a ripple of goosebumps trickles down my spine, and Johnny's voice enters me like a cold wind.

"Why are you here, Mom?"

"Because I need answers, Johnny."

"Isn't it enough to hear me? To know I'm all right?"

"How can you say you're all right? You're dead."

"Dead isn't so bad, you know? There are worse things. You can be more dead when you're alive. And we're talking again, aren't we? Finally."

"Why did you run away from me, Johnny? Why did you shut me out for so long?"

"You know why. You didn't want me to have the only life I ever wanted. You were always scared of my music, scared of my voice."

"I was right to be scared, wasn't I? Look what happened."

"You can justify being afraid of anything, but it wasn't music that killed me. You were always afraid of the wrong thing."

"What should I have been afraid of?" A prickling unease crawls over my skin, and Johnny's voice gains volume, urgency.

"Mom, you need to get out of here. Now."

"Why? What's the matter?"

"Hurry—you don't have much time. They're coming."

"Who?"

"You stirred up trouble, being here. Big trouble."

"Then help me! Tell me who killed you. Tell me why it happened."

"I can't, Mom. You have to go. Don't stop to change. Run!"

And then he's gone. There's nothing left of his voice but phantom sparks in the air, and these disappear, one by one.

My blood pounds in my ears, every particle of my skin pulsates with heat, and the glowing rocks at the center of the circle seem to throb in time with the beat of my heart.

"Peace to you, my friend," Russell murmurs, and everyone but me shouts in unison: *"Ho!"*

The heat is suddenly unbearable, and I rise and aim myself at the flap in the door, overwhelmed by heat and the rise of an anguish so great I can't hold it in for one more second. Falling clumsily against Phil, he offers a hand to steady me. I take it and put my foot down on someone else's foot. Several hands reach out to guide me forward, and I press on, struggling over the other sweating bodies until I finally burst through the flap.

I'm out, walking on stones toward the river, so hot I can't think. My skin steams like a pot of boiling water. Stumbling to the river, I lie down flat in the shallows, where the water is only three or four inches deep, and the coolness flows around my head. Ten or fifteen yards away, Sally and the men start to sing in the sweat lodge.

Every time I hear Johnny's voice I have to say goodbye to him all over again, and when he tells me to leave, the sting of rejection is almost unbearable. How can he not need me? How can I love him this much and have so little claim on him? He pushed me away for five years, and he's still pushing me away. Telling me to run and hide—it's another wall, another way to shut me out.

Everyone knew him better than I did, even strangers like Russell and Sally. They know more about his secrets than I probably ever will. I think of Maggie, saying, "You can dig up all kinds of shit about his life, but he's *dead*." Why won't Johnny tell me what she meant? What truth is so terrible that a mother can't face it? The worst has already happened.

The water pushes against the back of my head as tears

crawl down my cheeks, and the heat inside me slowly leaks away. Suddenly I'm cold, chilled to the bone. I try to get up, but can't move. It seems absurd, but I can't even lift my hand. For a few seconds I squirm, trying to get a purchase on the slippery rocks, trying to push myself up, but my muscles are useless.

A shadow creeps over me until the moon and stars are blotted out, and when I look up I see a hooded figure standing above me. In the dim light I'm not even sure if what I see is real.

"Give me a hand," I say out loud. "I can't move."

There's no reply, but I feel fingers under my armpits, lifting me. They seem real, but the features of the face above me are obscured, like a ghost.

The stones no longer scrape my back, and I realize I'm being dragged deeper, toward the center of the dark current. We're going the wrong way, and the hands gripping my arms are immovable.

"Help!" My throat is raw from heat and smoke, and the people in the sweat lodge are singing too loudly to hear me.

Suddenly a hand covers my face and bears down. I thrash under water, and the river tugs at the long dress and tangles up my legs in a wet cocoon. I fight, but the hand is too strong. My diaphragm tightens with pain as pinpricks of light appear behind my eyelids, and a thread of bubbles escapes from my mouth.

Desperate, I twist, open my mouth and bite down hard on a thumb, bite so hard it makes my teeth hurt. The hand leaps from my face, and my body is yanked into the fast moving current of the Rio Grande.

The river seizes me and I go under, kick up and go down again. Swollen with snowmelt and the runoff of late spring rains, the Rio Grande is a muddy, icy torrent. Fence posts, fields, trees go spinning by as the water pulls me into its dark mouth. I come up gasping and call out, but my voice is lost in the sound of the river. Rocks knock against my legs as I go tumbling by, but the water is too fast, and I can't stop. Underwater there's no way to tell up from down in the black night.

The river hustles me past curves and over rapids, until something sharp snags me and a branch bends, then cracks under my weight. Slamming into the half-submerged trunk of a tree, I cling to it with the last of my strength. The bark is slick, and the sharp points of broken branches cut me as I work my way along its length. My arms are weak as water-logged weeds, and the cold leaves me feeling boneless and hollow. It's too damn cold. The river is winning.

"Help!" The wind whips away my voice.

I crawl up on the trunk, shivering, clinging to the tree and trying to keep my legs up out of the water, freezing, but alive. "Help," I say, over and over, almost to myself, while the river and the canyon walls shine silver in the moonlight, and the stars glow in a sky that's almost blue because the moon is so bright, and even though I'm freezing I realize this is a beautiful night, this is a beautiful world, and I don't want to leave it.

Time loses its shape in the lapping of the river against the trunk of the tree between my legs. Slowly I work my way along the slimy bark, ripping my dress to shreds on the broken stubs of branches, edging closer to the bank while my shivering takes on a rhythm of its own, like another pulse. In a kind of netherworld where my body remains numb and nothing is real, I finally pull myself up along the sharp ladder of broken limbs to the shallows. There are rocks under my feet, but I'm too weak to stand.

Bleeding from a hundred small cuts, freezing, bruised, but

alive, I crawl up out of the water, onto the bank, and keep crawling forward until I see the dark shape of a house, and a light in the window.

Chapter Six

Someone chafes my hand and whispers my name. *Johnny,* I think, and squeeze the hand holding mine as my eyes flutter open.

Tom stands by the bed, his eyes full of worry. Early morning sun shines through a window. I'm lying in a strange room, groggy, sore, but alive. A middle-aged woman in white cotton pants and a white T-shirt leans against the mantel of a stone fireplace on the other side of the room. The light hurts my eyes, and I close them.

"Elena?" Tom bends closer, gives my hand a little shake. "Can you hear me?"

I feel like I just came out of surgery, but I open my eyes and push myself up on my elbows. That makes the pain in my eyes spread through my head, but I stay up, even consider standing.

"Hold on there," Tom says. "Why don't you rest a minute?"

"I'm fine." Struggling to sit, I swing my legs off the bed, but the light gets unsteady and before I can rise to my feet Tom scoops up my legs and lowers me back down.

The woman walks over to the bed and looks down at me, her eyes full of concern. "Take it easy, sweetheart. You got dinged pretty good in that river."

I raise my hand, feel a bandage on my forehead. "Who are you?"

"Jeannie Archuleta. You knocked on my door last night."

"She said you were soaking wet," Tom says in a low voice.

"I thought you were a goner—blue with cold, and shaking like a leaf," Jeannie says. "Right before you passed out you gave me this guy's name, but I figured a good night's sleep would be the best thing for you, so I waited until this morning to call him."

"What happened, El?" Tom asks.

It starts coming back to me, the hands over my face, pushing me down. My gaze drifts around the room as I hesitate, reluctant to tell him the truth, knowing it will lead to questions I can't answer. "Somebody tried to drown me last night."

Some kind of eyebrow signal passes between them. "Who?" Tom asks.

"I don't know."

They wait for more, but I don't know where to begin, and I have an uncomfortable feeling that no matter what I say, Tom won't be satisfied. An oak clock on the mantel ticks out the seconds as their eyes remained expectant, fixed on me.

"What the heck were you doing down here?" Tom asks.

The thought of Alison flashes through my mind, the look on her face when she left me there. The way she walked off, her back straight, pissed off at something. Or frightened, maybe.

"I found a map in Johnny's closet, with yesterday's date on it, and I thought it might be important, it might tell me who he was spending time with before he . . ." I close my eyes to make the room stop spinning. "Anyway, I came down here and found some people who knew him. They were having a sweat lodge ceremony."

"Russell Black Crow?" Jeannie asks, and I open my eyes and nod. She lays a hand on Tom's wrist, and he looks at her.

"One of my neighbors is a Lakota Sioux, and he hosts a sweat lodge ceremony about once a month. He's a good man, a good friend." She turns her gaze back to me.

Tom grips my hand. "Tell me exactly what happened."

A fresh wave of fatigue hits me as I realize Tom thinks this will all be resolved by interrogation and logic, and I don't know if I have the strength to oblige him. "The sweat lodge was too hot. I went to the river to cool off, and somebody came up behind me and shoved my head underwater."

He nods, slowly, thoughtfully, and his voice is calm, but his eyes burn into mine. "Was it a man or a woman?"

"They were dressed in black. I couldn't see a face."

"Who else was in the sweat lodge with you?"

"Four men and a woman. It wasn't any of them, though. I could hear them singing after I left."

"Who knew you were coming down here?"

Seeing his expression arouses a flutter of caution in me, and I decide to keep Alison out of this. But my mind leaps to the car she said was following us, and I realize whoever it was could have come back. There was a full moon. It would have been easy for them to spot her car parked in the clearing. Maybe they saw the fire, or heard us singing in the lodge, and then all they had to do was wait for me. I think of Johnny, warning me to run, but it still doesn't make sense. Why would someone want to drown me?

"There was a party at Jack and Maggie's," I say. "There were twenty or thirty people there. Anyone could have followed me."

"Do you want to call the police?" Jeannie asks.

I think about it. Was there a time when going to the police would have been a natural reflex, an act of faith? That faith is gone. Talking to Detective Gallegos, reading his irritated, bored expression—that look incinerated whatever hope I had left in the police. Ever since Johnny was killed, Gallegos has treated me like an adversary, the hysterical mother of the victim, someone who has to be excluded from the investigation. Every piece of information the police give me is second-hand, and as far as I can see, they're no closer to solving Johnny's murder than they were on the day they found his body. If they can't find a killer, how will they find whoever assaulted me?

"I can't give them a description. It was dark, and I couldn't see anything. It could have been anyone."

Whatever Tom is thinking remains veiled behind those blue-black eyes. "Did you talk to Johnny last night?" he asks.

"Who's Johnny?" Jeannie asks.

Tom goes on staring at me, as though trying to convey some message that doesn't arrive.

"Yes, I talked to him. What's your point?"

He turns to Jeannie. "Our son was killed recently."

The shock registers in her face. "You're Johnny Waters' parents? I read about him in the paper. I'm so sorry." Her eyes are alert as she glances at me, then Tom, assessing the undercurrents in our conversation.

"I didn't make this up," I say to Tom. "Somebody held my face underwater until I bit him. Or her."

He nods, as if he's come to a decision. "Let's get you to a doctor, then."

A little zing of alarm passes through me at the thought of going to a doctor. I've had enough doctors to last a lifetime. Slowly I sit up from the pillows and let my legs slide over the edge of the bed. There are big patches on my shins that are gray-blue with bruises, and my head aches, but nothing feels broken. "I think I'm okay."

"I checked your temperature and blood pressure last night

and this morning, while you were sleeping," Jeannie says hesitantly. "I think you'll be fine. You just need to rest."

"You're a doctor?" Tom asks.

"A paramedic. I work with the local fire department."

"All right," he says, turning back to me. "Let's go home."

I'm wearing an old plaid flannel nightgown that must belong to Jeannie. "My clothes are up near the sweat lodge—I don't have any shoes." I look up at Tom. "My purse is there too. We have to go back."

Jeannie walks out of the room, then comes back with a pair of old garden clogs. "You better wear these if you're going back to Russell's. There's a lot of cactus along that path." She puts her hand on my back and rubs it a little, a motherly gesture that makes me weaken for a moment, but I can't afford to show Tom how shaken I feel or he'll pack me off to the ER.

The clogs are too big for me, and my legs feel like rubber as I slip them on and hobble out to the driveway after Tom. The cottonwoods by the river murmur in the breeze, and the shadows underneath the trees fill me with a new, unpleasant anxiety. Every sound makes me wonder if I'm being watched, and whether whoever attacked me might try it again.

Jeannie follows us, and once I'm settled in the passenger seat of the truck, she leans through the open window to talk to me. "Russell helped me sandbag the pasture this year during the spring flood—I couldn't ask for a better neighbor. You should talk to him about what happened to you. He might be able to tell you more."

"Thank you," I say, and reach for her hand. "You saved my life last night."

"Don't worry about it. Just get some rest."

She holds her palm up in farewell as we drive down a long bumpy driveway and turn onto the dirt road on the west side of the Rio Grande. From there it's a mile to the bridge at

Embudo, and soon after we turn back on the highway and head north, the chile stand marking the trail to the footbridge appears on the left.

"Stop up here," I say. "We have to cross the footbridge."

Tom crosses the highway, pulls over on the wide part of the shoulder and switches off the engine. In the sudden silence my stomach tightens at the thought of crossing the loose, weather-beaten sheets of plywood on the footbridge, so close to the river that almost swallowed me last night. Everything out the window looks odd, unsettling, dangerous somehow. A car streaks past us, too fast, way too fast. Tom waits patiently for me to move, but I can't seem to make myself get out.

Finally he takes my hand in his and gives it a squeeze. "Let's forget it, El. Let's go to the police and tell them what happened. They can look for your purse. You don't have to do this."

"I don't want the police." I remove my hand. "They're no help."

He stares out the window at the river. "You know what I think? I think you should go back to New York and take some more time to recover. This isn't healthy, all this running around looking for a killer."

Instantly, heat flares inside me, and I say the thing that will hurt him the most. "Maybe I miss him more than you do."

He gives me a long, even look that makes me feel worse than anything he could say, then turns his gaze back to the river. "I know this is a hard time for you, but this vigilante crap, driving off in the middle of the night, looking for clues—it scares me, El. You could get killed."

"If someone was threatened enough to follow me down

here and try and drown me, they must be afraid I'll find out the truth."

"By talking to his ghost?" His voice is gentle, but skeptical.

"Maybe. Why not?"

"These villages are full of addicts and ex-cons—what happened to you might not have anything to do with Johnny."

"I can't just sit at home and grieve! Can't you understand that? I'll go crazy if I do that. This is the only thing that's keeping me sane right now. If it scares you, well, frankly, I don't care. I need to know why Johnny died." My throat closes, and I shake my head, angry at the useless tears that fill my eyes. Maybe I'm just kidding myself, and this is all a bunch of big talk. Maybe I'm not really brave enough to do this.

That thought propels me out of the truck, and I slam the door behind me and start walking toward the trail to the footbridge. A few seconds later Tom's door opens and closes, and his footsteps crunch over gravel as he catches up.

At the top of the steep slope overlooking the muddy rushing water of the Rio Grande, I pause, and Tom silently takes my hand. My anxiety ebbs a fraction as I feel the warmth of his rough calluses pressed against my palm, and I take a deep breath. "My purse is just across the river."

He continues to hold my hand as I shuffle down the slope in Jeannie's loose clogs. The sight of the river chills me, and I tighten my grip on him as we cross the footbridge. The planking clatters underfoot, and the guy wires stretch with every step, making the bridge bounce and sway. Queasy, I keep my eyes glued to the other side as I hurry across.

Leading Tom up the path, I step carefully over the broken fence, pick my way slowly past a few smashed beer bottles and patches of cactus. The river shimmers on our right, a high, flat, fast-moving snake of water. The rusted corpses of a couple of junked cars lie half in and half out of the water along the steep bank, the farmers' protection against erosion.

When we arrive at the sweat lodge, the tarps are missing, and only a willow cage remains over the pit where they placed the hot rocks. Tom examines the fire pit with interest as I head for the clump of juniper where Sally and I changed last night. My purse and clothes lie hidden in the space at the center of the ring of trees, and I dress quickly in my jeans and pullover, then stuff Jeannie's clogs and nightgown in my bag.

Feeling steadier in my sneakers, I walk to where Tom waits for me by the riverbank, and watch him shy stones into the water for a few minutes. It's been ten years since I last saw Tom skip stones across a river. He still moves with the same grace, tilting his body and cocking his arm, releasing the stone with a deft twist that makes my heart lean toward him. There was a time when this stretch of the river was our personal playground, our sanctuary, and seeing him here almost feels like we've stepped back in time, except for the knot of anxiety in my chest.

Sunlight plays across the deep green leaves of the cottonwood trees arching over the water, and dragonflies hover in the shallows. It's an idyllic scene. The river is deceptively calm above the ripping current, and I take a deep breath to shake off the fear I feel standing next to it.

When Tom bends down to pick up another stone I clear my throat, and he looks up. I point to the nearest adobe above the flood plain. "I think that's Russell's house."

Tom begins walking purposefully in that direction, while I follow more slowly. The windows in the low adobe are dark in the midmorning brightness, but when Tom reaches out to knock on the front door, it swings open before his hand touches the wood.

Russell stands on the threshold, dressed in overalls and no

shirt, his long silver hair loose over his shoulders. "Elena! I'm glad to see you. Where did you go last night?"

My smile feels strained. "Could we come in and talk to you for a few minutes?" I tilt my head toward Tom. "This is Johnny's father, Tom Waters."

"Good to meet you, Tom." Russell turns his sharp eyes to the purse in my hand, then looks up at me. "I'm glad you got your purse. Sally wanted me to take it inside, but I was afraid you'd think it was stolen when you came back."

"Elena fell in the river last night," Tom says. "She was swept a mile downstream. I'm surprised you didn't send anyone out to look for her."

I put a restraining hand on his arm. "It's not his fault, Tom."

Russell's face remains expressionless as he digests the information. He lifts his chin toward the dark room behind him. "Maybe you better come in."

We follow him to a small dark kitchen and sit at a table while he fusses with a kettle on the stove. Bunches of brown, withered herbs hang from the ceiling, with clumps of dirt clinging to the roots. The kitchen smells musty, like a cellar, and through an open back door I can see an attached greenhouse, crowded with plants.

"We thought the heat was too much for you," Russell says. "That happens sometimes with newcomers. They leave, they come back."

"Did you see anyone follow me out?" I ask.

He puts three cracked mugs on the table in front of us and gives me a puzzled look. "We all came out together, after we finished singing."

"There weren't any strangers hanging around when you came out? Anyone who looked suspicious?" My hands have tightened into fists, and I put them in my lap.

"The only strangers I saw last night were you and your friend."

"What friend?" Tom's voice is sharp.

"Alison," I tell him. "She drove me down here, but she didn't want to sweat with us, so she left."

Russell pours a liquid that smells like licorice from the kettle into our mugs. "Maybe you better tell me what happened to you, Elena."

"After I left the sweat lodge, I lay down in the shallows of the river. Someone came up behind me and dragged me out deeper and shoved my face underwater."

A stillness comes over Russell's face. "Who?"

"I couldn't see his face. Or hers. It could have been a woman. I bit his thumb. That's how I got away."

He puts the kettle back on the stove and returns to the table. "Was it a big thumb? Little?"

I shrug, feeling foolish. "Medium."

A fat gray cat walks into the room, waving its tail like a wand, then leaps on Russell's lap, and he strokes it absentmindedly as he looks at me. His inspection is frank, the look of someone who's willing to listen without judgment. "Could you taste anything when you bit it?"

"I was underwater. I tasted the river."

"There was a full moon," Tom says suddenly. "Why couldn't you see his face?" He says this gently, the way he might question a child.

Reaching for my mug, I clutch the warmth of it in both hands as I close my eyes and try to remember exactly what happened. Uncomfortable sensory details begin to surface as I cast my mind back to the moment when I was in the river. First there was that odd paralysis brought on by the chill of the water, and then those hands, lifting me up by the armpits, dragging me to the deeper current. Then I remember wet fabric under my fingers as I thrashed in the water.

"I think there was something over his face, like a stocking, or a ski mask. And he was wearing a sweatshirt, a black sweatshirt, with the hood up." When I think of the river, and those hands pushing my face under the water, it's like a sliver of ice sliding down my back. Irrationally the thought of Alison flashes through me, a memory of her large hands, her square-tipped fingers, smoothing the map we found in Johnny's closet across her knee.

The cat stares at me, pupils wide in yellow irises, then blinks and looks away.

After a long silence Russell taps the rim of his cup. "This tea is made from osha root. Good for the lungs, good for stress. Johnny helped me collect it, up near Angel Fire. He liked to drink osha after a sweat. Go on—it'll make you feel better."

Obediently I take a sip of the strong, honeyed tea. "Sally never told me how she met Johnny. Do you know?"

"Sally makes Indian costumes. Very expensive, lots of beading, hand-stitched doeskin. It can take her a year to make a coat. Johnny ordered one for his next tour, and I guess they got to talking about Lakota traditions."

Tom turns the mug in his hand but doesn't drink. "Did he come here regularly to sweat with you?"

Russell leans back in his chair, which lets out an alarming creak, and the cat leaps off his lap. "Enough to learn the songs. He had a quick ear."

"Sally told me he always prayed for strength," I say. "She said it sounded like he was getting ready to do something that scared him. Something dangerous."

He grunts. "Sally has a big mouth. What we pray for in the sweat lodge shouldn't leave the circle."

I stare at him, unmoved. "Johnny's dead. Telling his secrets won't hurt him now."

Russell studies me for a beat of silence. "I think you know better than that, Elena. Johnny's spirit is alive. You heard him speak to you last night, didn't you? There were sparks in the air. When a spirit is strong, there are sparks."

Tom's mouth tightens, and when he speaks the edge is back in his voice. "I really don't think it's a great idea to encourage Elena to believe she can talk to Johnny."

Russell turns his mild gaze on Tom. "Our people have been talking to spirits for thousands of years. It isn't a bad thing to be comforted by those who leave us."

Tom pushes his chair back from the table, stands, carries his cup to the sink and pours the tea down the drain.

"I thought I was hallucinating those sparks," I confess.

Russell's eyes are calm. "What did Johnny tell you?"

"He told me I was in danger. He told me to run."

"I'd say he was right," Russell says.

"I'd say this is horseshit," Tom says, bracing his hands on the sink. "You should have looked for her last night. She could have died."

Russell takes a sip of tea from his mug, then puts the mug down on the table. He folds his hands in his lap and closes his eyes for a moment, as if he wants to consider his words before he speaks. When he finally opens his eyes again he looks directly at me, with that same open gaze, warm and comforting as a touch.

"We respect suffering in our culture. Deprivation, thirst, heat, solitude, any kind of physical trial—these can give the seeker important visions. To interfere with your quest for a vision would have been unthinkable for us. If someone in our circle embraces suffering, we support the choice for the gift it can bring." His black eyes remain fixed on me, and again I have that sense of timelessness, that deep familiarity with the light behind his eyes. "I believe you're wiser now than you were yesterday, Elena. You touched your enemy."

"And he almost killed her," Tom says. "You count that a success?"

"Of course. She's still alive, Tom. If she was destined to meet him, I'm glad she met him here. This is a good place. A holy place. She was protected here."

"She could have drowned!"

"But she didn't. Elena won her first battle, left her first mark. And the river carried her to safety."

"No thanks to you," Tom mutters.

Russell's lips curve in a smile, but his gaze remains on me. "Help will come when she needs it. We have given her our most powerful gift."

My throat feels tight. "What gift is that?"

"Our blessing. Our protection. Our prayers for you to find the help you need along the way." Slowly he pushes himself up from his seat and rises to walk over to Tom, who continues to grip the sink with his back toward us. Russell places a hand on his shoulder and speaks in a low voice. "Elena has chosen this path, and she takes this journey not only for herself but for all of us who loved Johnny. For you, Tom. And for me."

Chapter Seven

As I stand in the driveway and contemplate Tom's house, the past creeps up and leans over my shoulder, breathing memories into me while the leaves on the cottonwoods chatter in the morning wind, and a horse whinnies in the pasture beyond. This was my home for ten years, and I loved it. Walls two feet thick, warm in winter, cool in summer. Back then it was a trim adobe surrounded by lush, healthy flowers and shrubs, and it hurts to look at the yard now, like looking at a neglected child. There used to be a set of lawn furniture, not to mention a lawn, and a jungle gym that Tom spent one long Christmas Eve assembling in the garage. All these accessories have vanished, and the house looks like it belongs to a bachelor who never even thought about having kids. The flowerbeds are overgrown with cheat grass, the windows are dirty, and the honeysuckle I planted along the east wall is gone. For a moment I wonder if it died or if Tom dug it up, just to get rid of the last trace of me.

Tom unlocks the front door and we walk into a living room that's almost bare. No couch, no recliner, no rugs, no piano. All that's left is a wall full of books, a desk, a computer, an old-fashioned floor lamp, and a Taos day bed with a Pendleton blanket folded at one end. Across the room the kitchen still occupies the east wall, and smells like stale coffee. He's kept the big oak table that used to be the heart of our house, but otherwise there are few reminders of the past.

The light falls across the floor in the same dappled pattern, though, and motes of dust float in the shafts of sunshine. When I focus on the dust dancing in the light, I can almost see us, out of the corner of my eye, the way we were back then: the rugs covered with blocks and crayons, Johnny's kindergarten watercolors taped to the walls, the rooms filled with the sweet domestic squalor of our family. I can almost see Johnny, sitting at the piano, feet not touching the floor, pounding the keys with a terrible intensity that seemed like such a gift at the time.

In our old bedroom the windows face east and south, and at this hour, morning sun spills across the bed. When I look out into the back yard I see a charred hole in the weeds, where a blackened piece of metal lies propped up against a heap of charred wood. Long strands of wire curl around the metal, filaments that have twisted in the heat of the fire. With a jolt I realize I'm looking at the sounding board for our old piano.

"I took an ax to it," Tom says, standing next to me, looking out at the fire pit.

"That was a good piano," I say sadly. "We paid a lot for it."

"Too much, probably." He examines my face. "Do you play anymore?"

"Sometimes. Not since he was killed, though."

"You were good, El."

I smile, touched by his effort at praise. "Nothing like Johnny." Out of curiosity I crack open Tom's closet door and see the TV parked inside, gathering dust. "When was the last time you pulled out the television?"

Tom scratches his nose. "A year ago, maybe. I watched the election results."

"For president?"

"Yeah."

"He's been in office two years, Tom."

He shrugs. "Two years, then."

On the top shelf of the closet I see a fat pile of manuscripts, and a few dozen copies of his first book. "Did you ever finish your novel?"

"Right before Johnny died, I sent it off to my old editor at Dutton, and they bought it. It's coming out next September."

"Tom, that's wonderful! Why didn't you tell me before?"

He shrugs and slides his hands in his pockets. "Timing, I guess. We had other things to deal with." A glimmer of a smile hovers at the corner of his mouth. "It's hard for me to believe it's coming out, to tell you the truth. I didn't want to tell anybody about it until I had the real thing in my hand."

"Congratulations," I say. "By God, you did it. You pulled it off."

His eyebrow quirks up. "And it only took eleven years."

I toe off my sneakers and pull back the covers of the bed while he watches, then crawl under the covers without taking off my clothes. The bed is soft, and smells deeply familiar. I settle back against the pillows and look at him. He looks okay. Tired, with those shadows under his eyes, but okay. Perfect, in fact, from my point of view.

Tom stands calm against the wall with his arms folded, watching me. His ankles are crossed. He always had lovely feet, lovely hands, and a graceful way of leaning against a wall. I watch his shoulders, his long legs, his soft hair and dark blue eyes, and wonder why we ever broke up. We know each other. That's why I want him here. We know each other and nothing has to be explained. No one else could understand the depth of what I've lost. No one else knows how much Johnny was a part of me, despite the distance between us. Just looking at Tom brings back a comforting memory of being married to someone I loved, the way it felt before everything went to hell.

After a long silence, Tom walks over to the bed, sits on it and smoothes a stray lock of hair from my forehead. "You sure you don't want a painkiller? I have some Darvon."

Curled up on one side, I stare at his hand on the bed, only inches from my face, and loneliness weighs on me like a stone over my heart. It's been too long since I dared to touch someone, to break out of this self-imposed exile. Suddenly the urge to kiss Tom is a living thing inside my chest, and I take his hand in mine and trace the creases in his palm.

"Are you going to tell me my fortune?" he asks.

I bring his palm to my mouth and kiss it.

"Elena," he whispers. "What are you doing?"

"Come here," I say.

"I am here."

"Closer." Desire mixes with a kind of panic, a fear that he'll leave. I take his hand under the covers, under my shirt, and spread his fingers across my bare breast. I'm not even embarrassed that my skin is ten years older—and the difference between a thirty-two year old breast and a forty-two year old breast is a noticeable difference. I'm still alive, and I feel sexy. For this one little moment I want to do something sexy and dangerous and wild with my ex-husband. I want to feel his hands everywhere on my body. It's a purely selfish, physical need, like hunger.

"Please," I whisper, leaning closer to him, smelling the warm smell of his clothes, taking everything I can get while I can get it.

He removes his hand. "I can't, El." His voice is husky, soft.

"Sure you can." A sweet hot longing rises from the soles of my feet, shooting up my legs.

He laughs, in spite of his armor, but shakes his head. "It took me too long to get over you. I can't go back to that kind of pain."

His back and his arms are the most beautiful things I've ever seen in my life. What do we have to live for that's so important we can't forget ourselves this one time? Everything he says just makes me want him even more.

"I won't tell a soul," I whisper.

"That's not what scares me."

The phone rings, shattering the silence. Tom walks into the other room to pick it up, and I hear his voice through the wall. "Elena" comes up more than once, along with "could have died," "no doctor," and "won't listen." The conversation goes on for several minutes, and I stare at the ceiling and look at spider webs as the one-sided dialogue wanders from "I don't know" to "I'm not sure," into "Maybe," and finally, "We'll see."

Tom appears at the bedroom door, holding a cordless phone. "It's Maggie. She wants to talk to you."

I hold out my hand, and he passes the receiver to me. "Maggie?" I say.

"Tom just told me what happened. Are you really okay?" She sounds breathless, worried.

"I'm okay. A few lumps and bruises, that's all. Did Alison get home all right?"

"Yes, thank God, although it was awfully late when she got in. El, I was petrified when you didn't come back last night."

"Maggie, I'm sorry about Santa Fe. I know you wanted to go—"

"Oh, God, El, that doesn't matter at all, as long as you're really okay. We'll do it another time."

"I feel terrible about worrying you and Jack like this."

"Don't give it another thought. You want to take a nap there? We can send the car around for you later. And the backpacking trip up Santa Barbara Canyon is definitely out, right?"

My hand tightens on the phone. *Johnny would have gone if he were alive.* It's crazy, I know, but I can't help feeling that I can't afford to wait, that I have to go where he would have gone, enter the life he would have lived, or I'll never understand why he died. "I'm fine. I'll be ready to go in the morning, I promise."

"Hold on—Jack wants to say something."

Muffled voices come through the phone, and then I hear Jack's voice. "Hey, kiddo, how are you feeling?"

"I'm fine. A little bruised, that's all."

"We could send over our doctor."

"Thanks, Jack, no, I've already been checked out by a paramedic. I'm fine, really."

"You sure you're still up for the trip?"

"I'm positive. Some time in the mountains, out in the sun, under the trees—it'll be good for me. I'll be ready to go in the morning."

Maggie's voice crackles through the receiver. "I'll send Alison over to pick you up this afternoon."

"Tom can take me back to your place."

"No, you stay there, take a nap, and I'll make sure she's there by two o'clock. Is Tom still there? Let me talk to him."

Tom takes the phone and walks into the living room, while I lean back on the pillows, lift the covers over my face and burrow more deeply into the bed. The sheets smell like his shaving soap, a green herbal bar he used to buy at the local health food store. I close my eyes and pretend he's going to come back in here and climb into bed with me any second now. But the minutes tick by, and the long, hushed conversation in the other room rustles on and on.

When Tom finally reappears he looks embarrassed, and I wonder if I've been the topic of more than one conversation with Maggie.

"What did she say?" I ask.

"She's worried about you, El. We all are." His voice is careful, and he can't quite meet my eyes. "Maybe you should pass up this trip. If you take some time to rest you might feel better."

"I'm fine, Tom. Really." My voice becomes soft, pleading. "I know it must have scared you, getting that call from Jeannie. I'm sorry I made you worry, but I can't just sit at home. Don't ask me to do that, Tom."

His reply is hardly more than a whisper. "You don't have to punish yourself."

Maggie's words, like a cold breath on the back of my neck. "What do you mean?"

He comes closer and sits at the foot of the bed. "Every time you said Johnny ran away from you, I let it slide. But he didn't run away from you, El. He left because you kicked him out."

"That's a lie."

"I'm not saying it was a bad thing. Maybe it was the best thing you could have done for him."

I look away, too angry to speak, while Tom rubs his face with his hands, then looks me in the eye. "He was sixteen, and he knew what he wanted. What was so terrible about that?"

This is a conversation we probably should have had five years ago, and my pulse accelerates as I open my mouth. "You have no idea what he was like. You don't know what happened between us."

He spreads his hands. "Then tell me."

"The last year he was with me, he stopped going to school. I couldn't make him get up, couldn't rouse him out of bed until late afternoon. He put a padlock on his door and wouldn't give me the key. And the people he hung out with, my God, they scared me to death."

"The kids from Juilliard?"

"They weren't kids—they were in their late twenties, early thirties. One of the girls—Krista , she played drums in his band—she was Johnny's best friend." The thought of Krista still makes me shiver. She was thin, pale as a cadaver, with hair as stiff as a man's toupee, dyed a lifeless artificial blue, shaved at the sides. Her tongue was pierced, and she wore a nose ring. The first time I met her she sat on my kitchen counter and lit up a joint without asking me if I minded, then used my favorite cup as an ashtray. Oh, I hated her. I hated her shifty little mascara-encrusted eyes, her black tattooed tears, her pointy, shiny, blood-colored nails.

"Krista was a dealer. Cocaine, mostly, but I think she could get just about anything. They went everywhere together. I couldn't stop him, Tom. He wouldn't listen to me. It was like I didn't even exist anymore. All he wanted to do was play music and hang out with Krista and sleep until four or five in the afternoon."

"Then you did the right thing. Kicking him out was your only option. You don't have to feel guilty about it, El."

"No! I never told you this. I never wanted you to know. He left because of me, because of what I did." I twist the sheet in my hand, unwilling to look at him. "One night I was late getting home from work. When I walked in the door, Johnny came flying out of his room. He was crying. Krista was lying on top of his bed with an empty syringe stuck in her leg. Her face was blue, and she wasn't breathing."

"Jesus." Tom's face is pale, and he reaches out to cover my hand with his.

"I had to give her CPR." The memory of her mouth is still with me, the dark, fetid taste of cigarettes and un-brushed teeth. When her eyes fluttered open I felt relief, at first. The rage came later.

"Did she recover?"

"She was conscious when I went to the kitchen to call an ambulance, and by the time I got off the phone she was gone. I called the police and told them about her. They said they'd pick her up."

"What did Johnny do? Leave with her?"

"No. He stayed. I told him he had to quit the band, told him we'd move to Brooklyn if I ever saw him with her again. I told him I'd called the police."

Tom purses his lips and lets out a puff of air. "I'm sure that went over well."

"He went berserk." My throat constricts at the memory. "He told me he hated me, not because I was his mother, but personally, as a human being. He said I'd never been loyal to anybody, and didn't deserve to have a son. He said he'd rather die than turn into somebody like me."

Tom's eyes are dark, troubled, waiting for me to go on.

"Johnny kept yelling at me, and he wouldn't let up. He was standing so close to me his nose almost touched mine, and he was spraying my face with spit and the vein in his forehead was throbbing—he looked insane, Tom. My God, the noise that came out of him would have killed the houseplants if he'd kept it up. Mrs. McGarrity in the apartment upstairs started pounding on the floor with her cane. And then I lost it." I stop talking and rub my chest as if I could rub out the ache in there.

Tears fill my eyes, and my voice wavers. "I slapped him, Tom. I hit him so hard he fell on the floor."

I don't dare look at him. I go on, stumbling over my words. "Johnny lay on the linoleum and smiled at me like he'd won the war. And he had. I didn't deserve him anymore. I'd cracked. I'd done the one thing I swore I'd never, ever do to him."

"Did you talk to him about it?" Tom asks softly.

"I didn't say anything. I went to the bathroom and knelt down on the rug and stayed there for a minute or two, shaking. I didn't know how I was going to face him. But when I came out he was gone, and his note said he was on his way to Taos. On his way to you."

Tom lets out a long, low groan. "Why didn't you tell me all this five years ago, when I might have been able to do something about it?"

"Don't you get it? I was afraid! I thought if you knew what happened you wouldn't let him come back, and I wanted him back." My voice has run down to a whisper. "I was sure he'd come back."

Tom leans forward, elbows on his knees, his hands loosely clasped in front of him. "He was pissed off when he got here," he says in a small voice. "But he wouldn't talk about it. He looked like a vagrant after hitchhiking all the way from New York. That's what tore me up, thinking about him out there, sixteen years old, hitchhiking across the country."

Every word that comes out of his mouth pierces me with fresh guilt, but I need to hear this. Tom's never talked about it before.

"Johnny lived with me for three months. Three months, and I couldn't take it. He wanted to fight all the time. Told me I was a failure, told me I was weak. Played the piano like it was an animal he was trying to beat up. Noise, just noise. I couldn't stand it. There was no way to talk to him, no way to reason with him. Everything had to be a fight. He wouldn't eat the food I made for us, wouldn't do anything to help me around the house. When he wasn't banging on the piano he was yelling at me. It was like he was determined to stomp me to a bloody pulp before he could walk out the door and live his own life."

"I know what you mean."

"And his friends scared the shit out of me. Lowriders, *pachucos* with homemade tattoos and hairnets, gangbangers, guys who kept switchblades in their boots and guns in their coats. They'd pick him up and he'd vanish for days. I heard rumors about raves up in Taos Canyon where Johnny'd play with one band or another, jamming for hours, strung out on God knows what. He was arrested twice."

"For what?"

"Drunken driving and vandalism. A bunch of those idiots he hung out with decided to spray-paint graffiti all over the chief of police's house one night, while he was inside, asleep."

"Did you punish him?"

"I never hit him, if that's what you mean, but I wanted to, lots of times. I tried to ground him, but that was a joke— he'd walk in and out of here like he owned the place. I yelled at him. Finally I threatened to throw him out if he didn't clean up his act, and the next day he was gone. Three days later Maggie called and told me he was over at their house and wanted to stay. I barely saw him after that." He stares out the window, chin resting on his hand. "El, I was so excited when I saw him here. I thought I was getting my son back. I told all our neighbors he'd moved back in with me." His hand drops, and he looks up at me, his face taut with grief. "But he left me too. It wasn't just you. Something was eating him up inside."

"Why?" I ask. "Why was he like that? You never hurt him."

"I've asked myself that question a million times. I don't know what I did wrong. I don't know."

The remorse I feel is almost unbearable, and I try to think of the right words to say. But there are no right words. Nothing can fix this. Knotting the sheet in my fist, I squeeze until my palms ache. "But it's my fault he's dead, can't you see that? If I'd just stopped listening, if I'd plugged my ears and walked away, he'd be alive now."

Tom's voice is rough with emotion. "You didn't kill him. Some asshole with a gun killed him. Not you."

"Every choice I made brought him closer to that bullet. Johnny was right. I was always afraid of the wrong thing!"

He rakes his hand through his hair until it spikes up from his forehead. "What are you talking about?"

"I'm talking about you! I left you because I was afraid. I was afraid Taos would never be enough for Johnny, and you wouldn't leave it." A strangled sob escapes me. "Do you know how stupid that makes me feel? This is where he finally blossomed. What if I'd stayed here, and we raised him together? Wouldn't everything be different?"

Tom shakes his head impatiently. "Don't do this, El. It'll make you crazy."

"But it's true! I feel so ashamed of the choices I've made I can hardly breathe."

"You have to let it go. You did what you did, and it's over."

It's not over. A savage desire remains in me, and I feed that desire every night. I feed it with images of Johnny as a baby, nursing from my breast, Johnny walking off to school, banging his Batman lunchbox against his leg. I feed it with images of the man he would have become, the future we would have shared. I feed it with the image of a black bullet hole in his chest. And for the first time in my life, I can understand how someone can want vengeance more than food, or breath, or love.

There are afternoon shadows on the wall when I wake up, and as I roll over in Tom's bed, a jarring moment of déjà vu shimmers through me. This used to be our favorite time of day for making love, in the early afternoon, when Johnny was down for his nap and the sunlight fell across the bed just like this, warming our bare skin. Instantly I vault back twenty years to the way it felt to be married to Tom, to belong to him, to be completely wrapped up in marriage and motherhood.

Tom's figure was always vivid in my mind, right down to the muscles of his legs, defined into plump, hard cords of flesh. Abdomen, arm, back and shoulder muscles are still visible on him, as visible as they were when we were just starting out together. In spite of the new lattice of lines around his eyes and mouth, every expression on his face, every posture, every movement is deeply familiar. And yet he remains a mystery, too, concealing hidden depths. There's something hard, hawk-like, and ultimately unknowable about him. I'm attracted to that veiled core in him, the part that can explode into passion.

My clothes are too hot under the sheet, and I shrug them off and kick them to the floor. When I look down I see my pale breasts tipped with pink, the foreshortened, rounded triangles of my thighs, the plum-colored bruise on my hip. I look at my body and think about all the times I had sex with Tom in this bed, and my skin begins to tingle, electrified by memories of his flesh pressed against mine. Some heat-seeking radar in me can feel him, close, only a few feet away in the next room, and the warmth of knowing he's nearby builds in me like a fever. Desire washes over me like a long hot tongue, and I fling my pillow on the floor, embarrassed by my own longing for what I can't have.

It's almost two o'clock. Alison will be here any minute, and I get up and dress quickly, eager to escape the spell of the bed. Outside the window, hummingbirds buzz each other in the hedge of trumpet vine. Beyond the neglected, derelict yard, beyond the line of trees along the *acequia*, the tall blue silhouette of Taos Mountain fills the window.

The view draws me to the window, and I prop my elbows on the sill and stare out at the valley. Somewhere out there the person who killed my boy is washing his car, or drinking a beer, or watching TV. My throat thickens with a deep, primal eagerness to lay my hands on him, wrap my fingers around his neck and squeeze. Somehow I'll find him. There has to be something the police overlooked.

In the front room, Tom reads the *New Yorker* with his feet up on the desk, a pair of spectacles perched low on his nose. I could look at him all day, he's so familiar, so worn and worried and handsome.

"So you wear glasses now?" I ask.

He looks up at me over the tops of his glasses, then folds them into a shirt pocket as he swings his legs off the desk. "Alison's not here yet—you want a cup of tea? A sandwich?"

"Maybe." I'm a little hungry. Amazed that I'm hungry. Amazed that I'm still moving, calm above the surface of my life, surviving. "A sandwich would be good."

He goes to the kitchen, pulls some bread from a cupboard and almond butter from the refrigerator. I sit at our old table and watch him spread almond butter on a piece of bread, then cut up a banana and arrange the wafers on top.

When he hands it to me I take a bite. It's good. He takes a paper towel from the roll above the counter and puts it next to me, then pours a glass of milk and places it on the table before he sits down next to me. For the next few minutes I chew, remembering the comfort of food.

"I'm glad you're hungry. You're too thin, El."

"I know," I say, my mouth full.

"You want some chips or something?"

"This is enough," I say, licking my fingers. And then I look up and see his eyes watching my mouth, my lips, and I put the last bite of the sandwich down on the paper towel. His eyes burn into me, filled with a powerful loneliness, a powerful longing.

We rise slowly to our feet, as if we're already connected. His eyes remain locked to mine, dark eyes from another world, another decade, another century. He reaches out and draws me into the curve of his body and I'm instantly aroused, as aroused as I used to be back in college when I could feel the heat of his gaze on the back of my legs. A thrill of desire flows up my spine as he pulls me closer, leans down and kisses me on the lips. Our eyes remain open for a second or two, watching each other until my eyelids close and the warmth of his mouth becomes everything. His lips are soft. Like silk. Like water. My hands reach for his face, and I fit my body to his body and feel the length of him pressed against me, warm, hungry, wanting me. A wild heat spreads through my chest, through my whole body as he tightens his grip on my waist.

The sound of tires crunching over gravel floats through the open window as a car purrs into the driveway.

Tom releases me, looking like he just lost a bet with himself. I run my hands over my hair, straighten my shirt, take my purse from the chair and walk on wobbly legs toward the door. Outside the house a car door opens, then slams, and footsteps approach.

I can feel him follow me. Tom puts his hands on my shoulders, turns me around, then kisses my forehead. A gentle, chaste, paternal kiss. Not what I wanted, not at all.

"Go," he says, and pushes me out the door.

Chapter Eight

"Maybe you should think about going back to New York," Alison says as we pull out of the driveway.

At first the words don't seem ominous. She says them so lightly, as if she's only stating the obvious. And my mind is half on Tom, and the way my lips tingle from the imprint of his mouth, and the flush of pleasure it provokes somewhere deep inside me. That man can kiss. Part of me wants to gallop right off the edge of caution, dragging the rest of me toward a future that looks too much like the past.

"I can't go back," I say, half to myself.

"You're going to go on looking for whoever killed Johnny?"

With a jolt I come back to her question. "I have to."

"Why doesn't Johnny tell you?"

There's a sarcastic edge to her voice that makes me turn to look at her. She's wearing black jeans and a sleeveless black top that exposes her midriff, and a small silver ring gleams at her navel. Her sunglasses hide her eyes, and her hands grip the leather cover of the steering wheel tightly as she whips around the curves of upper Ranchitos Road.

"Sounds like Maggie's been talking," I say.

"She told me you can hear Johnny. If you can hear him, why doesn't he tell you who shot him?"

She sounds angry, but why? My eyes linger on her hands, on her thumbs. Her fingernails have been painted a flat, opaque black. "Your mom said it was late when you got back from Embudo last night. 'Awfully late,' she said."

Alison fiddles with the radio, selects a hard rock station and pumps the volume.

I put my hand over the power knob and shut it off. "Talk to me, Alison."

She slumps back in her seat, lips compressed. "My mom doesn't have a clue about time. You know that."

"How long did you stay at the river?"

"I went home right after I left you."

"Then you were home by eleven, right? That's not late. Why would your mom think that was late?"

"I don't know. Maybe she didn't know I was home. I don't tell my mother when I come and go." Her tone echoes the stubbornness in her voice last night, when she refused to go into the sweat lodge with me, and I wonder if it has anything to do with why she sounds so pissed off now.

"I wish you'd stayed with me in Embudo," I say.

"So I could sit around with a bunch of Indians in a hut, sweating my brains out? No thanks. They gave me the creeps."

The surliness seems like a cover for something else, but I can't tell what it is and I know there's no way to shake it out of her. When she was a little girl she'd get that hard look to her jaw, and her mouth would tighten the way it does now, until her lips almost disappeared.

Alison turns left on Paseo del Pueblo Norte, and we cruise in silence past the Indian pueblo land to the east. Outside my window miles of sagebrush and wild grass dissolve into the blue rise of Taos Mountain. The peak gleams in the afternoon light, immutable, lofty, serene. The thought drifts through me: I could stay here. Forget Manhattan, forget the job. Manhattan was where I failed at mothering, where I failed as a human being. What's left for me in New York? The market on Forty-second where I get my baby Gruyère and biscotti? The little café where the waiters all know my name and start making my decaf non-fat latte as soon as they see me walk in the door? How many years has it been since I went to a Broadway show, or MOMA, or Lincoln Center, or an art gallery? For me the city has shrunk to the horizon of my computer screen at work. Why go back to New York when I could go on breathing this thin, clear air, go on gazing at horizons that extend for a hundred miles? The landscape looks so real here, so sharp and clear and vivid. The bones of the earth are exposed, and the light is indescribable. No wonder Johnny chose to live here.

"Johnny was miserable in Manhattan, that last year he spent with me," I say, gazing at the line of cottonwoods along the Rio Pueblo. "Then he came out here and moved in with your family and everything changed. He blossomed. Why do you think that happened?"

"He got famous, that's what happened," Alison says. "Fame can perk you right up."

I lean my head against the glass, watching the cows graze in the fields. "Something was bothering him, though, even after he moved out here and built a career. He wouldn't talk about it. I wish I'd pushed him to tell me what it was. I always thought there'd be time for us to get past it, you know? I thought we'd be close again."

"You don't have to beat yourself up about it," she mutters.

"I'm not." I twist in my seat to study her profile. "But I'm curious. I want to know what happened to him. Not just how he died, or why, or who shot him. I want to know about his life. I want to know how he transformed himself from an angry, bitter, screwed-up kid into the person he turned out to be."

"He entered the machine, that's what happened. My parents put him into training, and he trained hard. He knew he couldn't show up stoned or drunk or too tired to work, because he'd be out on his ear. Johnny was ready to get down to it, and he did."

"But why didn't he do that in New York? He could have trained there. He had the program at Juilliard, and his teachers were crazy about him."

"No," Alison says firmly. "This is different. The camp my parents are running here, it's serious. It's big business. And it costs more money than you could believe to groom a star. My mom spent a fortune on publicity and promotion—she has a knack for it, a kind of sixth sense for marketing without overexposing the talent. It's like perfect pitch in this business. And my Dad knows music, knows trends before they happen, what's on the way out, what's on the way in, what songs are going to make it, what won't. The things they did for Johnny—there's no way he could have done it for himself."

"It sounds like a hell of a lot of pressure on Johnny."

She gives me a look, eyes unreadable behind her dark glasses, lips tight as a seam. "It was. It was never easy for him to live up to that level of expectation. You get that much energy pushed on you, it can explode." Her voice drains away to a mumble. "Trust me. There are things about Johnny's life you really don't want to know."

A tingle of fear slides down my back, the same fear I felt when Maggie hinted at the same thing. "Allie, whatever I find out about him can't be worse than his murder. Please, tell me. I want to know. I need to know."

"Johnny was in the wrong place at the wrong time, that's all. And the sooner you get that and go home, the better off you'll be."

The reflection in the curved surface of her sunglasses reveals nothing but my own distorted face. "I can't just sit around in Manhattan, waiting for news—the detective on the case won't even talk to me anymore. I'll go crazy."

"You don't think it's crazy to jump in the river in the middle of the night? You could have died! Is that what you wanted?"

I try to keep my tone light. "I was attacked, Alison. It wasn't something I planned."

She gives me a contemptuous glance. "Sure."

"What's the matter with you?" I snap. "Why are you acting like I'm guilty of something?"

By now her face is flushed with anger. "I know about the overdose, Elena."

It's a sucker punch, and I should have seen it coming. I turn away, lean my forehead against the cold glass and stare at the blur of sage, but I don't see the landscape sliding by the window. Instead I see the green walls of my room on the fifth floor of St. Andrews Hospital, and the harsh disinfectant smell of that room fills my head, an olfactory hallucination that makes my pulse start to race.

"It was an accident," I say.

"You ate too many pills. No one forced you to do that, did they? No one *attacked* you?"

It was dusk when Tom called to tell me Johnny was dead. Ten past six on a Monday night, March twenty-first. The first day of spring. Salsa from a radio next door drifted through the wall, while the refrigerator hummed at my back. I held the phone pressed tight to my ear and flicked the light switch on and off, on and off, over and over, trying to grasp what Tom was telling me. Someone's laughter came from upstairs, and a horn blared in the street. Normal sounds. Ordinary sounds. But I would never be normal or ordinary again.

"I was in shock, Alison. Can't you understand that?"

"Sure I understand. You wanted out."

"It wasn't like that. I had a headache. It felt like someone was pounding a nail through the center of my forehead." Just thinking about that pain now makes me shiver. It was the worst thing I'd ever felt, worse than childbirth, and it ripped through my skull like a river of acid.

"There was a bottle of brandy in the kitchen, and I had a drink. Maybe two or three drinks, I don't know, maybe more. And then I took some Tylenol," I say.

"You took a hundred extra strength gel-tabs, for Christ's sake! They had to pump your stomach. You think I don't know about that? My parents paid a fortune to keep it out of the papers." Her voice is thick with tears.

Extra strength gel-tabs. Even the sound of those words can make me shudder. I remember the sensation of eating them, how hard and round and bright and shiny they were, like candy. "Pain Reliever," the label said, but after I ate a few handfuls the pain grew worse and spread like a fast licking fire to my belly. The cramps that followed made me groan so loudly that one of my neighbors called 911.

For seven long days I lay in a hospital bed, too stunned to weep, forced to drink a tall glass of antidote every few hours. It was a thick, foul-tasting poison of another kind, designed to unbind the toxin from my liver, but it felt like a punishment for all the things I'd left undone, all the things I'd neglected to do. Of course I should have gone to Taos when Johnny ran away from me, at the first sign that he wasn't going to return. I should have kidnapped him. I should have taken him back.

My hands are sweaty, and I wipe them on my jeans. "I promise you, Alison, I don't want to die. I'm okay. I'm really okay. I'm just trying to get through the days like everybody else."

"By throwing yourself in the river? Look, I don't care what you do to yourself. Go ahead. It's really none of my business, is it?" Her voice wavers and cracks on the last sentence.

"Listen to me. This is important. Last night, when I was clinging to that dead tree in the middle of the river—it was beautiful, Alison. It was the most beautiful night I've ever seen. Even though I was freezing and stuck and didn't know if I'd make it out alive, it was so beautiful it felt like a dream, with the moonlight shining on the rocks, and the water flowing around me like silver. You know what Tolstoy said? He said life was God, and to love life was to love God. And last night I could feel what he meant. It felt like the whole world was alive, everything, the rocks, the water, the sky, the stars, and I was alive and maybe I had no right to be alive, but I was, I am, and I want to stay that way. Oh, I know it sounds crazy, but Allie, please believe me. I want to live."

We draw up to the tall iron gate of the compound and come to a halt. Alison raises her sunglasses and glances at me, revealing the shadows under her eyes, the blasted look of grief. An ache of tenderness washes over me as I reach out and stroke the hair back from her forehead.

"I'll be careful," I say, and take her hand in mine, clasp her palm to my palm and intertwine our fingers. "I promise." And then I nod in the old way, up and down two times, each move exaggerated, a cartoon of reassurance.

The pool is still, empty, a perfect rectangle of sapphire blue, shimmering in the June sunlight. The windows on the backside of the main house are dark, shuttered against the heat. Even the birds are silent, and the entire compound seems deserted until I see Maggie in the shade of the portal, sitting in a wrought iron chair with her back toward me. She's wearing cream linen slacks and a sleeveless ivory blouse, and her hair glows like the gold bracelet on her wrist.

Maggie's shoulders are shaking, and it takes me a moment to realize she's crying.

When she hears my footsteps, she leaps from the chair and whirls around, hand over her heart, eyes wide as she catches sight of me. And then her expression changes from shock to relief, and she walks toward me and crushes me to her body. "Oh, El, thank God you're all right. I was so worried."

Her body is warm, solid, comforting, and I hold her for a minute until she settles against me, then releases me with a final squeeze. With a nervous laugh she dabs her lower lids, a practiced gesture to avoid smudging her eyeliner. "I'm sorry." Her blue eyes gaze up at me, wide and fragile as she blinks away fresh tears. "You know you're my best friend on earth, don't you? If anything happened to you, I don't know what I'd do."

Between the two of us, Maggie was always the strong one, the sturdy one, and to see her this upset makes me queasy, as if the earth were moving underfoot. If she was thinking about me, why did she look so shocked when I appeared? Something about her emotion feels off, and I can't help feeling as though I've walked in on a grief that's more raw and private than her fear of losing me.

Maggie seems to read my thoughts, and lets out a shaky laugh. "The truth is, I've been going out of my mind because I can't find Jack. The phone's been ringing off the hook, musicians are pissed, he's already missed six appointments today, and we're supposed to leave tomorrow for the hike. Other producers are sniffing around the bands we have under contract, filling their heads with talk about Jack going through a mid-life crisis, telling them to bail out now. And I can't find him anywhere. He just skipped out without a word."

Maggie takes my arm and draws me closer. "And when you didn't come back last night . . ." She draws her hand down the side of my face, cups my chin tenderly and looks into my eyes. "I couldn't take it if anything happened to you now. I mean it. Please, stay close to us. Don't take any more crazy chances. No more midnight rides, okay?"

"I'm all right, Maggie."

She pulls herself up, takes a deep breath, pats my arm and smiles. "I know, honey. It'll be good to get away from this crazy place for a few days, get up in the mountains, away from everything." She searches my face anxiously. "You're sure you're feeling well enough for the hike tomorrow?"

I roll my eyes. "How many times do I have to say it?"

"Okay, okay. I know I'm just an old mother hen, but I worry. I promise I won't ask you again. You know we have all the stuff you'll need, right? Boots, tent, pack, water bottles— just let me know if there's anything else you might want and we'll go get it for you. You need anything, just ask." Wordlessly she reaches out to hold me again, and folds me into her arms.

"Maggie, take it easy." I laugh and pull away. "Alison already gave me the third degree. I don't need any more mothering today."

She tilts her head and studies my face. "Really? What did she say?"

"Apparently she thinks what happened to me last night was a cry for help. You didn't put that idea in her head, did you?"

She lifts her hand, palm out. "I just told her what Tom told us. She must have drawn her own conclusions."

"Well, tell her I'm not about to do anything stupid, would you? From now on, I'm on vacation."

A look of relief flickers across Maggie's face. "Good. I'll

tell her." She glances at the house and lowers her voice, as if someone might overhear us. "So what else did she say?"

I study her, wishing I had her talent for worming the truth out of anyone who might have information she wanted. "She said there were things about Johnny I really didn't want to know."

Maggie's face tightens in a smile, but her eyes remain watchful. "Really."

"It sounds like the two of them were pretty close. Alison said they went out a few times."

"They dated for a while," she says in a low voice. "Then it was over, and she wouldn't talk about it. But I think she was really in love with him." She glances again at the house. A flutter of movement in one of the windows catches her eye, and she straightens her shoulders and takes a step back from me. Her face becomes a pleasant mask as her voice returns to a normal volume. "You sure you don't want to borrow any camping gear?"

I shake my head, taking the hint. "I need to shower and change. I'll see you later, okay?"

"I'm counting on it," she says.

When I open the door of the guesthouse, the air inside holds the scent of a stranger, the palpable sense that someone else is here. A creak emanates from the bedroom, and I stiffen.

"Who's there?" I call out.

There are footsteps, and Jack fills the doorway to the bedroom, clothes disheveled, eyes puffy. He's barefoot, and a pair of tasseled loafers dangles from his left hand.

"Ah. You're back," he says, wiping at his eyes with his cuff. "Sorry, El—I thought you were still at Tom's. I was trying to catch a nap."

"Jesus, Jack. You scared me to death. What's wrong with your own bed?"

He gives me a rueful smile as he drops his shoes and slides his feet into them. "Too many people know where it is. I didn't think anyone would find me out here."

Something about the expression on his face makes me look at him more carefully. His eyes look bleary, and his face is pale, haggard with strain. He stares at the floor for a few seconds, as if he's lost in a daze, and then to my utter amazement his face crumples, and he covers his eyes with both hands as his shoulders start to quiver.

Helpless, I walk over to him and lay my hand on his shoulder as his body quakes with grief. What the heck is going on around here? In all my life, I have never seen this man cry.

Jack shakes his head violently, as though to deny the tears, then wipes his face on his shirtsleeves. "I can't believe I'm doing this in front of you, of all people. As if you don't have enough on your plate! God, I feel like a shmuck."

I stroke his back for a moment. "Hey. You're allowed."

His bloodshot eyes seek out mine. "I just can't believe he's gone."

I nod, feeling the ache, not wanting to feel it.

Jack takes a deep breath, then stares out the window with his arms crossed tightly, hugging himself. "Right after Johnny died, everything went down the tubes. Maggie won't admit it, but we're finished. The business, the marriage—I'm done, El. I can't go on like this."

At a loss for words, I stand there, holding the silence.

Jack heaves a deep sigh, his gaze fixed on the perfectly framed view of the mountain. "Christ! Listen to me." He gathers himself with visible effort, squares his shoulders, and for the first time really looks at me. "What about you? Are you okay?"

"I'm fine."

"You're sure?"

I smile. "I'm fine, Jack. I promise."

"And you're sure you want to go camping with us? It's not too late to cancel."

"I'm looking forward to it."

"Birthdays," he mutters. "I'm getting so fucking old, it's a pain in the ass. Every year I think, I can't walk up that goddamn mountain again, please, don't make me do it. But that's the beginning of the end, isn't it? You flake out on a little camping trip, next thing you know you start boring people at parties with talk about your bad knees, your high blood pressure, your fucking cholesterol count. You start spiking your bourbon with Maalox."

"You're only forty-two, Jack. You have a few years left."

He sighs. "At least it's not the monsoon season yet. You remember the last time we all went up there?"

There's no protection against memory. Anything can trigger it—sight, sound, smell—or the mention of a camping trip that took place ten years ago. Johnny was with us the last time we walked up Santa Barbara Canyon, and it grips my heart to remember how he shuddered on the trail when the thunder boomed, then looked back at me to make sure I didn't notice. He was ten years old, slim and blond and beautiful. Strangers used to walk up and tell me he was the most beautiful child they'd ever seen.

Jack takes in the look on my face. "I wouldn't blame you if you were angry at us," he says quietly. "He died on our watch."

"It wasn't your fault."

"He took risks, El, and we couldn't stop him. He went jogging at night in a county full of drunks and guns. Everywhere he went, he took crazy chances."

There's no argument I can make, because we both know it's true. Johnny always lived in extremes, moving too fast, talking too loud, sleeping twelve, thirteen hours a night or staying up for days at a time. He could eat enough for a football team or skip meals for a week. Ever since he was born, he courted disaster.

"Do you think he wanted to die?" I ask.

His face softens. "He wanted to live. He just wanted to live on the edge."

The gentleness of his expression reminds me of the first time I met Jack all those years ago, when he was a fresh-faced eighteen-year-old who barely needed to shave. The air seemed to crackle around Maggie when she saw him for the first time, and from then on, no other boy existed for her.

Jack was shrewd enough to realize Maggie possessed exactly the kind of ruthless charm that would become such an asset to him later. He had the golden ear, but she had the golden tongue, and an amazing ability to ingratiate herself with those in power. Eventually Maggie would learn how to purr into a phone and put together deals with the big boys in the record companies, multimillion dollar contracts that would have been impossible without her powers of persuasion. Jack hated the politics of the music business, the casual graft and ego-stroking necessary to land a deal. With Maggie on his team, he didn't need to be a salesman. Jack loved music, and Maggie loved Jack. Until now, they'd been the perfect team.

The silence thickens between us as I stand there, still holding my purse, suddenly exhausted and ready to be alone. Should I offer him a cup of tea? I don't want to make him tea.

I want to shower and change, but I can't do these things if Jack is brooding in the living room.

After a minute or two he walks to the piano and presses a black key, and the mournful sound fills the room. He sits on the piano bench and looks up at me. "Maggie said you talk to Johnny."

Inwardly sighing, I turn away to sling my purse on the couch. "You're not going to ask me to talk to a shrink, are you? Everybody around here seems to think I need one."

Jack looks down at the piano and rubs the ivory of middle C without depressing the key. "I don't think you're deluded, El. Anyone else, yeah, maybe, but you were always pretty down to earth. If you say you hear him, I believe you."

Surprised, I stare at him. "Thanks."

His voice is soft. "So what does he say?"

I look out at the mountain, at the clouds hanging in the bright afternoon sky. "Little things. Comforting things, mostly." I make a wry face. "He says I should stop trying to find out who killed him."

Jack is still, listening intently. "Good advice."

"I can't give up, Jack."

He gives me a small, closemouthed smile. "I never expected you to."

There's another awkward pause as I wait for him to make some gesture toward leaving, but he doesn't move. I contemplate the door, then Jack, who shows no sign of ever wanting to get up off the piano bench.

Slowly, reluctantly, I say, "I can come back later if you want to finish your nap."

Jack rubs his face with both hands. "No, I should get out of your hair. But thanks for listening to me, El. You get some rest." He rises from the bench and walks over to me, kisses my cheek, gives the room one last glance, and then he's gone.

As I look around the room, I realize for the first time that it's spotless. The books Alison and I took down have all been replaced on their shelves, and the kitchen is tidy, the faucets gleaming. In the bedroom the bed is made and the coverlet shows only a slight hollow where Jack lay down for his nap. Everything else in the room has been straightened, put away, vacuumed and dusted.

I walk back out to the living room, feeling oddly uneasy, unable to settle down. First Alison, then Maggie and Jack—they were all acting jumpy and weird. This has to be about something more than my escapade last night.

The glow of a tiny red light gleaming in the bookshelf of the living room catches my eye, and when I walk closer I see it's the power indicator light for a tape player. Jack must have turned it on. A cassette fills the window of the tape compartment, and out of curiosity I press the "Play" button.

Suddenly Johnny's voice floods the house. Loud, enthused, as real as if he were alive and standing next to me. The hair on my arms lifts into a wash of goose bumps.

"The physics of the piano are totally different from the guitar—the guitar limits you to the rhythms it offers," his voice booms.

My heart knocks against my ribs, and I shut off the power and stare at the machine. A few seconds later I turn it back on, adjusting the volume as the tape rolls on.

"A piano is a beast. It's huge, eighty-eight keys, and it has a big, wild sound. When I'm composing it feels like it could bite my fingers off."

The voice of his interviewer is young and feminine. "You've been compared to any number of singer/ songwriters, from Jerry Lee Lewis to Thom Yorke. How would you describe your music?"

Johnny's voice is quiet, thoughtful, slightly deeper than

the speaking voice I remember, and my eyes fill with tears as he goes on talking. "I was born in a small town—Taos, New Mexico—and I grew up on popular music. Every Saturday night I sat in my bedroom and wrote down the titles of the Top 20, cheering for my heroes, hissing the villains. I knew I wanted to be one of those guys. All I ever wanted was to write songs that were real, songs that could thread their way into people's lives, so they could feel their own memories, their own ideas."

He clears his throat, and I can hear the fatigue in his voice, the wear and tear from singing for hours at a stretch, in smoky clubs, in freezing air conditioning, in open air stadiums. It clutches at my heart, that fatigue, and I stand there, pinched by longing, drinking in the work-roughened voice of my boy.

"If I dig inside myself and find out who I am, I think that makes my songs useful for other people, helps them find out who they are."

The woman's tone is delicately flirtatious. "You're so young—only twenty-one—"

"Twenty-two in July."

"Aren't you amazed by the fame you've already achieved?"

"I'm amazed all the time."

"But you keep on touring, writing, singing like there's no tomorrow."

"Tomorrow—well, there are no guarantees about tomorrow, are there? I might get hit by a bus. In the meantime I want to sing as if this is my last night on earth."

The tape spools to an end and clicks off. Overwhelmed, I sit in the chair at his desk, tears pooling in my eyes. Twenty-one, I think. Dead at twenty-one. It's a long time before I can move.

The house is silent, but after a while the silence begins to feel spooky, and my skin crawls with the feeling that someone, somewhere, is watching me. I go to the kitchen, open the pantry door and stare at shelves full of cans and boxes. No one's hiding in there. The coat closet in the hallway next to the living room reveals nothing more than an ironing board and an iron on the shelf overhead. Feeling foolish, I grip the handle of the iron and heft it in my hand. My mind flashes to the hand that pressed my face underwater last night, and I tighten my grip on the curved plastic handle. The iron is reassuringly heavy, and I hold it in front of me as I go back to search the bedroom.

No one lurks behind the bathroom door, or hides behind the pebbled glass of the shower door. The linen closet holds only linen, and when I peer under the bed no one stares back at me. No feet skulk under the floor-length curtains, nobody crouches behind the dresser. I'm alone in the house.

Then I notice a narrow door in the bedroom, a door I never saw until now. It's closed, but not all the way. Unlatched, it sticks out half an inch from the wall. My fingers squeeze the handle of the iron as I tiptoe toward it with my elbow cocked, the iron over my head, ready to strike whoever is inside. I fling open the door.

Johnny stands there grinning at me.

Gasping, I stumble back and sit down hard on the bed as the iron drops from my hand. The breath goes out of my lungs, and my body hums with shock.

It's a life-sized cardboard cutout, a full color blowup of his figure. I stare at the young man in front of me, a man who looks like an older brother to the boy I remember.

Decked out in a long leather coat—Sally's?—Johnny's bare chest gleams with sweat, and his blond hair looks wet and hangs in strings. In his ragged Levi's and knee-high boots, he's taller than I would have expected. His jaw seems larger, hardened in a man's face, and a world of experience is written in his eyes. His face looks sly, sexy, his lips twisted in the same crooked grin I remember, his eyes full of secrets.

I sit on the bed for a long time, looking at his image. This powerful figure bears no resemblance to the autopsy photos, and a chill steals down my spine at the sight of him, so whole and real and tangible, standing there looking at me.

Outside the window there's a sudden loud scraping sound, and I bolt from the bed and peer through the curtains. A gardener rakes the gravel path, his face hidden by the shadow of his hat.

My heart hammers like a fist on the door, and I flee the bedroom. A burst of adrenaline detonates in my veins as I rush out the front door and race across the lawn, desperate for the reassurance of another human face.

The back door to the main house is unlocked, the kitchen empty. Walking quickly past broad granite counters, I push through two swinging doors into an enormous formal dining room. There are Flemish tapestries on the walls, chairs upholstered in silk, a table made from some exotic dark wood, and a long Oriental runner on the floor.

No one is around: no maids, no Jack, no Maggie, no Alison. Where is everybody? I trot through the dining room, down a hallway, past another vacant room, then another hallway, on and on, through acres of empty space. Panicked by the deserted house, I sprint up the curved staircase in the foyer, cross the thick carpet of the landing and head for the first closed door.

Knocking produces no response, but the door swings open to reveal an immense bedroom, full of light and color, a soft, inviting space. Two couches face each other in front of a large marble fireplace, with an easy chair and ottoman angled to catch the view of the mountains. Several faded kilims adorn the floor, and a king-sized bed with a delicately embroidered satin duvet is sheltered under swags of silk.

"Wow," I say, under my breath.

Tentatively I move under a curved arch into a large adjoining room, a room that's bigger than my living room back in Manhattan, but it must be Maggie's dressing room. The walls are an exquisite expanse of bird's-eye maple, and one side is dominated by a huge mirror with an ornate gilt frame. When I touch a gold handle on the wall, a door springs open silently and a light goes on inside the cabinet, illuminating about a hundred pairs of women's summer shoes, elegantly arrayed on cedar shelves.

And then I hear Maggie's voice as she walks into the bedroom from the hall. "That son of a bitch expects to get away with this kind of *shit!* I won't put up with it!"

Automatically I shrink back against the door of the cabinet, which closes without a sound. Slinking to the corner of the dressing room, I press my back against the wall.

"Maggie, you know we can't get rid of him. We have to handle this some other way." It's Jack's voice.

"Screw handling it!" she shouts. "I'm so fucking sick of this, Jack. All this pretending. I can't stand it! We have to let him know he can't control us."

From my niche in the corner of the closet, I can see both of them in the mirror, facing each other. They could see my reflection too, if they turned only slightly, but they're focused intently on each other.

"How do we do that?" Jack's voice is weary. "Tell me. I'd really like to know. If you have any ideas, I'm all ears."

Maggie sits down heavily on the couch and stares out the window. "I'll leave. I swear to God, I'll leave."

Jack stands behind her and puts his hand on her shoulder. "What about Alison?"

There's a long silence, and then Maggie says in a small, whipped, utterly defeated voice, "I know."

My pulse drums in my ears as I stare at their reflections. There's no trace of sorrow in either of them now. They're a team, with a common enemy.

"Does Elena know?" Jack asks. My heart nearly stops, I'm listening so hard.

"I don't think she knows anything," Maggie says. "But she suspects something's not right."

"What do you think we should do?"

"We have to go on pretending."

"Do you want me to talk to him?" Jack asks.

There's a long pause, and then a muttered response. "It won't do any good."

Jack kisses the top of her head. "I have to go back to the studio—Jerry's been up all night doing the rough mixes. The band finished the backing tracks for fourteen songs, put final vocals on three and guide vocals on six more. I promised I'd give them a listen."

"Go," she says, and he walks out the door, closing it softly behind him.

A rush of heat passes over my face as I watch her. Why do they need to pretend in front of me? Why are they worried about what I suspect? I walk out into the bedroom, feeling like my head is on fire.

Maggie bolts from the couch when she sees me. Her mouth opens, but nothing comes out.

"What's going on, Maggie?"

"What are you doing here?"

"Why did you say you'll have to go on pretending?" There's an angry hum in my head, like a swarm of bees looking for something to attack.

Slowly, she lowers herself to sit on the ottoman and leans

133

forward, grasping her knees in front of her, then starts rocking back and forth, her face blank. Finally she looks up at me. "Elena, I really wish you could forget everything you just heard."

I kneel on the carpet in front of her and clutch her arm. "For God's sake, Maggie, just tell me what this is all about."

She looks away from me and goes on rocking, back and forth, lips quivering, her breathing uneven in the dense silence between us. My pulse drums in my ears as I wait for her to speak, and I squeeze her arm as if I could squeeze the truth out of her.

When she finally opens her mouth the words come slowly, reluctantly. "We're being blackmailed."

I let go and sit back on my heels. "Why?"

Her gaze shifts to the window, and when she speaks again her voice is almost inaudible. "I can't tell you that, El. Trust me, it has nothing to do with you."

"Then why did Jack ask you if I knew anything?"

Her voice hardens. "Because you've been acting like a goddamn detective ever since you got here. Tearing apart the guesthouse, running off to Embudo, pumping Alison for information. And now I find you hiding in my closet, eavesdropping on us! Look, I know you've been through a lot, but you have to believe me. This has nothing to do with you."

Her objections mean nothing to me, not now, not with so much at stake. "Who's blackmailing you?"

There is a tiny hesitation. "He's a reporter." Maggie's shoulders sag. "One of our musicians did something really stupid, and now we're paying the price because this sleazebag from the tabloids found out about it. Jack wants to go on paying him, but I think it's just a matter of time before it all comes out." She slides a covert glance at me, then shifts her gaze to the view.

The earnest look on her face takes me back thirty years, to my parents' apartment in Brooklyn; when Maggie projected a heartbreaking sincerity whenever she lied to my mother to get us out of trouble. Maggie's a wonderful actor, and she always lied well, fluently. She knows how to lie with a catch in her voice, as if she's confessing. Or she can lie with a cool, defiant anger, and most people believe her.

But I know this woman. We started out in a playpen together, skinned our knees together, learned our multiplication tables together, dropped out of college together. We have the same battle scars. We struggled through childhood, braved our enemies, fell in love with our husbands and bore our children together.

I know things about her nobody else does, and I know that she's lying.

She looks at me, and reads the disbelief in my eyes. Something flashes across her face, something so fleeting I almost miss it, a wild and despairing gleam of panic. Her eyes fill with tears as she shakes her head slowly from side to side. But I know Maggie too well not to see the thoughts that flicker, race, and dive for cover. "I can't talk about it, El. I really can't. If you care about me at all, you'll drop it."

Her voice is firm. She lifts her chin and her eyes hold mine. We go on staring at each other for five or six seconds, and the silence widens like an abyss between us. Gradually her mouth tightens into the same compressed line I saw in Alison's face an hour ago, and her eyes become opaque, flat, almost hostile, as if a thin steel barrier has shuttered down between us.

Slowly I rise from the floor, and Maggie lifts herself from the ottoman and stands in front of me with her arms crossed tightly against her chest, drawing herself up to her full height.

One look at her tells me that whatever secrets she's keeping, they'll remain hidden behind the locked door inside her.

Chapter Nine

In the morning Tom drives me to the trailhead in his battered old Ford pickup. Jack leads us up the deeply rutted Forest Service road in his Range Rover, through Ponderosa pines and dark stands of Douglas fir. The tall trees cast long shadows over the road, crowding out sunlight and erasing the horizon as we ascend. At ten thousand feet, the breeze coming through the open window carries the chill of the forest, and I hug my arms against my chest, nagged by a sense of dread as the truck jolts and grinds its way up the dirt road.

Tom steals a glance at me when he thinks I'm not looking. "You want to tell me what's bugging you?"

"What makes you think something's bugging me?"

"You've hardly said a word since we got in the truck."

I stare out the window and try to shake off the uneasiness lurking in the pit of my stomach. Maggie tapped on the guest-house door this morning to tell me Tom was waiting in the main house, but otherwise she and I haven't spoken since yesterday. I've tried to tell myself it's all right, it's probably nothing, that Maggie would tell me if her secret had anything to do with Johnny's death. But still I feel the hard knot of doubt tighten inside me, like a screw being turned by an unseen hand. The strain between us feels palpable to me, and I know Tom must have noticed it when we loaded the vehicles with our gear.

"When was the last time you were up here?" I ask Tom.

"With you." He glances at me, then leans back with his elbow slung out the window, turning his eyes back to the road. "They stopped inviting me after you left. I guess they thought it'd bring back some painful memories. Jack and I hardly see each other anymore, to tell you the truth. He's a busy guy these days."

I stare at his profile, wondering how much time Tom has spent with Maggie in the last ten years. She used to defend Tom every time I talked about leaving him; defend him to the point of really pissing me off sometimes. I remember how she'd listen with a pained expression whenever I complained about him, how she'd cut me off, smother my arguments and refuse to admit he might be less than perfect. It still bothers me, remembering how chummy they seemed on the phone when they were discussing me.

"And Maggie?" I ask quietly. "Do you see much of her?"

He gives me a quick, assessing glance before he turns his gaze back to the road. "Maggie's been great. If it weren't for her, I wouldn't have known anything about Johnny's life. She made sure I knew his tour schedule, what he was studying, things like that."

"She's been lying to me."

He gives me a sharp look. "What are you talking about?"

"Yesterday, she and Jack were talking in their bedroom, and I overheard them."

"What were you doing in their bedroom?"

The suspicion on his face makes me want to pinch him. "I was looking for Maggie. Their bedroom door was open, so I walked in there and then they came in and started talking about somebody they couldn't control. They didn't know I was standing in the dressing room. Jack asked her if I knew what was going on, and she said she didn't think so, and they'd have to go on pretending in front of me."

Tom glances at me, then stares out the windshield. "Did they see you?"

"Jack left, and then Maggie saw me. She claims they're being blackmailed. She told me it was none of my business."

"Maybe she's right, El."

"I don't believe her."

"So what are you going to do about it? Pull out the thumbscrews?"

"I think whatever they're hiding has something to do with Johnny."

"If you're right, the police will find out what it is. Let them take care of it."

"The police are useless! Gallegos doesn't even bother to return my calls any more. We can't depend on the police, Tom. We have to hire a detective."

His hand tightens on the wheel. "*We* have to?"

"We have the money. We need to do this."

"Forget it. I think it's a mistake."

"Why?"

His shoulders tighten, and he hunches forward, hands tight on the wheel. "You're determined to make yourself a target, aren't you?"

"Because I want to find out the truth?"

"Because there's a killer out there, Elena. Do you think whoever shot Johnny won't come after you, too, if you go on like this?"

My ribs tighten with apprehension. "I'm not afraid."

"Well, I am. I don't want you to pursue this." The truck rolls to a standstill in the middle of the dirt road, and Tom switches off the ignition and stares straight ahead for a long moment before he turns to look at me. His eyes soften then, and he reaches out to touch the curve of my cheek. "You're not bulletproof, you know."

His fingers are warm, and I lean into them.

"It scares me, sometimes, how much you're like him." He presses his thumb lightly to my lower lip. "Same bull-headed stubbornness." There's a longing in his eyes, and sadness, too.

I take his hand between my palms. "Doesn't it bother you, knowing his killer is out there, walking around free? It bothers the hell out of me. Why won't you help me find out what happened to him?"

"Johnny's dead, El. We can't change that. No matter what kind of self-destructive crap you put yourself through, it won't change a thing. You went to Embudo looking for a fight, and it almost killed you. And if you go on looking for trouble, I can guarantee you, it'll come."

He reaches forward to switch on the ignition. The truck rumbles and coughs in response, and he puts it in gear and gives it some gas. A passing cloud obscures the sun, and we drive the rest of the way in silence.

The six of us walk through a long, narrow meadow that stretches for miles, ascending steadily through scattered aspen groves, slowly approaching the blue peaks in the distance. By now Jack is so far ahead he's just a moving speck, flickering in and out of the trees. For most of the day he's been in the lead, his stride aggressive, as if he wants to put some distance between himself and the rest of us. Maggie struggles to keep up with him, but her pace is uneven, her head bowed. I lag a few hundred yards behind them, while Tom, Alison, and Mike bring up the rear.

The mountains are always so much larger and more massive than I remember. A billion years ago the rock faces of these mountains lay miles below the surface of the earth, where layers of sediment were heated and compressed until they formed enormous slabs of quartz. And then these slabs slowly went to war with each other, riding tectonic plates that shoved up against each other until the bedrock quartzite rose to fantastic heights. Millions of years later, erosion finally exposed the glassy white veins of quartz, and in some places, the spine of the mountain range has crumbled to form white chutes that sparkle like diamonds.

It's beautiful, here. Green, tranquil, sunny as a postcard, with patches of late spring snow in the shadows under the trees. But the view is no competition for the bleak thoughts crowding my head as I rehash Maggie's explanation for the conversation I overheard in her bedroom. I'd love to have a talk with the reporter who's blackmailing them, if there really is a reporter. If whatever Maggie wants to hide from me has nothing to do with Johnny, why can't she tell me about it? And why did Jack and Maggie look more like conspirators than a couple on the brink of divorce?

The straps of the backpack dig into my shoulders, and I cinch the waistband tighter to put more of the load on my hips. Step by step, breath by breath, mile by mile, I push myself up the long, rolling incline of the meadow, studying the wildflowers that stretch for acres on both sides of the path, a lush kaleidoscope of false hellebore, cranesbill, primrose, and osha. Recent rains have spawned colonies of puffballs and amanitas, and clumps of columbine are more prolific up here than I've ever seen them before. The last time we were up here I taught Alison and Johnny the Latin names for the trees: *Picea engelmanii,* Engelmann spruce, *Abies concolor,* White fir, *Pseudotsuga menziesii,* Douglas fir, and *Populus tremuloides,* aspen. The kids were nine and ten years old then, the golden age, when they were both still young and innocent.

We were all innocent. Maybe I'm gilding the memory, but back then we moved up the mountain easily together, talking, laughing, the kids running back and forth between the adults. Jack and Maggie, Tom and me, Johnny and Alison; one tribe, one extended family, so close it seemed like nothing would ever divide us.

I remember how it rained mercilessly after we arrived at our campsite on the ridge, forcing us to stay inside our tents for two days. Of course the kids didn't care—they ran around in yellow slickers, busy with their own made-up games that seemed to consist mostly of loud instructions to each other. Maggie and Jack and Tom and I played Hearts for six hours straight in our tent, sprawled out in the familiar stink of sweat and wet wool as the rain beat steadily against the tent walls. I remember how Maggie's head rested on Jack's lap, the way he threaded his fingers through her springy blonde curls as he measured his cards. The tent felt like a dim cave that grew warm from our commingled bodies, and I remember thinking, this is how it should be. This is how people should live, in soft, domed spaces where they can feel the warmth of each other's breath. All our problems were reduced to mosquito bites and blisters and cooking on a Coleman stove in the middle of a relentless downpour.

In between hands we talked about Johnny and Alison, who were both going to Taos Elementary. There was a bully at their school who was giving Johnny a hard time, and Maggie and I spent hours discussing how I should deal with the situation. It's odd to remember how worried I was about that little eleven-year-old bully; how he would keep me awake at night.

When the sun came out we took pictures, and these are still the best pictures I have of us. Our arms circled each others' waists, my head rested on Maggie's shoulder, and all of us were backlit by the evening sun, our bodies shining in wet yellow slickers, our faces glowing with affection.

Things come back. The memory of Johnny's face. The way the tuft of hair on the top of his head stood up like a feather, how I'd lick my fingers and pat it down.

Grown and gone in the blink of an eye.

You wash a mountain of diapers, make an endless round of box lunches, attend the P.T.A. meetings and Little League games, recitals and fund-raisers. You deal with chicken pox, measles, mumps, earaches, and every bout of flu. You hold him through the nightmares and thunderstorms and fevers of childhood.

You do all that, and he dies anyway.

Why? What kind of universe is it where your child can be murdered?

I trudge forward, every step a punishment, my lungs tight with grief and altitude and the struggle to go on, wondering why I should ever love anyone again, when love brings so much pain.

"You know why," Johnny says.

"I don't want to hear it," I say, and the exhilaration of anger almost lifts me off my feet.

"If that were true we wouldn't be talking."

"Why should I listen to anything you say? You're dead. You got to be a rock and roll martyr, and that's what you always wanted, isn't it? You took a bullet in the chest and you can't tell me why. You don't care what it's done to the rest of us who have to pick up the pieces."

His voice is quiet, no more than a whisper, but firm, clear, insistent. "Look around you, Mom. This is what you wanted, right? To walk where I walked, see the things I saw? So look."

The wind picks up, and the aspen leaves clatter in the breeze. When I lift my head, I see how far I've fallen behind Jack and Maggie.

"Look behind you," he says.

A hundred yards down the path I see Tom plodding toward me, head down, his pace slow and even. His boots are caked with mud and his pack looks like it weighs about a hundred pounds, but he continues steadily onward.

Where does it come from, his endless patience? He's so calm and silent and good, so receptive to whatever life brings or takes away. How does he do it? I stand there watching him, filled with a grudging admiration. That patience looked like a liability ten years ago, but now it looks solid and honest and so mature it brings on a twinge of remorse. For the second time in two days, I admit it: I never should have left him. I should have stayed in Taos.

"He's a good man. And he still wants you."

"He's worried about me, that's all."

"It's not worry, Mom. He never stopped wanting you."

"Then why didn't he call me? Why didn't he tell me how much he missed me? He'd call to talk to you, but he never had a thing to say to me."

"You hurt him more than he was ever willing to show. When I was little and he had me in Taos for the summer, I could see how much he missed you. It nearly killed him to lose you."

"He wasn't the only one who got hurt."

"Tell him that," he says, and his voice wavers and disappears into the world that owns him now, a world I can't enter.

When Tom gets closer he catches me watching him, and I see the hesitation in his face, if not his stride.

"You okay?" he asks. With his black hair hidden under his hat, his face looks like an older version of Johnny's, a face that makes me want to draw my hand across the dark stubble on his cheek.

"I'm fine," I say.

"Want me to take some weight for you?" Tom holds his hand out toward me, fingers outstretched. He gave Johnny those fingers, long pianist fingers, capable of spanning an octave and a half, large enough to hold our newborn in his palm.

Wordlessly I give him one of my water bottles, and he tucks it into his pack. His long, lean face looks so familiar, so earnest and dignified under his battered hat, that I reach out and touch his arm, squeeze it once and then let my hand drop, suddenly afraid of what it means to feel this tenderness, this uncertainty, this need.

We camp above tree line, on a windswept saddle overlooking the Truchas Lakes and the rugged terrain below North Truchas peak. Stars begin to appear in the dusk, and the evening air turns cold as winter. The moon appears at the edge of Jicarita Peak, then rises slowly until the full, luminous globe hovers above the summit, and the face of North Truchas glows as it catches the light.

I put on a hat and gloves to help Jack collect wood for a fire, then amble out on the ridge. Just below the saddle, near a scattering of low trees a hundred yards away, Alison and Maggie huddle close together, talking. Their voices rise, and I hear snatches of sound on the wind. "No!" Alison yells, and her hand chops the air in an agitated outburst. "She's going to find out . . ." Maggie's arms are crossed tightly against her chest until she holds her hands out imploringly, palms up. "We can't risk—" she says, and the rest is lost. Alison shakes her head vigorously, turns away from her mother, then lifts her head and sees me. She freezes. Maggie, looking up, slides a protective arm around Alison's shoulders, and Alison shrinks back against her mother as they both stand there, stricken, staring at me as if I were the enemy.

What the hell! I think, turning away and bending down to pick up another dead branch. When I look up again they're both hurrying back to the campsite, and after a few minutes I go back with an armful of wood to find the others have already gathered around the smell of food and the warmth of the fire.

After dumping the firewood, I lower myself to the ground slowly, then sag against a dead log as Mike passes out plates heaped with curried chicken and rice. Tom drops on the dirt beside me, his plate loaded. The group is silent, and everyone looks exhausted.

"I thought I was in great shape." In the stillness Maggie laughs, her voice bright as a new penny, a full-throated, merry laugh, but I can hear the strain underneath. "My trainer puts me through hell three days a week, but this is working a whole new set of muscles."

"Tomorrow I'm taking the ridge over to Middle Truchas," Jack says, looking up at the blade of granite teeth between North and Middle Truchas peaks. There's a treacherous thousand foot drop on either side of the narrow bridge that none of us have ever risked crossing before. Silently Tom and I exchange a look of skepticism at Jack's expense.

"Quit trying to be such a hot dog, Jack," Maggie murmurs. "You'll break your neck."

His eyes bore into her. "Don't tell me what to do, Maggie."

Everyone focuses on the food except for Maggie, who turns to me. "Elena, can we talk about what happened to you before you fell in the river?" Her voice is gentle, but my stomach tightens as I feel everyone's gaze turn on me.

I slip my fork into my mouth, take my time chewing, then swallow. "I'd rather not, Maggie."

Delicately she stirs the rice on her plate and lifts a forkful to her mouth, then pauses. "Tom told me you were talking to Johnny in the sweat lodge. Do you think you might have been in some kind of trance?"

I turn to Jack and point to the western sky. "See that star above Orion? I think it's Betelgeuse."

Jack leans back against the log and looks heavenward. "I see Orion's Belt—is Betelgeuse off to the left?"

"Jack," she says.

"Give it a rest, Maggie," he says.

We eat for several minutes in an uncomfortable silence, and then Maggie comes at me again. "The only reason I'm asking is because I worry about you, El. You know that. Isn't it possible you dreamed you were assaulted, the same way you imagine Johnny talking to you? Did he say anything that might make you think you were in danger?"

I roll my eyes at Tom, who shakes his head.

"Why can't we talk about what happened? At least tell me what you think Johnny said."

"I really don't want to talk about it now, Maggie," I say. "Let's just relax and enjoy the fire."

Her face hardens, and I brace myself for an argument, but her mouth closes and remains sealed.

Mike whisks away the plates as soon as we finish. Mike has been extremely quiet all day, efficient and helpful, flying below the radar of Jack's temper, but Jack looks visibly irritated whenever he catches sight of him. When Jack's not looking, Mike follows his brother with his eyes, more amused than intimidated.

Mike reaches into his pack and comes out with a large metal flask, which he kisses reverently. He pours a dark liquid into six plastic cups, and Alison takes the first one and knocks it back.

"Drop of scotch, anyone?" Mike asks, offering the next cup to Maggie.

Her lips tighten as she looks at him. "Brilliant, Mike. Give my underage daughter a couple shots of scotch. That's fantastic."

"For Christ's sake, relax," Jack says. "Alison can take care of herself."

I can see Maggie stifle whatever remark she was about to make, and Alison settles back against a rock and closes her eyes, ignoring her mother. Tom takes the cups and passes them along to the rest of us, and Maggie finally takes one, a removed, censorious look in her eyes.

After taking a sip of whiskey, Tom says, "Doesn't it seem a little odd that El found a map to the sweat lodge in the guesthouse? Why didn't the police find it?"

Jack grunts. "Maybe they did find it. Maybe they just weren't interested."

Tom clears his throat. "You had a team of lawyers in there the first time they searched the guesthouse, didn't you? Maybe they should go back and take another look."

Amazed, I turn to look at him. He's usually so good, so slow to say anything remotely critical of anyone, it fools me into thinking he's oblivious. But there's no mistaking the electric silence that greets this suggestion. Even in the darkness I can see Maggie bristle as she draws herself up and turns to him.

"If we invite the sheriff back to the house, he'll have a swarm of reporters on his heels. Do you have any idea how many people out there would love to drag our name through the mud?"

"What are you afraid of, Maggie?" Tom's voice is quiet, neutral.

"I'm afraid of becoming a punching bag for the media just so you can have your pound of flesh! What do you want from us? You want to make sure we all suffer as much as you do?"

Tom takes a long sip of his drink. "My son is dead," he says in a low voice. "And he was living with you when he was killed. I think that deserves some examination."

"I loved him too." Maggie's eyes shine in the firelight. "But

147

I'm damned if I'll punish my family because you need someone to blame."

A treacherous silence descends on us, and I swallow the rest of the whiskey in my cup as Maggie and Tom go on glaring at each other.

"We all do what we gotta do," Mike says, breaking the quiet.

"And what is it you do, Mike?" There's a savage edge to Maggie's voice as she turns on him. "Besides sit by our table and wait for crumbs?"

"Now, Maggie," Mike says. "You know you'd be lost without me."

"I'd be willing to give that a try, Mike, I really would." Maggie stands and tosses the remainder of her scotch on the fire, where it flares up in a blaze of blue light as she walks away.

A heavy awkwardness settles over the group in the wake of Maggie's departure. Jack, looking uncharacteristically cowed, rises to his feet and follows her. Tom quietly departs, and Alison melts off into the darkness.

Mike and I are the only ones left to sit by the fire, and he heaps dead branches on the embers until the flames roar and spit and change direction with the wind.

In spite of Maggie's outburst, he looks completely relaxed as he lowers himself to the ground and leans back against a rock with his legs stretched out in front of him. "Ten miles and two thousand vertical feet," he says with a sigh of satisfaction. "I'd say this calls for a toast, wouldn't you?" He wiggles his eyebrows at me.

My body still hums from the confrontation with Maggie. *"Salud."*

He lifts his cup and takes a deep drink. For a few minutes we watch the flames in silence, sipping whiskey and listening to the pop and hiss of green wood.

"You did good today, making it all the way up here after what happened to you in the river." Mike shakes his head. "Plenty of *pachucos* down in Embudo. Not a safe place at night."

"What's going on with you and Maggie?" I ask.

Mike laughs at the abrupt change of subject, then takes out a cigar, bites off the end and lights a wooden match with a flick of his thumbnail. He leans back and exhales with a grunt of satisfaction. "My personal opinion? She's always had a thing for me. But of course she can't admit it, and that makes her bitchy as hell."

I raise an eyebrow and let the silence speak for me. The moonlight glitters on the ridge, so bright the shadows on the granite look more indigo than black.

He goes on. "I guess the truth is she's still shook up about Johnny." He takes a ruminative puff on the cigar. "I meant to tell you before, I was really sorry to hear about his death."

I nod politely, sip my whiskey and watch the flames.

"He was a hell of a kid," he says quietly. "When the police called us with the news it was like a bomb went off. We were all flattened."

"Did you spend much time with him?"

He removes the cigar from his mouth, flicks it. "We crossed paths pretty regularly. I guess you know Alison was tight with him." Mike lets out a chuckle, and I sense the editing going on behind those shrewd eyes. "She tried to hide it, but that girl was crazy about him. Chased him all over the country, hell, all over Europe, going to his concerts, hanging out with him every chance she got. But I think he had his sights set a little higher, to tell you the truth. The kind of money he was making, he had his pick of women, that's for sure." He chews his cigar thoughtfully, then gives me a look of sympathy. "Maggie said you talk to him. Is that right? How's that work?"

The darkness, the whiskey, and the crackling warmth of the fire ease the vigilance I've been hanging onto all day. "I don't know. He comes to me, that's all. If I'm upset, or afraid, I can feel him nearby. Sometimes he comes early in the morning, before I wake up, or late at night, before I go to sleep."

"What's he say?"

"He talks about his life, and what it was like. He told me he was in love before he died. He says his death was all about love."

" 'All about love,' " Mike mutters, as if to himself. "Sounds like a song."

"Did Jack tell you I want to hire a detective?"

"No," he says, sounding surprised. "He never mentioned that. Why?"

"Because the killer's still out there, Mike. I want to set up a reward, too, for any information leading to a conviction."

Mike nods thoughtfully. "How much?"

"A million."

He lets out a low whistle. "You're going to pull in every wacko in the country with that kind of money. Have you talked to anybody at police headquarters about this?"

"Detective Gallegos won't take my calls anymore. Jack said he'd take care of setting it up."

"Good for you. Jack's the best."

Something dark flies across the clearing below us. An owl, probably. I shiver and stretch my feet out closer to the fire. "Whatever happened to the woman you were dating the last time I saw you?" I ask. "Marlena, wasn't it? I thought you guys were pretty serious."

Mike lets out a low laugh. "Marlena. Damn. I haven't

thought of her in a long time. Yeah, she was serious, all right. She was looking for husband material, and that's one thing you know I'll never be. She disappeared as soon as I got laid off."

The smell of cigar smoke drifts through the cold night air, different from the smell of the campfire, more dense, almost sweet, like a bonfire in a tobacco field.

"Maggie told me about that," I say, toasting my feet by the flames, kneading the sore muscles in my thighs. "What happened? Why did they fire you?"

"Oh, it was just the usual bunch of bullshit. Some junkie claimed I roughed him up when we raided his meth lab."

"Did you?"

"Damn right," he says, grinning. "I'd do it again, too. You have to stomp those roaches fast and hard or they're all over you with whatever they got, nail files, letter openers, pencils, broken bottles, whatever. It's a hell of a job."

"I thought you liked it."

He shrugs easily. "Sure. It was great while it lasted. You know what they say." He gives me a look, the bad little boy, mischievous and unrepentant.

"What?"

"Cops have the best drugs."

"Really," I say.

His voice drops to a whisper. "You bet. I still have some friends on the force. I can get whatever I want."

I frown at him. "You're not serious."

"Sure. I mean, it's purely recreational. I'm not dealing or anything—I'd never do anything that stupid. If I ever got busted here in New Mexico and had to do any time at all I could kiss my ass goodbye. There're at least a hundred drug runners in the state pen because of me, and they're not the forgiving kind. No way I'm taking that kind of risk."

He exhales a plume of smoke, then raises the flask and holds it out to me. "You want a little freshener?"

At first it doesn't register when I see the bruise, no more than a smudge, a semicircular darkness on the knuckle of his thumb. My eyes remain fixed on it as my skin goes icy on the back of my neck, between my shoulder blades, and fear stitches a long cold seam down my spine. When Mike sees me staring, he lowers the flask to the ground.

"What happened to your thumb, Mike?"

Casually he holds it up and examines it, then shrugs. "Must have banged it somehow." His eyes meet mine for a fraction of a second, and even in the firelight I can see something flicker behind them, some glimpse of fear or guilt, a flash of knowledge that makes every hair on my arms stand straight up.

Breathe, I tell myself. Don't show him you're afraid. But my heart clenches like a fist and plummets as I reach for the flask and pour myself a drink. I take a deep swallow and feel it burn going down.

Mike relaxes slightly as he watches me drink. He swirls the whiskey in his cup and takes a sip, but his gaze never leaves my face. "You and Tom—you guys divorced now or what?"

"Divorced. It's been ten years now."

The cigar glows like a hot eye as he draws on it, then releases the smoke. "He looks at you like he might still be interested."

"He's worried about me. It's not quite the same thing," I say, unable to keep my voice from wobbling.

Mike takes the cigar out of his mouth and taps off the ash. "It's natural to want to hang onto somebody, though, especially after what you've been through. I bet there are some mornings you don't even want to get out of bed." He settles back on his elbow, his eyes licking me. "Maybe you'd feel better if you had somebody in there with you."

Frozen, I stare at him, every inch of me tingling with the urge to jump up and run away. My stomach tightens as I feel his eyes lingering on my legs, my breasts, and I hunch forward, clutching my cup.

Mike turns the cigar reflectively in his mouth for a few moments as he studies me with his sharp eyes, calculating unknown factors. "It's been a long day," he says at last. "And I know you've been through a lot. I won't lean on you, but if you're like me, a little skin on skin would feel real good up here on a cold night like this. You want some company, I'll be in my tent." He rises slowly to his feet, hitches up his pants, gives me a wink and walks off, a swagger in his gait.

After he goes I pour myself another cup of whiskey with trembling hands. My body feels shaken, battered as an anvil. *Stop it*, I tell myself. This is Mike, someone I've known for two decades, Jack's brother, for God's sake, practically my brother-in-law. Besides, why would Mike attack me in the river, then proposition me here? It doesn't make sense. And what can I do about it? Scream? Point my finger? Make a citizen's arrest?

The flames begin to die, and I feed them twigs and watch them burn as I think about the things he said. The delicate, probing questions about Johnny, and what he's told me. Branches hiss and pop in the fire, and eventually my mind grows numb and my backside feels like a block of ice, but I don't want to go to bed. I don't want to lie in the dark and think about Mike.

The firelight lulls me with its warmth and light, hypnotizing me as the flames sear the wood and spit sparks. A log sizzles as a stream of sap bubbles and drips into the coals, sputtering and hissing until it disappears. My mind veers to

Johnny's body in the crematorium, in that terrible, flesh-charring heat, every bone and eyelash incinerated, his hands, his face, his perfect body turned to smoke and ash.

And then I see him on the other side of the flames, crouching lightly on the balls of his feet, examining me with calm, gentle, worried eyes. His father's eyes.

"You look sad," he says.

"I'm entitled, don't you think?"

"To a point. Then you have to move on."

"Did Mike shoot you, Johnny?" I whisper. "Was he the one who followed me to Embudo?"

He lowers himself all the way to the ground, wraps his arms around one leg and rests his chin on his knee as he stares into the flames. "Knowing who killed me won't change anything, Mom. Trust me. If you keep pushing, they'll come after you again."

"So it's okay that somebody shot you and got away with it?"

His eyes are thoughtful. "It happened, that's all. It happened, and now it's over. I never wanted to get old. I died when I was at the top, and that's a great way to go. I don't bear any grudges."

"I'm so glad it worked out for you," I mutter.

"What can I say? I loved it. All of it. Being famous, living that life—it was a rush. Wherever I went people lit up when they saw me. It's a jolt to walk down the street and see everybody perk up when you go by, and you know they're excited and happy just because you're there, breathing the same air, walking on the same sidewalk. Making that big sound with my body, listening to a crowd roar back at me—it was like riding thunder. The adrenaline, my God, Mom, it was unbelievable. And then I step into a limo big enough for twenty-two people, and it's just me, with a movie screen and stars on the ceiling and four bottles of Cristal on ice. Cruising London streets at three in the morning, checking out the lights, the crowds hustling from club to club. I loved it."

"*If you were alive you could still have it. Your voice could have lasted another thirty years. Somebody stole that from you, Johnny.*"

"*Thirty years! Jesus Mom, you don't have a clue. I might have lasted another two or three, maybe. Then it would have been a long slide down. That's the nature of the business.*"

"*But you'd still have your music. Don't you miss that?*"

"*Yeah. I have to admit, I do. Mostly I miss the way my body felt when I was singing. Like a bird. Like the wind. Alone up there, soaring on the sound. But the rest of it? Hell, no. Trying to sleep on planes and trains and boats and cars, always moving, millions of miles, two hundred and fifty gigs a year, hundreds of promo spots, hundreds of autographs to sign at the meet 'n' greets. Halfway through every tour I'd get so tired I could hardly see. Doing thirty, forty interviews some days, singing for four or five hours a night. I couldn't go on doing it forever, Mom. I left at the right time.*"

"*You didn't leave. You were shot. And if it's so great to be dead, why are you still here talking to me?*"

"*I'm not here because you need to know more about how I died. I'm here to help you see what you still have.*"

"*What I have doesn't matter, if I don't have you?*"

A rueful smile crosses his face. "*Dad looks at you all the time. Did you know that, Mom?*"

"*It's too late for us, Johnny.*"

"*Bullshit. You guys need each other. Go to him. Say you can't sleep. Say anything. Whether you know it or not, he's waiting for you.*"

"*Tell me if Mike had anything to do with how you died.*"

"*And then what would you do? Club him to death in his sleep? Come on, Mom. You're only going to hurt yourself if you keep looking for the killer.*"

I could push Mike off a cliff, I think.

Johnny shakes his head. "Don't even think about it. Please. Do me a favor—don't go hiking tomorrow. Stay in your tent."

"I don't want to stay in the tent," I say, suddenly afraid.

"Just promise me you'll stay here. You'll be okay if you stick around the campsite. Let the others climb the mountain without you."

The log breaks, releasing a shower of sparks, and Johnny disappears. Wobbly, light-headed, I rise, wishing I could step beyond the smoke and take his hand and let him lead me wherever it is that he has to go.

Tom's tent glows on the far edge of the ridge, a dome of light in the darkness, and the knowledge that he's in there fills me with such sudden longing that my throat contracts. I can't go to my tent and lie in the dark, not with Mike out there, not with Johnny's words lingering in me. Shivering, I walk toward the beacon of his tent.

The zipper sticks, and I fumble with the flap, then force my head through the opening. Propped on one elbow, reading a *New Yorker* in our old plaid sleeping bag, Tom blinks at me over the top of his glasses.

"Can we talk?" I ask.

"Sure," he says, and I'm grateful beyond words for the expression on his face as he opens the sleeping bag. "Come on in."

Struggling to unzip the flap of the tent, I finally open it the rest of the way, crawl in and zip it behind me. It only takes me a few seconds to pull off my boots and bulky down jacket and slither in next to him, into the enveloping warmth of the sleeping bag.

His arms encircle me, and I shudder at the sudden heat as I burrow my face into the cradle between his collarbone and neck. His skin is warm. With his heartbeat steady in my ear, I inhale the smell of his body, and it brings a familiar comfort.

His hands and feet were always hot when mine were cold. After I left him I had to buy an electric blanket.

"I can't believe Maggie lit into you like that," I say.

"Don't worry about it," Tom says. "Maggie's just a cranky girl."

"It's not Maggie who worries me."

Tom holds me close as I tell him about Mike, and the bruise on his thumb. When I finish talking, he lets a long moment pass, and then he says, "Why would Mike try to drown you, El?"

This is the crux of it, and I know he won't like the only answer I've been able to come up with. "Maybe he's afraid of what Johnny might tell me."

"Mike and Johnny got along fine, as far as I could tell. And a bruised thumb is kind of circumstantial, isn't it? It's not proof."

"I know it's only circumstantial," I whisper. "I can't explain it, and I know it doesn't make sense, but Mike scares me. And whatever Jack and Maggie are hiding—that scares me too."

Tom shifts slightly. "I have to admit, I've heard a few things around town that make me wonder about them." And then he stops talking. It used to exasperate me beyond words, how he'd stop in the middle of telling me something important.

I poke him in the ribs to get him started. It's an old habit, a married habit.

He removes my hand and holds it tight against his chest, then lowers his voice to a whisper. "Right after Johnny was killed, Maggie fired most of the household staff. They didn't do anything to deserve it, and they have no idea why they lost their jobs. I don't think they've hired any new people, either."

He's right—the main house is peculiarly empty. Alison always answers the door, and a crew of caterers came in to put on the party for the governor and clean up afterward. The gardener appeared yesterday, but left in his truck after a few hours.

A subtle, unvoiced anxiety has been in the back of my head all day, a fear I haven't been willing to face, until now. "Do you think Maggie and Jack had something to do with Johnny's death?"

His chest rises, then falls, releasing a small warm wind on my shoulder. "I don't know."

Closing my eyes to shut out the thought, I let my hand glide over the ripple of muscle in his arm, down to the ladder of his ribs, then turn over and press my cold flanks against his thighs. His legs are warm, and he wraps his arms around my belly. His lips almost touch my ear, and I can feel his breath on my cheek.

"You shouldn't have let me go," I whisper. "You should have moved with us, back to New York. Maybe he'd be alive now if we'd stayed together."

A pained silence fills the space between us, and I feel his heartbeat quicken. "There's no end to that kind of speculation, El. It'll drive you crazy."

Remorse tugs at me, but I can't stop myself from going on. "I'm already crazy. I'm so angry most of the time I feel like jumping off the edge of the nearest cliff."

"Don't say that." His hand traces the curve of my back from shoulder to hip, taking his time. "There's still a lot to be grateful for."

"Have you been with many women since I left?" I ask in a small voice.

"Sure," Tom says.

The stab of jealousy amazes me. It's the last reaction in the world I would have expected, and the shock of it makes me laugh. Tom laughs too, a bed laugh, intimate as touch.

He pulls the sleeping bag up over my breasts, keeps his voice low in my ear, teasing me. "It's not like I go out looking for action. They come up to me. They leave notes in my mailbox. I can't help it."

"Oh, get over yourself. You were always begging for it. That bleached-blonde who used to live down the street— what was her name? Debbie? Diane? You used to wash the truck with your shirt off and she'd hang out in our driveway for hours, watching you."

"It never took me hours to wash that truck."

"The way she used to smile at you made me want to take a broom to her."

His hand covers my mouth, and I pull it away. "Denise! That was it. Denise, with legs up to her chin."

"What about Sam?" Tom says, a smile in his voice.

"Sam who?"

"Sam Whiting, down at the Feed Bin. He never let you carry a bag by yourself out of that store. The minute you walked in there he'd drop everything and come running."

"Sam Whiting was a hundred years old."

"Baloney. He wasn't a day over seventy-five."

I lift my hand to swat him, and Tom catches my wrist and holds it away. Slowly, deliberately, he turns my body toward his and fits his lips to mine. His hand spreads across the small of my back and pulls me close, as if we're about to dance. In the darkness I draw my fingertips over the sandpapery stubble of his cheek, and his lips part mine. Our kiss sinks into a deep, slow exploration, and I relax into it, surrendering to the sweetness of his tongue, the warmth of it. I always loved the taste of his mouth.

When we finally break it off, we're both breathing hard,

and my skin is blazing. Without a word we start shedding clothes. Jeans get scrunched into a heap at our feet, while shirts, sweaters, socks, and underpants fly to the far corners of the tent.

When Tom finally slips inside me, he moves so slowly it feels like a secret, something precious and private, betrayed only by the gasp of his breath in my ear. Then the gentle rocking, the old, familiar harness of pleasure, lifting me until we strain against each other in long, rolling shudders.

I keep him in me, afterwards, stroking his back, and for a few minutes it doesn't matter how long we've been apart, if we can still feel this. He smells so good. His skin feels like silk as his body cups mine, a luxurious stretch of warmth, closeness, peace. And then his hands slide down my back to grab my bottom and pull me closer, and we go on, laughing because it feels too good to stop.

Time loses its meaning in the rhythm of his flesh pressing under and around and over my body, and the moon shines down like a lantern through the tent walls, illuminating the sleeping bag as it ripples over our intertwined legs and arms and hands and feet. After a long while Tom lifts his face from mine and we look at each other for a long time, seriously, carefully. And then we smile. He's such a handsome man. And in some inexplicable, deep, irreversible way, mine.

Chapter Ten

The sun climbs higher, shortening the shadows and warming the air, and I cradle my cup of coffee in both hands and study the view in every direction. Here by the campfire I can see the wide expanse of the Pecos Wilderness to the south, punctuated by the long green ribbon of Hamilton mesa, while Jicarita Peak rises to the east, a broad, bare summit.

Something clenched and lonely in me came undone in the night, in the hours Tom and I spent sliding in and out of each other. I haven't felt this good in years. Lazy now, limbs sore with use, every particle of my body seems stretched and porous. The tough, springy grass under my rump, the sleek curve of the cup in my hand, the coolness of granite as I lean back and look at the ocean of sky over my head—all of it enters me.

To the west I can see the others toiling up the broad-shouldered slope of North Truchas, an easy peak connected by a long granite bridge to the summit of Middle Truchas. The narrow, bony ridge—only inches wide, in some places—spans a treacherous abyss. I shade my eyes and see that Jack has already passed it by. Good for him. It would have been stupid to venture out there.

A broad, grassy slope—about as steep as a playground slide—leads to the North Truchas peak, and the silhouettes of the hikers are clear. Jack is in the lead, as usual, and even though he's tiny as a beetle I can see his pugnacious,

161

thrusting movements as he crawls to the top. Maggie and Mike struggle far below him, resting every few minutes. Tom and Alison hike close together, dawdling up the slope and taking frequent breaks to look around. When I wave, Tom sees me and waves back.

The day is fresh and lively, with a strong wind. Each rock seems bright, clear-edged, and the horizon glitters in the sun. It's hard to remember the urgency I felt last night, when I saw the bruise on Mike's thumb. Tom has a point—a bruised thumb isn't proof of anything, and besides, why would Mike want to hurt me? To believe he shot Johnny for no apparent reason, and then attacked me—it's ludicrous. I've known Mike for more than twenty years, since before Johnny was born, and the worst thing he's ever done in all that time is exactly what he tried to do last night, sidle up to me in a heavy-handed effort at flirtation.

In the piercing light of this perfect morning it's easy to dismiss the fears of last night. The more I think about it, the less likely it seems that Mike followed me to the river, and it shames me to remember how cheerful he was this morning, how quietly helpful when he offered me a spoon and a cup of coffee.

Damn, I feel *good*. Every few minutes I chuckle out loud at the beauty surrounding me, and euphoria blooms inside me. The colors of the mountains are unbelievable, rich and clear, and the air smells wonderful.

Suddenly my heartbeat accelerates from caffeine, and my pulse begins to flutter in a jerky rhythm that makes me uneasy. Is it the altitude? Or some kind of heart attack? Alarmed, I put the coffee mug down, press the flat of my hand to my chest and try to rub away the discomfort.

A wave of nausea seizes me, intense and unforgiving, like the onset of flu, and the earth seems to ripple under my feet. I freeze, unsure whether to walk, or stand, or sit. A little bomb of panic explodes in my chest, and I get up and aim myself toward the tent.

But the tent is red. Crawling into it and lying down in that color would be like drowning in a pool of blood. Is this a normal reaction? Am I thinking clearly? Was I afraid of red yesterday?

There's no doubt about it: I need blue. Sky, or water and sky are closer, up there, up the slope of North Truchas, where the others are strung out on the mountainside. My head feels strange as I walk toward them, and my skin is itchy, everywhere. Distracted, I pluck at my long sleeves, wondering if I have too many clothes on. My feet are hot. I take off my fleece pullover and let it drop, and the wind feels so good I take off one boot, then forget why I took it off.

A rush of energy fills me. Maybe I need to run. Running seems like a great idea. I go up. Breathing ragged, lungs burning, my bare foot hurts as I jog over gravel and weeds, but I can't stop. Colors everywhere I've never seen before, purples and greens that move like water under my feet, like the skimming movement of color in an oil slick.

And then I stop, uncertain, afraid. Something is happening to me, something terrible, an echo of something that happened a long time ago, in high school, with Maggie. A concert. Who was playing? I can't remember. There was wine. Maggie passed me a paper cup full of wine and I drank it. Acid wine, she called it. Acid colors, vibrant, amazing colors, like these, and I know I shouldn't be seeing them now. Did I take acid? No! But I'm stoned, wrecked out of my mind. What's happening to me? Tom will get mad.

Guilt makes me scurry from rock to rock, hiding from the others. God, it feels good to move. Scary, out of control, a little manic, maybe, but I can't sit still.

One of the first hits Johnny wrote was a song called "Sky's Gonna Bring You Joy." I hum it to myself: *Jump up, boy, gotta reach / Up boy, learn to leap / Nobody here can catch you boy / But the fall's gonna be so sweet.*

Going for the sky now, no choice, no doubt about it. The skinny ridge to the next peak has blue all around it. Big-man Jack with all his swagger, Jack is too chicken; he passed it by.

Suddenly the force of new knowledge breaks over me like a wave of light. I hate Jack. I have always hated Jack. What is his secret? How does he do it? Where does it come from, his undeniable power over people, over markets, over music? How does he latch on to the next new thing, suck it dry and toss it away when it's used up? It must be something very simple and obvious. My mind feels alert, focused, intent, alive to a new thought. There's something conniving about Jack, something hidden. He lives in camouflage. He has this way of letting his gaze fall on people when they attract his attention, but he doesn't smile, he doesn't reassure them. He judges them, measures them against some inner standard they'll never live up to, while whatever he is hides behind his eyes.

And he says he's going to leave Maggie, leave Alison, leave Taos. Break his family, break their hearts. How could he do that? Hatred rolls through me. I want Jack to die. I want to hit him with a stick, bash his head in, hard, until he's dead.

The thought leaves me breathless, and I stop, stupefied. How could I think about killing Jack? And then I wonder if this is how the murderer thought about killing Johnny.

Without hesitation, from thought to action. Bang.

Without regard for all the thousands of hours he spent at the piano, without a moment's pause for the music his throat, his lungs, his fingers could bring into being.

Bang.

None of that mattered. His childhood, his love, his joy, and oh, God, his smile.

Bang.

Precious breath, gone. What he was, what he saw, what he felt, what he knew—nothing mattered except that black desire to kill him.

What did it feel like to Johnny, that stunning rip of fire? For an instant I feel it, a pain in my heart, blazing there like a live coal in my chest. I can't stand it. I can't feel this and live.

The others yell at me as I bound uphill. My head hurts and my heart pounds like a jackhammer as I run out on the granite teeth, out on the ridge where the blue sky is everywhere, close, intense, soothing. As I run my mind clears; this is okay, this is what people do, it's perfectly all right. I'm hiking a little fast, that's all, I'm in control; I forgot a few things, water bottle, shoe, but that's okay.

The ground is so far away. Up on this tightrope of rock, there are forests below me, lakes, ridges, rivers, towns, cities, the rest of the planet. I'm on the edge, on a path with cliffs on both sides. Another burst of energy propels me up toward the top of a crag, where the sky is blue as deep water, as blue as Tom's eyes.

The chasm expands below me, breathtaking, immense. Rocks lie jumbled ahead, balanced on top of each other, tiny bits of moss in the crevices. *Don't look down, for God's sake don't look down, look at the next pillar of granite.*

Struggling, slipping, grabbing for handholds, I climb until I get stuck. I'm standing on a needle of rock. There's only one way to get to the next rock. I have to jump. If I jump . . . Holy Mary Mother of God, I'm a long way up.

A long slope of decomposing granite makes a dry waterfall on my right. To the left is another steep chute, with dazzling, glassy white pebbles going all the way into the valley below, cascading a thousand feet or more to boulders the size of houses, tumbled by an avalanche. I'm alone at the top of everything, standing on a tall rock with nowhere to go but down.

Think about geology, I tell myself. The angle of repose. If I can remember about the angle of repose I must be okay, my brain is okay, I'm not crazy, this isn't crazy.

The light wavers and I sit down abruptly, a loud buzzing pressure in my head as the air before me shivers like liquid, and my mind is so clear I can see everything. I can see through my hand, it's transparent as glass, and my bones are just shadows, not even there unless I imagine them holding me together.

Bright blue air, buoyant, like water. In the emptiness below me the wake of a hawk curls outward like a foam-edged wave. Oh, so beautiful. Air like water, only thinner. There are currents in the air, like currents in a river, and I know I could ride them if I tried.

And then a great rushing stillness explodes inside me, and for one expanding moment every particle in me and outside of me is the same. Union. No loss. No death. I stand, swaying, a part of the landscape, a part of Johnny, a part of everything.

I look down at the pedestal of rock where I'm standing, and the rock turns into a column of snakes, curling over my feet, undulating into loops and knots as they slither over one another, mating, all of them, joined in a ball of sex. I'm sinking into the center of the column, and one of the snakes has a tiny human face as it curls around my ankle. Johnny grins up at me and sticks out his forked tongue.

"Elena! Get down!" Far away, Tom is frantic, yelling at me, but his voice is no louder than the creak of the hawk's wing. The wind kisses my skin as I reach down to pluck Johnny from the writhing mass. "Let go," I whisper, and step into air.

Pain. Bad pain in my head, my elbow, my legs. Hurting, dizzy, I touch my face and my hand comes away red. Tom runs to me in slow motion, and the world spins as I close my eyes, wait for stillness, wait for the pain to stop.

Closer now, I hear Tom stumble, slide, jump up again, half-falling, half-running the rest of the way. Then holding me, talking fast. Words break when they come out of his mouth. I can't put them in order. He's telling me important things, but what are they? "Johnny," I say, and lift my hand, but Johnny disappeared. There's no snake in my hand, no face. One look at Tom tells me I'm scaring him, but the explanation won't come. There are tears in his eyes. Frustrated, I close my mouth, tears welling in my eyes. We cry.

Maggie's face stretches in a grimace, she's crying, and Jack looks angry, scared. Faces full of horror and pity float around me, looking down. Alison stares at me. Oh God, not Alison. I can't look at her. My fault. My fault.

Cut, blood on the rocks, face sticky, pain like knives in me. Tom wraps his arms around me and carries me, skidding on the gravel, down and down. My limbs flop and jerk against him. I want to come down now. My head hurts.

Blankness washes over me, not sleep, but over the edge, out of bounds, not awake, not real. I flicker there for a long time, listening to the others yell and hiss at each other, listening to the wind brush the mountain, listening, hurting.

A helicopter batters the ridge in great gusts of wind like bursts of gunfire, and the landscape throbs with the commotion. Bright blades circle, then stop. Two men with big red crosses on their chests and a woman in front with sunglasses and a helmet come out. She talks to Tom. To a little microphone wrapped around her face. To Tom. To the microphone. The two men run toward me, carrying a stretcher. Maggie's still crying. Jack turns away. Tom talks to me but I can't understand him. Love hurts, like a hole in my chest, and I try and try, but I can't understand him. And then they lay me down on the stretcher and put me in the mouth of the helicopter and the sky is dark metal now.

Tom holds my hand on the short, choppy ride to the hospital in Santa Fe.

The emergency room is loud, a bright fluorescent confusion of yelling, children crying, a hell of flashing color, red everywhere, splashed across white coats and walls and moving bodies. A man with a stethoscope around his neck leads us to a little room with no people in it. There's a big padded table and the man asks me to lie down on it.

The man with the stethoscope talks to me, but I don't understand the words as he unwraps the bandage the paramedics put on my head. His face stretches like rubber as he peers at the cut. Spikes of afternoon light come through the blinds and rove through the room, touching things. Hot. Like a hot hand, and I flinch when one touches my leg. The doctor's mouth moves, and bits and pieces of what he says float through the room like cartoon balloons of speech, stabbed and splintered by the light.

Part of me gets up and calmly crosses the room to wait for this to be over, while the other part remains frozen on the table, terrified, incapable of speech. Johnny materializes in the space beside the Other Me in the corner, and he looks so young! Eight or nine, wearing his blue striped T-shirt and brown overalls, his head a sunburst of yellow hair. He touches Other Me with his hand and she shrugs it away, refuses to look at him. She knows he's dead.

My forehead is numb. A shiver starts there and works its way down, making my whole body shudder. Spasms of cold, then hot. I want to take my clothes off. Banging, bright pain, behind my eyes.

". . . a few stitches on your temple . . . allergic . . . ?" The doctor opens a drawer in a cabinet by the door. There are metal things in there, hiding.

". . . not . . . to anything," Tom says.

A worm appears in the doctor's hair, a pink thread, lifting its blind head toward me, searching. ". . . Falling off the mountain?" he says.

The walls are dripping. There are worms crawling behind the paint, squirming up and down the wall, thousands of them, millions. They well up from the floor and ooze across the ceiling. Speechless, I sit there, shaking, while the Other Me folds her arms across her chest and watches the scene unfold, anger coming out of her head like red flames.

He swabs the cut, then takes a pencil flashlight from his pocket and shines the beam in my left eye. ". . . Count backward . . . ?"

He wants me to talk. I can't talk. I shake my head.

The light shines in my right eye. "Today's date . . . ?"

Groggy, I sit up and swing my legs off the examination table. I have to get out of here.

"Hold on . . ." the doctor says, moving quickly to my side. Firmly he lifts my legs up and lowers my back until I'm lying on the table. ". . . nasty cut on your . . . it can make you feel . . ."

Tom's face looms over me, his eyes huge with fear, while the Other Me in the corner comes closer and bends down to look at me too. Tom's mouth moves as he takes my hand in his, chafes it, squeezes it, trying to coax words out of me that I don't have.

". . . concussed," the doctor says in a low voice.

"But why . . . ? I saw her. It looked . . ." I see Tom's repeated, worried glances at me, the undercurrent of his thoughts—how is she now? And now? And now? As if this were some terminal condition.

My pulse beats in my ears as the walls throb. Frazzled, adrift, I barely listen as the doctor talks to Tom, but the Other Me, the one leaning over my head, she hears every word. ". . . may have been altitude sickness . . . conceptual reasoning . . . twelve thousand feet . . . Truchas thirteen thousand . . ."

Tom shakes his head. ". . . climbed that peak before . . ."

The doctor looks at me and shrugs as another worm slides out of his ear and inches over the whorls and curves of skin to find the thicket of hair above. ". . . sickness can still hit . . . no matter . . . New York, what, a few days ago?"

". . . right."

". . . sea level, so she went through . . . could be a factor . . . take some tests, find out what happened, and maybe we can . . ."

They all look down at me, Tom, the doctor, Johnny, Other Me. All together, peering at me with worry, disapproval, a great puzzlement. I close my eyes.

Chapter Eleven

Awareness returns slowly, like dim light seeping over the horizon after a long night, bringing shame and panic. My mind still feels strange, full of landmine that any stray thought might set off. A nagging feeling lingers in me that there's something important that I've forgotten, but I'm afraid to remember it.

The blinds are closed, but I see the slatted blackness of night through the cracks. The walls are no longer dripping, and my mouth is dry as a shoe. I'm lying on a hospital bed in a private room, with eighteen stitches in my left temple. There's a lingering smell of rubbing alcohol in the room, the smell of hypodermic needles and shots. In the past twelve hours it seems like every inch of my skin has been pricked and prodded and poked by men in white coats, until the entire surface of my body feels like one giant ache. Even my fingernails ache.

A newspaper crinkles in the corner of the room, and I flinch at the sound. Tom is there, sitting in a chair, lowering the paper to look at me. How long has he been here? I check my watch. Eleven. Eleven at night. Fifteen hours have passed since I drank that cup of coffee.

Tom comes over to the bed, takes my hand in his and rubs it gently, lovingly, but something in his gaze makes me feel like I'm on probation. "Feeling better?"

I swallow. "Thirsty."

He leans over, pours water from a yellow plastic pitcher, then hands me the glass. I drain it and hold it out so he can fill it again.

"When you told me you wanted to jump off a cliff, I didn't think you meant it, El." His tone is light as he refills the glass, but he examines me as if I'm a ticking bomb that might go off any second.

No matter how much I drink, I can't get rid of the foul taste in my mouth, but I'm too tired to brush my teeth. "I don't want to kill myself, Tom." There's an edge of rust in my voice.

"What were you doing up on the ridge, then? You've never gone out there before."

"I know. It wasn't anything I planned, believe me. Someone must have drugged me."

A tentative smile lifts the corner of his mouth, as if I might be joking. "Who?"

"I think it was Mike."

He gives me a quiet, passionless stare that says This Is Not Healthy And You Know It. "Why would Mike want to drug you, El?"

It was Mike, I'm certain of it. But it doesn't make any sense. Why would Mike want me to look like a lunatic? Because I've been poking around in the guesthouse, and he's afraid of what I've found, or what I'm about to find? Maybe he wants to get rid of me before I find it.

I meet Tom's eyes. "Mike was bragging to me last night about his access to drugs. I think he slipped something in my coffee."

He lets out his breath and looks away. "El, you can't be serious. You've known Mike for twenty years. Why would he want to hurt you?"

"He knows I talk to Johnny. Maybe that scares him."

A terrible grief softens Tom's face, and I know his sorrow isn't for Johnny. How can I blame him? No one will ever believe me, not without proof, or a motive, or some reason for this malevolence. A bruise on Mike's thumb. That's all I have to go on. But when I think of Mike I feel a current of fear, and a powerful urge to flee.

"Do you think they'll let me go home?" I ask.

There's a long pause before Tom answers. "I'm not sure that's such a good idea."

What is left unsaid sinks in, and I turn my face to the wall as a desolate wave of loneliness seizes me. Tom doesn't believe there's a threat to me out there. He believes the threat is in here, talking to him.

He shakes his head. "What happened between us last night . . ." His voice runs down to a rasp of guilt and regret. "I wanted you so much. Too much, probably." He lifts a hand, lets it fall. "I feel like an idiot. Like this is all my fault."

"Tom, this doesn't have anything to do with us making love. Come on. You know that."

He strokes my hand, his face pinched with exhaustion and a new kind of worry that makes me uneasy.

A brisk knock at the door makes us turn, and a shaggy, bearded man with horn-rimmed glasses enters the room, clipboard in hand. "You must be Elena," he says brightly. "I'm Dr. Sykes. Dr. Matheson asked me to talk to you." He studies his notes, then flips through the papers clipped to the foot of my bed. He smiles at me, then turns to Tom. "Would you mind leaving us alone for a few minutes?"

"I'd rather stay," Tom says.

"This shouldn't take long. Go have a cup of coffee. By the time you're finished we'll be all done here."

Tom tucks the paper under his arm, gives me one last sorrowful look, and leaves the room. When the door closes behind him my pulse accelerates, and I take a deep breath to shake off the anxiety stewing inside me.

"So," Dr. Sykes says, settling into Tom's chair. "I understand you had quite an adventure this morning. Want to tell me what happened?"

A long silence ensues, while the doctor looks at me with a neutral, kind watchfulness, and no hint of impatience. My palms are suddenly clammy, as if I'm about to walk out on stage and play a part I've never rehearsed. "I fell off the mountain, that's all. I must have slipped."

He nods, looking thoughtful. "Are you depressed, Elena?"

"No."

He consults his notes and reads for several long seconds before he looks up again. "Your son was murdered a few months ago. Doesn't that depress you?"

"It makes me angry. It makes me sad. But depressed? No."

"Are you hearing voices?"

My hand automatically reaches to cover my heart. Tom must have told him about my talks with Johnny, but telling this man the truth would mean a surrender I can't contemplate. "No."

"Have you experienced any sudden interest in religion, or the occult?"

I think of the sweat lodge, and Russell's words to me in his kitchen, and the fact that I talk to my dead son. My heart sinks as I realize Dr. Sykes probably interviewed Jack and Maggie, too. Twisting the bed sheet in my hand, I shake my head.

His gaze—warm, sympathetic, curious—flickers across my face. "Do you think your friends are conspiring against you?"

What can I say? My mind runs back to the conversation I overheard between Jack and Maggie, and the way Jack asked her "Does Elena know?" I think of Alison, arguing with her mother, saying "She's going to find out." I think of the bruise on Mike's thumb. The way he said "Cops have the best drugs." But these things would mean nothing to a psychiatrist.

"I fell, that's all. It was an accident, and now it's over. I want to go home."

Dr. Sykes removes his glasses and rubs his eyes. "Elena, your friends and your ex-husband told me you've been talking to your dead son, and they say you hear him talk to you. Ordinarily conversations like these are pretty common after the death of a loved one, but what concerns me—and your friends—is that these conversations seem to coincide with episodes of self-destructive behavior. You were recently released from a hospital in New York after an apparent suicide attempt, am I right?"

"It was Tylenol, for God's sake."

"You ate enough Tylenol to kill yourself. I think you knew it could kill you, didn't you?"

I stare at the far wall, the dead television, the green paint, the same green paint they used in St. Andrews. There must be one universally approved color for hospital rooms, this sterile, artificial green that has nothing to do with nature.

"Elena?" he says.

"It wasn't like that. It wasn't a decision." Nothing so coherent or purposeful, nothing I planned. It was like being sucked into a big black hole. It felt inevitable, like falling. "I was in pain. I just wanted to stop feeling pain."

"That's what suicide promises," Dr. Sykes says gently. "An end to it."

"I don't want to die," I say dully, hopelessly.

"It certainly appears that you wanted to die back then. Can't you admit that much, at least?"

"It was an accident."

"No." His voice is quiet, almost sad. "I don't think so, Elena. No one swallows that many pills accidentally."

"I was in shock. I'd just found out . . ."

"About Johnny. Yes, I know. And you wanted to escape the pain."

I make myself still, and numb, and send the feeling part of me deep inside. What Sykes sees is only skin, a shell of flesh, a woman in a hospital gown.

He takes a full minute to read from his clipboard, purses his lips and lets out a small, mournful puff of air. "It appears that you've had two more suicide attempts just in the past week."

"That's not true."

"You went swimming in the Rio Grande two or three nights ago, I believe." He looks down at the clipboard, then up at me. "According to your ex-husband, you appeared at a stranger's doorstep in Embudo a little after midnight. He says you were barefoot, disoriented, and hypothermic."

"Someone attacked me! Someone forced my head underwater, and I got away."

"But you never filed a police report."

"It was dark. I couldn't see their face—what would be the point?"

His gaze never wavers. "According to your husband and four of your friends who saw you, you deliberately walked off a cliff this morning. You could have killed yourself out there, Elena, and no one was anywhere near you. No one attacked you. Believe me, if I release you now and you suffer so much as a bad haircut, Jack Dalton would sue me for a zillion bucks."

The room seems to lurch slightly, and the walls close in around me as I sink back against the pillows. It's crazy, impossible, but I finally realize he wants to keep me here, even if it's against my will.

"Dr. Sykes, I'll talk to Jack, I'll make him see this is my decision, my choice. All I want to do is go home."

A small silence develops between us. "You have to understand, Elena, your friends are extremely worried about you. They want you to get better. And in cases like yours, when there's been an attempt at suicide and a reasonable fear it might be repeated, the state is allowed to step in and require an extended hospital stay."

"But I don't want to die!"

He nods. "I hope that's true, for your sake, but we need to be sure of that before we can release you. The way I see it, you have two choices: you can stay here and enter a locked ward on ICU, or you can sign some consent forms and receive treatment at a private rehabilitation facility in Ojo Caliente."

Rehab, or a locked hospital ward. Panic whispers along my veins, and my pulse starts to race. "What kind of treatment?"

"If you decide to go to the clinic in Ojo, we'll start you on an antidepressant right away, and Zyprexa, a fairly mild antipsychotic."

"What if I don't want medication?"

He leans back in the chair. "Do you want to have another episode like the one you had this morning?"

"What if . . ." I hesitate, wondering if my next question will give him even more ammunition. "What if I were drugged?"

His eyes are shrewd. "Maybe you were. I don't know. It could happen, I suppose. We won't know until the blood and urine tests come back."

"My son was murdered three months ago—don't you think it's possible someone wants to kill me too?"

Dr. Sykes lifts a shoulder, lets it fall. "You lived in separate states, and you hadn't even seen your son in five years. Where's the connection? What's the motive?"

I stare at him, unable to answer.

"I'll level with you, Elena," he says quietly. "About ninety percent of all the adult-onset paranoid-schizophrenics I've ever treated have your symptoms. They get disoriented, they get into dangerous situations, they do things that seem so out of character they're sure someone's trying to poison them. It's understandable—one minute you're fine, the next you're hallucinating. That's the way your disease feels, and the stress of losing your only child is certainly enough to bring on a full-blown episode. In a weird way it's perfectly logical to believe you've been drugged. But if I were you, I'd try out the medication for a week and see if you still think someone's trying to kill you."

Shaken, I stare at him. Up until this morning my mind has always felt like a sturdy house, spacious, open, accommodating, with solid doors and windows and walls. Up until now my mind has never failed me, even in the furthest extremities of grief and rage, but now it feels like the roof is collapsing and the walls are blowing around like sand in a dust storm. For the first time I wonder if Dr. Sykes might be right.

He goes on, his voice low, a rumbling, comforting purr. "The facility in Ojo Caliente is extremely luxurious, one of the best in the country. All kinds of famous people go there to kick their drug or alcohol habit, lose weight, deal with eating disorders, rest, reflect, take time out from lives that have become overwhelming for one reason or another. Everyone receives the highest quality medical and psychiatric care."

"I'm not famous," I say.

He smiles. "Mr. and Mrs. Dalton are on the board—otherwise we'd never be able to place you there. The therapist-patient ratio is four to one. You'll have a psychiatrist, a clinical psychologist, a psychiatric nurse, and a rehab therapist. There's also a fully equipped spa, with your own private outdoor hot tub, and therapists for massage, facials, pedicures, body wraps, whatever you want."

"Will I be locked up?"

"No. It's an open campus, with no locks on the doors or windows, but it's isolated, about nine miles from the nearest highway. And of course the compound is heavily guarded, to keep reporters out. This is not the kind of place you find listed in the yellow pages." He gives me a sly glance. "If someone really wants to get rid of you, this would be a safe place to hide."

I study his bland, good-humored face. Why is he trying so hard to steer me toward an expensive private clinic? "Do you work there?"

"I work for Mr. Dalton. I go wherever he wants me to go."

Confused, I struggle to understand the dimension of Jack's influence here. "Jack employs a full-time shrink?"

"And a full-time general practitioner—you already met Dr. Matheson. We look after the health of his family and the musicians who stay at the compound."

Slowly, I realize how much Jack must have already done to keep reporters away from the hospital, and an odd resentment mixed with relief drifts through me. "So you'll be my doctor in Ojo Caliente?"

Dr. Sykes nods, his eyes alight with satisfaction as he realizes I'm weakening. He stands, reaches for my hand and gives it a brief shake, like a boxer touching gloves before a match. "Right now you're my top priority."

He backs away from the bed, turns and strides to the door, white coat flaring behind him.

"One week," I call out as he opens the door. "That's all I'm agreeing to."

Dr. Sykes gives me a thumbs-up sign and disappears through the door. Before it closes all the way it opens again and Tom peeks in at me with an anxious look.

"Traitor," I mutter.

He comes back in the room, sits cautiously on the edge of the bed and takes my hand in his. "Don't look at me like that. It's only a week out of your life."

"Tom, I didn't walk off that cliff on purpose."

His eyes remain steady, fixed on my face. "I saw you, El." It's the kind of voice he'd use with a six year old.

"Do you really think I need to be locked up in a mental ward?"

"Think of it as summer camp. Besides, I'll come and visit you."

"I don't want to go, Tom."

"I know." He brings my hand to his lips and kisses my knuckles. "But I think this could be a good thing."

I close my eyes. "If this hadn't happened, we'd be in your tent right now."

"You know how many times I've kicked myself for agreeing to that stupid camping trip? It was insane to let you go up there after what happened to you in the river. I knew it was a mistake. I should have put my foot down."

"And we all know how well that's worked in the past," I say dryly.

"It's not funny, El. Do you have any idea what I went through, seeing you step off that cliff? And it's not like I didn't have plenty of warning. Ever since Johnny died you've been trying to get yourself killed."

I open my mouth to protest and he lifts his hand, palm toward me. "I know, I know. You were attacked, or drugged, or in shock, or some damn thing. I know you think none of this is your fault. But I saw you run up that ridge, El. I saw you walk off that cliff. Whether you were drugged or not, I can't get that picture out of my head."

Again I have that queasy feeling of wondering if Dr. Sykes might be right. Is this what it feels like to go crazy? Am I going to turn into one of those women who stand on street corners with all their belongings heaped in a shopping cart, talking to the air? I groan and pull the sheet up over my head. "I am not a wacko."

"I know that."

"I was happy, damn it. I finally got laid last night, and I was hoping we could do it again."

"Maybe it's more important to rest right now."

I pull the sheet down an inch and glare at him.

"One week," he says.

"One week," I say. "And then I'm coming to get you."

Chapter Twelve

Backed by tall sandstone cliffs, the clinic occupies high ground overlooking the lush Chama river valley near the village of Ojo Caliente, sixty miles from Taos. At first my body welcomes the distance, the isolation, and I lie down on the bed in my room and wake up nineteen hours later.

Sometimes it's soothing to be among strangers who require no effort, no reassurance. Everyone here has an inward, preoccupied air, a polite absence of curiosity, and the inmates, or guests, or clients, or whatever they call them, keep a wide perimeter around themselves as they pass me in the garden, or the foyer, or the hallways. Some faces are more familiar than others, faces I've seen on CNN, or sitcoms, or magazine covers, but for the most part they keep their eyes averted to discourage any interaction. The decibel level is hushed, like a monastery, and laughter is rare.

Sometimes it's a relief to be in a place where no one expects me to smile, but I'm lonely. I try to strike up conversations with people in the dining hall. The ones who aren't too drugged to talk are so quiet and polite that all my overtures whimper and die in the chill between us. It's like trying to play tennis with a sock. It's ninth grade all over again, when Maggie and I had different lunch periods and most days I ended up sitting by myself in the corner of the cafeteria, trying to look deeply interested in meatloaf and peas.

There are no visitors allowed in my wing. Unfortunately

they didn't spring that particular surprise on me until after I was admitted, or I might not have agreed to come here. Tom hasn't sent me any kind of message, and his absence hurts more than I want to admit.

My room feels like an expensive hotel room, with tasteful, busy wallpaper, a king-sized bed and rattan chairs next to a glass-topped table. There are flowered drapes and inoffensive paintings. When I'm not sleeping I sit on my balcony, staring at the vacant ranchland in the distance, too drugged to read.

Indifference. That's what the drugs bring. They steal my humor, my curiosity, my grief, and my anger, and these are all more terrible thefts than I imagined. Feeling indifferent is no substitute for being awake, aware, alive, capable of connecting one thought to another thought. How could I have ever taken that for granted? It amazes me to remember how much I wanted to stop thinking or feeling after Johnny died, how much I wanted to be out of my mind. Right now my mind is all I've got, and I can't go on lulling it with drugs or I really will go insane.

After three days of staring into space, I know the pills aren't doing me any good. If Dr. Sykes wants me to go on taking anti-psychotic medication for the rest of my life, he can go fly a kite. They might not let me out of this place for another four days, but I'm done playing their game. From now on, no more pills.

The only trouble with this decision is that it's almost impossible to slide the pills under my tongue while the nurse watches me take my medication. With her standing close enough to count my eyelashes, I have to tilt the white paper cup of tablets into my mouth, then drink a sip of water and swallow quickly enough to look completely innocent. If there's any doubt in her mind, she asks me to open wide and stick out my tongue.

On the nights when I manage to spit the pills out after she leaves, I wake up in a rage, so angry I feel I might fly apart. Then I want to hike out on the mesa to the middle of nothing and scream and scream and scream for hours.

Time passes so slowly I can't believe the clocks are really working. I've never been so aware of time, oozing like cold honey out of a bottle. By the fourth day, the face of my watch is depressingly familiar, and I look at it repeatedly in disbelief at the tormented slowness of seconds ticking out minutes, minutes ticking out hours, hours ticking out days. How could I be forced to stay here against my will? It seems surreal, impossible. And with every day that passes, I become more and more convinced that it's because Mike wants me out of the way.

After seven days have come and gone, my sentence is finally up, and I make my bed with vicious satisfaction, yanking the sheets, leaving no wrinkle unsmoothed, no inch untucked. Once I meet with Dr. Sykes, I'll never have to set foot in this room again. My mind simmers with plans. It's time to hire a detective, a ruthless, efficient investigator from Manhattan or New Jersey, someone with no connection to the Daltons or the police, a detective who can slip through town anonymously, uncovering the hidden link between Mike and Johnny, and the motive I can't see.

Dr. Sykes and I meet every morning outside the main residence, in a private arbor overgrown with wisteria. Every morning I struggle to sound dull and reassuringly normal, but he has a nasty habit of confronting me with facts he's gleaned from Tom, or Maggie, and truths I'd prefer to keep hidden leak out.

This morning Dr. Sykes looks hot, although it's only nine and the real heat of the day hasn't even begun. His spectacles slide down his nose as he consults my chart, and one hand absentmindedly rakes his thick brown hair until it sticks up like a rumpled patch of fur. We're seated in cushioned wicker chairs, and a server from the dining hall brings us two glasses of iced peppermint tea.

Dr. Sykes takes a deep gulp of the tea, then lets the clipboard fall in his lap. "I thought you should know your blood and urine tests came back. There was no sign of drugs, no sign of poison."

Astonished, I stare at him. "What did you test me for?"

He flips through the papers. "It was a standard five panel drug test, for cannabis, cocaine, amphetamines, methamphetamines, and opiates."

"And no drugs were found?"

"No."

"That's impossible."

"Why is it impossible?"

"Because I felt sick, and . . ." Crazy, I start to say, but I know it's a bad idea to admit it. I draw in my breath slowly and evenly, to avoid attracting his attention to the effort. I have a nearly overwhelming urge to start yelling, but I can't, not today, not when I'm so close to getting out. "What about LSD? Did you test for that?"

"No."

"Why not? Isn't there a test for it?"

"Yes, there's a test for LSD, but it's not reliable. Unfortunately it's not chemically similar to any of the other drugs we test for."

"Do it. Test me for it."

"No."

"Why not?"

Somewhere in the distance a dog barks, and Dr. Sykes looks toward the sound, then back at me. "It's too late, Elena.

The lab disposes of your blood and urine samples within three days, and it's been a week since they were taken."

"Take some more blood."

"If someone gave you LSD a week ago, your body has already processed it. It wouldn't show up."

I nod, slowly, trying to make sense of this. "Why didn't you look for LSD in the first place?"

"I told you. It requires a separate test, and it's not usually given unless we suspect prior use. It's extremely unlikely anyone would give it to you. What would be the point?"

"It would make people think I'm crazy, destroy my credibility. It would give you a reason to put me in here."

He takes a deep breath and lets it out in a way that lets me know I'm trying his patience. "And someone would want to do this because . . . ?"

Because then no one would believe me if I accuse Mike of anything, or ask the police to investigate a certain powerful family. When did this suspicion sprout in me, like a fungus, entwining itself in every thought, not just about Mike, but Maggie, and Jack, and Alison? Sometimes I wake up in the middle of the night and think, they know why Johnny died. They know who killed him, and they're covering it up.

Dr. Sykes stares at me, frowning. "Have you ever taken LSD, Elena?"

"Once, back in high school." Nervously I sip my tea, then wonder—why tea today? Usually they bring us ice water. I put the glass down. "What happened to me on Truchas—it was exactly like acid. For an hour or so I felt this euphoria build up, and the landscape seemed incredibly vivid. I was *wide*-awake. Then a crescendo of energy hit me, and it lasted for hours. Colors, hallucinations, distorted thoughts—I couldn't even talk. And then it went away. Maybe that's what happens during a psychotic outbreak, but it sure felt like LSD to me."

Musing, he scratches his beard and glances at the distant black speck of a raven riding a thermal. "But you heard this extraterrestrial voice, Johnny's voice, for several weeks before this last event."

A splinter of pain pierces my heart at the sound of Johnny's name, dropped so casually into the conversation by someone who didn't even know him.

Dr. Sykes smoothes the hairs above his upper lip slowly, thoughtfully. "I have to admit, it concerns me that Johnny warns you that bad things will happen to you, and then, seemingly inevitably, they do." He spreads his hands. "I have to wonder if you're manifesting these near-death experiences out of a subconscious desire to kill yourself."

I hold his gaze and enunciate every word, slowly, distinctly. "Dr. Sykes, I swear to God, I don't want to die."

He gives me a swift appraising glance. "And yet you jumped off a cliff for no apparent reason."

"I'm telling you, I was drugged."

Dr. Sykes takes off his glasses and breathes on the lenses, then buffs them against the shirt stretched over his belly. "So you still believe the Daltons are conspiring against you?"

The heat rises in my face, and I weigh my words carefully before I speak. "Maggie admitted they've been lying to me about certain things."

"There's a vast difference between lying to you and slipping LSD in your food. Do you really think your friends drugged you?"

Mike's amused, sardonic expression comes to me, the way he looked when he handed me a cup of coffee that morning. "Yes. Yes, I do. I think Mike Dalton drugged me. We were sitting around the campfire the night before and he bragged to me about his access to drugs. He said he could get whatever he wanted."

Dr. Sykes shifts uneasily in his chair, and glances at the circling ravens. I follow his gaze and realize they're not ravens, but vultures, gathering over a carcass in the valley. Thirty seconds pass. Maybe a minute. I know he's making judgments, decisions.

Finally he takes a deep breath and taps his pen against the clipboard. "I realize you're anxious to leave the clinic."

A wary stillness comes over me. Freedom is so close. Every nerve ending in my body stretches for it, but I have to be careful, tread softly, say the right words. "I feel fine, Dr. Sykes. I'm rested. I'm better. I want to go home."

"Home to New York?" he asks.

I pause, sensing a trick. "Sure."

"You're willing to leave the investigation of your son's murder in the hands of the police?"

A faint, warning tingle passes over my skin, and I lower my gaze from his face to his shirt, a white oxford with a gray stripe, while my mind churns furiously. This man works for Jack, and only Jack. "Of course."

He purses his lips and pushes them out while his pen taps the clipboard. "According to the night nurse, you're trying to avoid swallowing your medication."

"That's not true."

He gives me a skeptical look. "You think she's out to get you, too?"

"No! I didn't mean that. She's mistaken, that's all."

"Elena, I thought by now we'd see a marked improvement in your attitude. But several nurses have told me you resist your medication. You distrust your closest friends, and you distrust me. Believe me, we can make you feel better."

A deepening sense of unreality breaks through my caution, and I let out a laugh that threatens to escalate into something else. "By giving me more drugs?"

"We can calm those centers of the brain that suffer paranoid delusions. We can give you a sense of well being and safety. Why won't you let us help you?"

"You said I could leave in seven days! It's been seven days!"

He folds his hands in his lap. "Elena, I said we'd see. I never promised you anything."

I lean forward. "Dr. Sykes, I want to leave."

Something shifts behind his eyes, a kind of shutting off, a refusal to listen. "I'm sorry, Elena, but you can't. There's no way I could justify your release, given your present state of mind. In another week we'll review the situation and maybe things will have improved by then. Until then, though, I think you're better off in here."

The ignition of anger nearly lifts me off the chair. "You can't do that," I say, struggling to keep my voice low.

He turns his calm, implacable eyes back to me. "Elena, once you stepped off that cliff, you created a situation where the state has the power to determine your treatment. Believe me, it could be worse. The only reason you're allowed to stay in this clinic is because you're in my custody and you have powerful friends. Don't you see how lucky you are to be here? Or would you prefer to be locked up in a psychiatric hospital?"

Stunned, I stare at him, then lean back. "How long are you going to force me to stay here?"

"Until I'm convinced you're taking your medication willingly. You have to stay until I believe you won't be a danger to yourself."

I chew the inside of my cheek to keep from crying, and we sit for another minute in a silence that feels like one of those long, slow pauses on a roller coaster, when you creep up to the top of the first long dive. This can't be happening,

I tell myself, over and over. My whole body is numb, as though it belongs to someone else. Who am I kidding? It does.

For the next three days I search the compound for a way to escape. At first the orderlies are kind and helpful when I stumble into all the places that are off-limits to patients—the kitchen, laundry, staff quarters, and a maintenance shed—but after escorting me back to my room the fourth time, they tell Dr. Sykes I'm wandering a little too persistently, and he increases my dosage.

The nurses watch me like a hawk to make sure I swallow the pills. Each tablet is a little death, and they turn sleep into a dreamless coma that leaves me feeling weak, hazy, and lost. When I'm awake I feel like I'm underwater, moving in slow motion. Hours go by as time crawls from dawn to dusk, and I sit and stare out the window, thinking, *I can't go on like this.*

On the tenth day, the nurse gives me a perky smile as she brings in my morning medication. "You're doing so good, Miss Ellie!" she croons. A large-bosomed Irish woman in a starched white dress, she sits on the bed and hands me the paper cup of pills and a glass of water. "Haven't you been feeling better? You look better. I can tell you're taking your medication, just looking at you. For a while there we were worried." Her eyes fix on mine as I tip the cup to my mouth, then take a sip of water. She smiles as she places the empty cup back on her tray and puts the glass on the bedside table. Her fingers are warm as she takes my pulse. "You were sticking your finger down your throat, weren't you? Or maybe you were just spitting them out. Anyway, I'm glad you stopped. If they find out a patient's doing that, they put you on intravenous, and that's so uncomfortable, you know? So unnecessary."

The balloon of her meaning slowly floats across the haze of my consciousness, and when she leaves I go to the bathroom. For all I know, there are cameras behind the mirror, and I throw a towel over my head to hide the telltale finger. When I'm finished the pills float in the toilet, and I have to flush twice to get them to go down.

Hours pass, slow as sludge, a monotonous series of minutes, and I keep looking at the face of my watch, waiting for my head to clear. By early afternoon a familiar anxiety starts to build inside me, and when the nurse makes her afternoon rounds I swallow the pills obediently, without making a face. We watch each other for a moment, and then she nods, a pleased look on her face. Once she's gone I go in the bathroom and bring them up again.

The next day, the old anger starts to kick in, fueling my determination. Too wired to sit, I pace my room, snapping my fingers, seething with plans. I sit down, then spring back up again. Pacing is better than sitting. I try to think.

When I go to lunch I walk slowly, eyes lowered in drug-glazed look of indifference, and when I get back to my room I take up pacing again, full of a revved-up energy.

By now I know there are guards at the entrance on the south side, and a high wall surrounds the rest of the facility, except to the north, where the residential buildings press up against the natural barrier of a tall, nearly vertical sandstone cliff. A few utility trucks are parked in the lot back there, along with several Dumpsters.

If I want to get out of here without a chemical lobotomy, the north side is my only chance. But how can I scale the cliff? It's at least a hundred feet high, a sharp, unforgiving drop, and the thought of trying to climb it makes my mouth go dry. Even if I manage to get up there, I have no idea what kind of terrain lies beyond that wall.

Tom took my hiking boots and clothes from the hospital, and they've given me white pajamas to wear here, with paper-thin slippers and a blue robe. Other patients wear regular clothes, and walk around in rubber-soled athletic shoes that I covet more than world peace. Whenever I bring up the possibility of getting some exercise, Dr. Sykes insists that I'm here to rest, and exercise would only slow the healing of my concussion.

So how far can I get with no cash, no ID, and no shoes? *Tom*, I think, automatically, but he can't visit me in this part of the compound, and I haven't seen a phone since I arrived.

The thought of Tom grips me with a sudden, fierce homesickness. I'd give anything to see his weathered, sorrowful face, his crooked smile. I wish we could talk. If only I could hold him for a minute. If I could trace the long cords of muscle in his back and feel his palm between my shoulder blades, pulling me closer, this would all melt away like a bad dream. I can feel him out there, worrying about me. If I ever get out of here, I'll go straight to his house.

Or should I?

What if Tom brings me back here? I've been here for eleven days, and as far as I can tell, he hasn't even tried to reach me. Back in the hospital, I remember how he paused when I asked him if he thought they'd let me come home. How he said "Maybe that's not such a good idea." He must think I belong in here.

And then the sliver of doubt works its way deeper into my thoughts. What if he had something to do with what happened up there on the mountain? He brought me a bowl of granola that morning. What if he dropped a pill in it? What if he's the one who's trying to hide something from me?

I think of how he spoke on the phone to Maggie the day he picked me up in Embudo, how his voice was hushed as he walked in the other room to keep me from hearing what he was saying. I think of how he stopped the truck when I told him I wanted to hire a detective. What if the worry in his eyes wasn't for me at all? What if he was concerned about himself? What if he was worried about what I might find out?

I stop pacing. He and Johnny fought all the time, he'd told me. They'd fought for months before Johnny moved out. *It was like he had to stomp me to a bloody pulp before he could walk out the door and live his own life.* What if that hostility smoldered for five years and finally exploded? It falls into place with the quiet click of a padlock opening. Who else would Johnny protect like this? Who else could have lured him out of the compound, met him at some secluded location and then . . . ? But why? Why would Tom kill him after five years?

Could Tom know more than he's telling me about Johnny's death? I think of how he confronted Maggie by the campfire, how she left in a huff. Could they have staged the whole thing for my benefit?

I close my eyes and think of Tom's body pressed to mine, heartbeat to heartbeat. How we melted into each other, shuddered against each other, rocking like newlyweds in our old tent. Was he saying hello or was he saying goodbye? I think of his silence, and all the things it might conceal.

No, I tell myself. It's impossible. I can't think about it now. I have to focus on one thing at a time and move on. Whatever Tom has done or left undone, I'm alone now, and if I have any shot at all of escaping from this place, I'll have to get out of here by myself. Clothes, shoes, and money: that's all I really need. A map would be good, but I can wing it without one.

The cicadas start up outside, a shrill, buzzing sound in the afternoon heat. I walk to the window, press my forehead to the glass and look out at the imposing face of the cliff to the north. The only way to get what I need is to steal it. And this is the time to do it, when everyone is asleep or dozing in group therapy.

Chapter Thirteen

Out in the hall cameras swivel as I walk by, sleek white videocams with red eyes that follow me as I exit the building and enter the wide central courtyard. The other residences are arranged in a rough U-shape around the broad rectangle of green, and I study the windows of the first and second stories as I shuffle along the sidewalk leading to the west side. The buildings on the west end are more richly landscaped, with large sycamores, cottonwoods, lawns edged in lushly blooming perennials and trellised roses. The windows look bigger, the balconies more spacious, with double French doors instead of sliding glass. Obviously the wealthiest clients stay there.

Moving slowly across the courtyard, I enter a side door in a large building on the west side, far away from the mezzanine. I try to look vague and harmless as I wander down the hall, avoiding eye contact with the ever-vigilant videocam perched in the corner of the ceiling. Potted palms and bouquets of fresh flowers on marble-topped tables create a scent of luxury in the broad, carpeted hallway, and every twenty feet or so a large window offers a view of the grounds, flanked by a pair of high-backed wing chairs with a table between them, and a fan of brightly colored magazines arranged on top.

Casually leaning against the wall, I dawdle down the hall, testing the handle of each closed door behind my back. It seems to take an unbearably long time to wander down the hallway, lean against each door and surreptitiously press one handle after another. Finally one gives in to my pressure, the door opens, and I take a deep breath and slip inside.

A sour smell pervades the darkness, and at first the room seems empty. With the drapes closed against the bright summer afternoon, it's hard to see anything but dark humps of furniture, but then my eyes adjust and I detect an odd silhouette in the doorway to the bathroom. In the deep gloom, I can't tell what it is.

"Hello?" I whisper. "Anyone there?"

There's no response. Tiptoeing over to the drapes, I brush one side open, and light streams into the room from the glass paneled door to the terrace. When I turn around I see a young girl strapped to a wheelchair, staring at me over her sunken chest. Her eyes are huge, luminous with fear, and uncombed strings of dark hair frame her face. Her legs look like broomsticks, and her spandex shirt should be skin-tight but it hangs on her frame like laundry.

Caught in the crosshairs of her gaze, I step back, too startled to speak.

Her biceps spasm with effort as she stabs at something behind the bathroom door. There's an emergency call button in the same place in my bathroom. A red light goes on above the door to the hall.

Suddenly the girl opens her mouth and screams, a sharp, serrated edge of sound in the stillness, loud enough to summon an army of security guards.

Frantic, I grope for the doorknob behind me, one of those old-fashioned glass knobs, and I can feel every facet as I twist it and jerk the door so hard it flies from my hand as it bangs open.

I bolt outside, searching desperately for cover, but the terrace offers nowhere to hide, forcing me to vault the low railing and race around the corner to the back of the building, ducking past a hedge of trumpet vine. Breathless, heart skittering in panic, I head for a large, leafy sycamore with a branch that curves low to the ground. Scrambling up on the lowest branch, I cower behind the trunk as two men dressed in white run around the corner, heading my way. The men hustle down the side of the building without looking up, moving quickly and purposefully until they disappear around the next corner.

For a few seconds I perch there, frozen, clutching the trunk and wondering how long it will be before they come back. I can't stay here. Maybe I should climb back down and make a run for it, but I still need shoes, and money, and clothes.

A heavy branch above me curves toward a balcony on the second floor, and my stomach churns as I evaluate the drop to the ground if I fall from up there.

Each leaf of the sycamore is larger than a man's hand, and the thick layers of greenery flutter in the breeze, screening my movements as I knee myself up from one branch to another, climbing until I reach the limb that goes to the balcony.

My knees are killing me, and my hands start to sweat as I straddle the branch and realize I'll have to stand up on it if I want to get to the balcony. There's no way I can inch along on my belly—there are too many spiky clumps of leaves and smaller branches in the way. The branch I'm sitting on is at least eight or nine inches across, but looks narrow as a tightrope when I stare at the ground twenty feet below.

A golf cart whirs up the sidewalk, and I shrink back, hugging the trunk as it rolls to a halt underneath me, and four men in security uniforms jump out. Two of them go north, while the other two head south, patrolling the perimeter of the building.

A cold drop of perspiration trickles from armpit to waist as I stand up on the branch and let go of the trunk to step out on the limb. My whole body wobbles as the branch gives slightly. Grabbing the branch for balance, I climb the slope of the limb on all fours, quivering with fear.

Every time I look up, the balcony looks impossibly far away, and the bough sways alarmingly as I lurch forward. My ankles are weak as water, and my trembling legs make the branch vibrate under my feet. Finally the gap narrows to a few feet, and I plunge toward the railing, gasping as my feet slip from the bark and my hands catch the metal grille.

Shaking with adrenaline, I pull myself up and climb over the railing. Two orderlies appear at the corner of the building on the sidewalk below and rush toward me, talking into handheld receivers. I crouch by the teak chaise longue next to me, eyes closed, breathing stilled, waiting for the sound of their footsteps to fade away. When I finally dare look over the edge, I see them disappear around the other side of the building, their heads down as they listen to their walkie-talkies.

As soon as they turn the corner I edge past the chaise and press my forehead against the glass door to peer inside. The apartment is spacious, much more luxurious than mine, with a white leather sectional couch and armchair and a big-screen TV. A massive stone fireplace rises to a twenty-foot cathedral ceiling, and tall, healthy-looking plants line the wall of windows to the south. No one appears to be inside, and when I twist the knob, the door silently opens.

The air in the suite smells terrific, as if there were extra oxygen in the room, and a humidifier near the plants exhales a steady plume of mist. The kitchen on the north side of the room features a wall full of steel cabinets, broad black granite counters, and a large butcher-block table. I head over there and start opening drawers, hunting for cash, or a rope, or anything I can use later.

A toilet flushes beyond the wall, and I freeze. A tall, elegant looking man with a pencil mustache appears in the doorway to the bedroom, staring at me in astonishment. His hair is silver, the line of scalp so straight it could have been parted with a knife.

"May I help you?" he asks politely.

My cheeks burn. "I was looking for . . ." What? What could I possibly be looking for that wouldn't make him toss me to the men outside?

His face echoes the question as he takes in my pajamas, robe, and slippers, and he tightens the sash on his quilted satin smoking jacket as I cautiously advance.

"Please don't call for help." I lift my hands and show him my empty palms. "I don't want to hurt you."

A small smile tweaks the corners of his mouth as he looks down at me. "How very fortunate."

"I know this must seem crazy," I stammer, wiping my forehead with the back of my hand. Every cell in my body feels jittery, shivering with vibrations I hope are undetectable. It's stress, I tell myself, stress and withdrawal from the goddamn pills, not to mention a concussion that still makes the top of my head feel like it's being squeezed in a vise.

His eyes sparkle with amusement as he crosses his arms in front of his chest. "I never let sanity stand between myself and the promise of an enlightening conversation."

"I'm in trouble," I tell him. "I need help. I want to leave this place and they won't let me go. There are people . . ." A deep, shuddering sob escapes me, like a hiccup. "I need shoes, and money, and clothes. These pajamas are all I have, and if I try to leave here looking like this, anyone who sees me will think . . ." I bite my lip, unwilling to finish the thought.

He examines my face, eyes soft with concern. "Forgive me, but you look as though you could use a boost to your blood sugar. Would you like a glass of lemonade? Perhaps a cracker or two, with a bit of Stilton?"

"No, thank you. I don't need a lot of money. Just enough to take a bus or a cab back to Taos."

"Dear lady, how on earth did you arrive here? Don't you have a family looking out for you?"

All the air goes out of me, and despair rises in me like a bitter tide. This was a stupid idea, an absurd idea. "Sometimes having a family isn't enough. Sometimes families fall apart. Sometimes they die. And sometimes they just stop believing in you."

He cocks his head to one side, listening intently, a spark of sympathy in his face. "They do indeed."

I stare at the floor. "No one wants me to talk about it, but I have to know . . . I want to know how it happened. Why it happened. No one can tell me why my son died. And now everybody thinks I'm crazy, the doctors, my friends, even my ex-husband."

I laugh helplessly at how deranged this sounds. "Believe me, I know how this looks, but I'm not crazy, I swear. It's just that I'm coming off a dosage of five hundred milligrams of Zoloft and ten milligrams of Zyprexa and another two or three or four hundred milligrams of whatever it is they give me every night, those little white pills. Do you have to eat those little white pills?" My voice starts to wobble.

"Little white pills." He closes his eyes and taps a finger on the side of his nose. "You're probably being treated for anxiety. Xanax? Ambien, perhaps? I rather like Ambien. You don't happen to have any with you, do you?"

"I'm sorry, no. I never thought anyone would want . . . my name is Elena, by the way."

"Elena," he says solemnly. "I'm Richard." He extends his right hand, and holds mine for a long moment. The warmth of his large, soft palm reminds me of my father, my poppa, and I have to stifle the urge to collapse against the satin lapels of his dressing gown and let someone else take care of me.

"I can't take the pills anymore. They make me so fucking tired." I flap one hand at the idea of going back to my room and lying on that bed in the blur of that pharmaceutical death. Tears spill down my cheeks and drip off my chin, wetting the front of my robe.

Richard clicks his tongue against the roof of his mouth as he takes a crisp white handkerchief from his pocket and holds it out to me.

I wipe my face and hand it back to him with a shaky smile. "I'm sorry. I know this must look a little desperate."

"Yes," he says. "Anxious, upset, angry, sad, perhaps, but most assuredly not crazy."

The pity in his face makes me pull myself away and wander to the other side of the room, where I finger the fronds of a maidenhair fern. Automatically I test the soil for dampness.

"I used to think I was normal," I say, pressing the dirt more firmly around the roots. "I thought if I worked hard and treated others kindly and paid my taxes and wrote Christmas cards and didn't break the law, then nothing too terrible would ever happen to me."

"Life is rarely that simple," he says gently.

"I fell apart," I whisper.

The silence is full of unspoken questions, and his eyes remain locked on me, full of sadness.

Somewhere under my heart I know what happened, what I

did, but I can't look at it squarely. "I was in shock. I didn't know what I was doing."

"You were bereaved."

"Yes."

"You wanted to stop feeling bad."

"Yes."

He walks toward me, lifts my hand and looks at the inside of my wrist. I pull it away. "Was it pills, then?"

Guilt wraps its vise-like fingers around my throat, and I swallow hard. "Yes."

He lets out a long, regretful sigh. "The long pink bath, now, that's infinitely more peaceful, although the visual aspect must be a bit daunting. Like bathing in wine. But that's how I shall go, when I'm ready. Lots of aspirin in the system to thin the blood, and perhaps a few glasses of cognac to soften the exit."

The green, pencil-thick branches of the Euphorbia next to the fern are covered in a fine layer of dust, and I use the hem of my robe to brush them clean. "Are these your plants?"

"My sister brought them. She's fond of greenery, but I'm afraid I'm hopeless with it. At home I have gardeners who deal with the landscaping, and one of my maids is wonderful with the houseplants. Personally, I never enjoyed the feeling of soil on my fingers."

The fiddle-leaf philodendron beside the Euphorbia looks healthy at first glance. "See how the tip of this leaf is beginning to turn yellow?" I say, holding it up. "That's usually from over-watering. It isn't really the water that damages the plant but water molds, fungi that thrive when water stands too long around the roots, especially when the soil is warm. It would probably benefit from a little neglect." I pinch off a withered stalk.

A rapid, aggressive pounding comes from the front door,

and Richard raises an eyebrow as we stare at each other. He looks toward the bedroom, then back at me. The invitation is unmistakable. Running on tiptoe, I close the door behind me and press my ear to the wood.

"Mr. Hahn?" The voice is loud, official.

"Yes, gentlemen?"

"We're sorry to disturb you, sir, but we received word that a female intruder was spotted in the building. We'd like to search your rooms, if that's all right with you, sir."

There's a hint of a smile in Richard's voice. "Good heavens, I assure you, there is no woman hiding under my bed."

"Then you won't mind if we just take a look for ourselves, will you sir?"

"By all means, come in."

Are you out of your mind? I yell silently. The bedroom door has no lock. I run to the bathroom, looking frantically for a place to hide. The linen closet is stuffed with sheets and towels, and the shower door is made of beaded glass. I race back to the bedroom, press myself against the wall next to the door and pray.

"It's not often I receive visitors," Richard says. "Can I get you fellows a drink? Of course I don't have anything from the grain or the grape, but I make a rather refreshing lemonade."

"No, thank you sir. We just need to check the rooms and we'll be out of your hair."

"Have you been in law enforcement a very long time?"

"We're not law enforcement, sir, we're just security guards. Although Harry here served on the force for a few years, didn't you, Harry?"

"And are either of you available as, shall we say, a *personal* bodyguard? There are times when I do feel frightfully ill at ease here, when I'm in need of some physical reassurance, if you know what I mean. And now that you say there's a crazed female on the loose, well, I'd be delighted to hire both of you, you know. Absolutely delighted."

I suck in my breath and turn my face to the hinges as the door swings toward me and all three of them crowd into the bedroom. The door grazes my breasts and starts to spring back.

"And the nights are the worst, you know," Richard leans against the door, pushing it against me. "That's when I ache for the companionship of bright, intelligent, fit young men like yourselves. And in time, who knows? Perhaps my company could be a reward in itself."

"No one's in the bathroom," Harry mutters to his partner.

"We're sorry to have bothered you, Mr. Hahn," the partner says. "We'll get out of your way now. You ready to go, Harry?"

Richard's weight lifts from the door, and their footsteps fade and disappear as the front door clicks shut behind them.

After a few seconds Richard reappears in the bedroom, cheeks pink with excitement. "So many visitors in a single day . . . I'm agog."

Lightheaded with relief, I let myself sink down on the bed. It's eight feet wide, with dozens of little pillows piled against the headboard, and the spread is made out of some sort of fur.

"Chinchilla," Richard says, sitting beside me, stroking the silky ribs of fur. "I do hope you're not one of those people with a 'Fur Is Dead' bumper sticker on your car. This was pieced together out of my mother's old coats."

"Thank you for hiding me," I say.

He gives me a wry grin, eyes sparkling in his elegantly chiseled face. "I adored it. You've been a breath of fresh air to me, my dear." He walks past me to the dresser, where he extracts a few bills from a drawer and hands them to me. "I believe you said you needed money."

I stare at the money in my palm. He's given me five hundred dollar bills. "One is enough," I say, and hold out the rest.

His eyes never leave my face as he folds my fingers around the money and guides my hand back to the pocket of my robe. "How did you hurt yourself, Elena?"

The stiff bumps of the stitches on my temple aren't as sore as they were a few days ago, but every mirror reminds me that I look like someone who walked away from a car wreck. "Hiking. I had an accident."

Delicately his hand reaches toward my face and traces the cut, his eyes full of compassion. "Are you feeling well enough to escape?"

"Yes. I want to leave tonight."

"You know the entrances are electronically sealed?"

"I know."

"The access road to the clinic is patrolled by security guards. You'll surely get caught if you try to leave that way."

"I won't go by road."

"You're going up the cliff?"

"That's why I need shoes."

He nods thoughtfully as he smoothes his silver mustache with an index finger, then turns to the closet, bends down to retrieve a pair of white wingtips, and unbuckles the shoetrees inside them. "My feet aren't quite as small as yours, but perhaps these will be better than nothing."

The wingtips have slick polished soles, perfect for ballroom dancing, and they're several sizes too large for my feet. "You don't have any sneakers? Or any shoes with rubber soles?"

Richard smiles apologetically. "I'm afraid I've never been much of an outdoor person."

"Do you have any clothes you can spare?"

"Of course. Let me see what I can find." After rummaging in the closet for a moment, he whisks a light gray and white striped seersucker suit from the rack and tosses it on the bed. "This might fit, if you make a few adjustments. It was always too small for me, but vanity never dies. When I was a young man of sixty it fit me perfectly, and I could never bear to throw it out."

I hold the suit up to my shoulders. "I can return it to you, and the shoes, and the money, of course."

"Don't be silly," he says. "We'll never see each other again."

I let the suit fall. "Why are you helping me?"

He takes my shoulders in his hands and kisses me gently on the forehead. "You remind me of my sister, I suppose. And, to tell you the truth, I always enjoyed the illusion of rescuing others. Especially when I'll never see them again."

"I'd like to repay you."

"Nonsense. You don't even know where I live when I'm not serving out my time here. And I prefer it that way, frankly. Don't give it another thought."

After I bundle the clothes under my robe, we walk to the front door, and Richard opens it and looks up and down the hallway. "The coast is clear," he says, eyes twinkling. "I believe that's the appropriate term?"

"Thank you," I whisper, and kiss him on the cheek. He shoos me out, looking pleased and slightly flustered, then closes the door.

I shuffle past the security cameras with my head down, clutching the shoes and clothes to my chest under the cover of the robe, trying to minimize the obvious bulk. The fire exit door is unlocked, and I take the stairs two at a time, anxious to put some distance between myself and the guards. Once outside, I resume the slow walk of the heavily medicated, arms pressed tight against my middle, praying that the shoes don't fall out in the middle of the courtyard. Across the lawn a golf cart filled with security men whizzes around the corner of a far building, and I keep my eyes riveted on my slippers as I scuttle forward, praying they won't turn in my direction. The band of tension around my chest eases slightly when the cart heads for the main entrance of the west wing.

The nurse on duty in the mezzanine of my building is arguing quietly with one of the patients as I glide past them. Gratefully I open the door to my room, slip inside, then sag against the wall as I drop the clothes to the floor. Wingtips, I think, staring at the shoes. I probably need a set of lock picks and a few hand grenades, but instead I have wingtips and a seersucker suit.

The room is silent, empty, but I look up, alerted by something out of place, something I can't define, and a tentacle of fear grazes my skin before I can pinpoint what's wrong.

A faint scent of smoke clings to the air.

It conjures an image of Mike, lounging by the fire, the hot eye of his cigar staring at me. A chill passes over my skin as I walk to the screen door to the balcony, sniffing for the source. The smell comes from the patio underneath, and when I peer over the railing I hear the click of a door closing below me.

The smoke remains, but the smoker is gone.

Chapter Fourteen

At three in the morning the clinic is hushed and dark, and I dress without turning on a light. The pant legs of the seersucker suit are too long, the waist too big, but I roll up the legs and use the sash from my bathrobe for a belt, and they fit well enough. With toilet paper in the toes of the wingtips, money in my pocket, and Richard's suit hanging on me like a Halloween costume, I'm finally ready.

The night shift workers chat down the hall in low voices as I strip my bed and knot the sheets together. Noiselessly I slide open the door to the balcony, tiptoe outside and tie one end of the sheet to the railing. The ground is at least twenty feet below, and I swing one leg over the rail and test the knot. It holds.

Scared to go on, but more frightened by the thought of staying, I push off, then suppress a gasp as my fists scrape the floor of the balcony on my way down. The sheets end at least twelve feet above the patio below, and I dangle there for a moment, dreading the jump.

A second after I let go, my shoes smack the brick, stinging the soles of my feet, jarring my bones. I crouch there, shaken, half-expecting the shrill bark of an alarm.

From the patio it's a two hundred yard dash to the north side parking lot, and I streak across the dew-soaked lawn, clinging to the cover of the chamisa on the edge of the grounds, praying I'll be long gone before anyone sees the sheets tied to my balcony.

The night is alive with the rustle and trill of insects, and moths swarm in the yellow pool of light from a security lamp in the parking lot. Five vans and a truck are parked back here, all bearing the logo of the clinic. One by one I test the doors of the vehicles, just in case someone got careless and left the keys in the ignition, but they're all locked. Running low past the Dumpsters, I enter the shadows beyond the security light and head for the steep slope of rubble at the bottom of the cliff.

In the darkness I stumble up the slope and run my fingers across the dirt face of the cliff, searching for a foothold, a place to start. Rotten from winter rain, the sandstone crumbles easily under my hand. With only touch to guide me, the cliff feels like a wall with no openings.

Finally I find a long crack, wedge my foot in it and hoist myself up. The wingtips slide around like boats on my feet, so I jump back down, take them off, tuck my socks inside, tie the laces together and sling them around my neck.

Barefoot, I try again, working my way up slowly, painfully, blindly reaching for toeholds, handholds, a root, a rock, anything. After gaining only five or six vertical feet, the earth collapses under my weight and I fall.

Precious minutes of darkness slip away, and I can't get higher than six or seven feet off the ground. The west end of the cliff ends in an impassable snarl of cholla cactus, and the east side abuts the compound wall, high as a two-story building. After an hour my pants are ripped and filthy, my palms are bleeding, and frustration wells up inside me, with fear looming right behind it.

There is no way out.

I have to go back.

Bitterness sparks tears of frustration as I realize I have to go inside before I'm discovered. I'll have to go in the emergency exit and pray the alarm doesn't go off, and run like hell if it does. Filled with an overwhelming sense of failure, I turn away from the cliff.

The roar of an engine bursts the silence. Automatically I throw myself down and press my cheek to the dirt, flattening myself into the shadow of a large cholla. The engine revs in the darkness, falls into a stuttering idle, then roars again. When I peer through the skinny arms of the cholla I can see an orderly in a white coat and a baseball cap, his head under the hood of a van, down close to the engine. He tinkers with it, feeding it gas, and the engine growls in response.

The side door of the van is open, a black square hole facing me, and I race toward it before I can stop myself, before I can think of the consequences if I'm caught. The man in the white coat keeps his head under the hood, adjusting the idle. The shoes bounce off my shoulder, but I don't stop to pick them up as I rush forward over fifty yards of dirt and gravel and pavement in my bare feet, hurrying to get to the van before he looks up.

Breathless, I pause at the dark opening and climb inside, careful not to rock the van, but a toolbox catches my shin and I crumple to the floor. Howling silently, I roll to one side, grab my ankle and try to muffle the sound of pipes and other bits of plumbing rubble clinking beneath me. The noise of the engine covers the sound of metal striking metal, and the orderly revs the motor again as I wriggle over sharp edges and hard, bone-digging surfaces to the darkest corner in the back, where the smell of machine oil is thick.

The van shakes as the hood slams down. Footsteps approach, and the side door slides shut while I cower in the shadows. A few seconds later the door on the driver's side opens, and the man in the white coat jumps in and puts the van in gear. We start to move.

The vehicle tilts as it follows the turn out of the parking lot, then speeds past three S-curves. We slow down at the main gatehouse, then accelerate down the straightaway to the access road. The darkness is complete. No moon, no stars penetrate the murk in the back of the van. Shielding my watch with one hand, I press the stem to illuminate the dial. It's already four in the morning. Soon it will be light, light enough for him to see me. What do I tell him then?

The van jolts over a speed bump, then turns onto the access road. Here the pavement is smooth, and the driver guns it until we're hurtling down the access road at what seems like a dangerous speed. I brace myself against the metal walls as the pipes around me rattle and bounce, making a racket, but the driver never glances in the rearview mirror, and the darkness covers me like a cloak.

Eventually the van slows, then makes a sharp left turn and picks up speed again. We must be on the highway, going north. Why is he going north when the larger towns are all to the south? We must be headed for Taos.

A nagging, sick feeling in my stomach blooms into suspicion. This isn't right. Why did an orderly leave the clinic at four in the morning? Why was the side door of the van open? This is all too easy, and I curse myself for leaping in here without thinking. Blindly I grope the floor of the van for a chunk of metal I can use as a weapon.

Thirty minutes later, the stars begin to fade as the sky lightens, and the ink-dark blackness in the van changes to gray. Crouching in the shadows, my hand tightens on an L-shaped piece of pipe that fits in the palm of my hand. If he sees me—if he threatens to make me go back—I'll hit him. I'll hit him and run.

A few minutes later the van slows and makes a sharp right turn. My heart bangs against my ribs, and I tense, fearing the moment when he looks up and his eyes meet mine in the rear-view mirror.

The van covers another few miles, then slows, bumps onto the shoulder and comes to a halt. The driver switches off the engine, and the sudden silence seems ominous. No traffic. No city sounds. We're in the middle of nowhere.

In the pre-dawn twilight I can see the silhouette of the baseball cap on his head, the slope of his shoulders as he reaches into a compartment between the two seats. There's something familiar about those shoulders.

He pulls a dark object out of the compartment, turns, removes his cap and smiles at me. "Hello, Elena."

Speechless, I stare at him, confused, and then my gaze drops to the gun in his hand.

"Thought you were getting a free ride?" Mike says, grinning at me, friendly as ever. "Well, that's okay. I won't make you go back there."

He holds the gun casually, keeping it aimed at my head as he climbs into the back and opens the side door. "After you," he says, waving the gun toward the opening.

My blood jolts as I step out of the van and see the rim of the gorge, a dark line of basalt in the gray of the mesa, and the bridge where Tom and I scattered Johnny's ashes. A few lights twinkle in the distance, ten or fifteen miles to the south, but otherwise there are no signs of life, no sound of cars or people. To the east the Sangre de Cristo Mountains hover like shadows above the dark ocean of sage, and the sky is the color of tin. Silence reigns in the pre-dawn chill.

"Mike, I'm glad to see you," I lie, babbling to distract him. "But don't you think the gun is a little over the top? Nobody from the clinic followed us out here, did they? Why don't we get back in the van? You can drop me off at Tom's."

Mike gestures to the bridge, his voice brisk, business-like. "Let's walk, shall we?"

My hand tightens on the knob of metal in my coat pocket, but I can't throw it at him, not with the barrel of the gun nudging me between the shoulder blades. Barefoot, I walk in front of him as slowly as I dare, the sidewalk cold and gritty under my feet.

"You've been watching me," I say, thinking of the smoke.

"Every minute. The security people lent me a monitor to keep an eye on your door, but then you went off the balcony. Couldn't believe it when you dropped right on my patio. Good thing I heard you land, or you might have gotten away after all."

I can hear the smile in his voice as he prods me with the barrel of the gun between my shoulder blades, pushing me forward. My breathing quickens, and my legs tingle with the need to run, but I know I can't go fast enough. We're on the bridge now, walking toward the center of the span.

"Can't we go somewhere and talk about this?" My voice is hardly more than a squeak. "We could make a deal. I have money. I could get you out of the country, set you up in a new life, a good life. Or we could just go our separate ways and forget this happened."

"You ever get depressed, Elena?" Mike asks in a conversational tone. "You ever wake up in the morning and think it's just not worth the trouble to get out of bed?"

"No," I say, and grip the railing. How can I get away from him? The bridge is all straight lines, a perfect shooting gallery. I'd never make it to the other side. Even if I did, the highway is surrounded by miles of stunted sagebrush, with no trees, no houses, no cover. "How did it happen, Mike? You didn't mean to kill him, did you? Everybody loved Johnny."

The words come out in a rush. "You must have known Jack would turn you in if he found out you had anything to do with his death. So you took his body and dumped it out on the highway. That's what happened, isn't it? You made it look like a drive-by shooting, some random thing that had nothing to do with you." And it would have been easy for him, I think grimly, with his background. He'd know what clues the cops would be looking for.

Mike's voice is low, only inches from my ear. "I really think Johnny's death was too much for you, Elena. Everybody says so. In fact everyone thinks you're so depressed you'll probably end up killing yourself."

By now we've almost reached the middle of the bridge, and I glance at the void below us. Six hundred feet of nothing but air, and a river that looks like a thread. As I look over the railing, vertigo hits me like the sleek curve of a wave. I can't let myself drop into that abyss. I close my eyes and try to swallow, but I can't.

"Come on," he says. "You're a big girl. You're brave. Think about it. The end to all your suffering. The end to all your grief. It's the ultimate escape, Elena."

"No," I whisper, then plant my feet, hook my elbows around the steel railing and hang on with all my strength.

Mike comes around to face me, a reproachful look on his face. "Here I've gone to all this trouble, and you don't cooperate. You want to go back to the clinic and let Sykes turn you into a walking vegetable? I don't think you realize what an opportunity you're missing here."

"Wait," I say. "Mike, please. Just tell me one thing. Did you drug my coffee?"

"Hell, no," he says, smiling easily, scratching his cheek with the barrel of the gun. "I put it in your orange juice."

"It was LSD?"

He nods. "Two hits of the finest windowpane I could score."

"Why was it so important to make me look crazy?"

He tilts his head, appraising me with that same easy smile, but his eyes are flat, opaque. "You got any more questions before you jump? Or are you gonna make me shoot you?"

Trembling, I tighten my grip on the rail. "Down in Embudo, in the river—that was you, wasn't it? As soon as I saw that bruise on your thumb, I knew it was you. You wanted it to look like another botched suicide attempt, didn't you?"

"This is a hot spot for jumpers, you know. Three so far this year, six last year. No one's gonna think you didn't kill yourself, Elena. After all, you tried it before. Hell, you spent a month in a psych ward in New York, didn't you? Everybody's gonna think it was all too much for you."

My voice is hardly more than a whisper, and I can't draw a deep breath. "Johnny told me he wasn't killed on the highway. That must have scared you, because he wasn't, was he? You shot him somewhere else. The guesthouse, maybe. Maybe you left some clue, some evidence there, and you thought Johnny would tell me where to find it."

"We took care of the guesthouse before you ever got there," he says, looking over the railing.

The meaning of that *we* sinks in as he stuffs the gun in his pocket. Hurriedly I go on talking, anxious to keep him engaged in conversation. "It must have terrified you when I told you I wanted to hire a detective. And the reward! There must be somebody out there who knows something that would incriminate you. A million dollars might be a little too much temptation."

"Elena, it's been fun knowing you," he says. "You've been a good person, a good friend. Don't take it personally. None of this is your fault. You were just in the way." He comes toward me, smiling, slides an arm around my waist, then hooks the other arm under my leg and hoists me up above the railing.

A scream rips the air and it takes me a second to realize it's coming from me. I hang onto the steel bar, kick at his face and miss. He shoves my legs over the top. Still gripping the top slab of metal with my arms, my toes scramble wildly for a foothold on the outside of the guardrail. Under my feet the chasm is surreal, impossibly deep.

"Let *go*," Mike says, and hits my hand hard with the gun.

A burst of pain explodes in my hand and streaks up my arm. Whimpering, hugging the rail, I edge along the outside, bare toes gripping the concrete rim of the walkway while my heels hang over six hundred feet of air. My only chance is to get under the bridge and slide down a steep diagonal beam, down to the great arch that supports the span.

Mike walks toward me as I crouch down, grab the bottom of the railing and lower one leg toward the chasm below me to feel blindly for the beam. When he sees what I'm doing, his steps quicken until he's standing over me. I lower both legs and scrabble frantically for a purchase on the beam until they connect with the strut under the bridge.

Mike lifts his foot and stomps down on my hand.

Screaming with pain, I let go of the railing.

My body slams into the steel beam below. Knocked breathless, I skid down the steel beam to the arch that supports the bridge, then pitch forward on my belly and hug the slope of the arch with both arms. My legs quiver with fear as I wrap them tightly around the foot-wide slab of metal. I look up and see Mike straining over the railing, looking for me.

Our eyes connect, and I scrunch forward, shaking uncontrollably, clutching the narrow girder.

Zzzzippp. A bullet bounces off the steel, and the beam vibrates like a bell in my arms. Inching forward as fast as I can, I struggle to reach the cover of the next diagonal.

Mike throws a leg over the railing. He's coming after me. Moving carefully, he swings onto the girder, slides down and lands on the arch, light as a cat.

I scrabble forward with my belly pressed to the cold metal, wriggling toward the next beam. *Think,* I tell myself. *Stop panicking and think. Be like Tom. You can think your way out of this.*

When I look over my shoulder I see Mike walking up the arch toward me with the ease of a steelworker, seemingly unperturbed by the abyss.

I lurch forward, hand over hand.

When he speaks, his voice is terrifyingly close. "You just couldn't leave it alone, could you?"

Dizzy with vertigo, I take the L-shaped chunk of pipe out of my pocket, look over my shoulder and heave it at him. It misses by a yard, falls into the great nothing below us. A bullet whines over my head, and I scramble forward, finally reaching the diagonal beam. *He won't shoot me,* I keep telling myself. *He can't afford to leave any bullets in me. He wants me to jump. He wants it to look like suicide.*

Shaking, my arms and legs quiver like jelly as I pull myself up and swing behind the twelve-inch girder. The wind begins to blow from the north, and the bridge sways lightly in the breeze.

Another bullet screams into the metal, making it ring. Every instinct tells me to jump away from that sound, but to jump would mean falling six hundred feet. As I look around the girder I catch the flash of his teeth in his smile, and the smile enrages me.

"You son of a bitch!" I shout. "Tell me what happened, God damn you!"

When I peek around the edge of the metal strut that separates us, he lifts the gun and points it at me. "Sorry, Elena. I wish I could. I really do, but I made a promise, and I always keep my word." His voice is unnervingly calm.

Standing, hugging the girder, I pray. A sudden, strong updraft blasts my back. The baseball cap blows off Mike's head, and his hair streams up in the wind.

"Take off . . ." the wind whispers.

"This is where you dumped his ashes, right?" Mike shouts over the wind. "He's down there waiting for you, Elena. Once you let go you'll be able to talk to him as much as you want."

"Take off . . . !" Johnny hisses.

My legs quake, vibrating with terror. "Shut up!" I scream, and another bullet ricochets off the metal.

"TAKE OFF YOUR COAT!" Johnny yells, as the wind rises to a howl.

Finally I see. I understand. But terror almost makes me faint as I take one hand away from the beam and struggle to get my arm free of the coat sleeve.

Mike walks toward me, balancing easily on the curve of the arch.

Holding the girder with my other hand, I shrug the coat off. The wind catches it and makes it flap in my hand like a furious, living thing.

Mike lunges toward me, and I let it go. The coat flies toward him, slaps his body and wraps itself around his head, blinding him. His hands go to his face, and as he tears it away his body leans to the right, just an inch too far, and he staggers.

For a long, horrifying moment he wavers there on the high beam, reeling back and forth, fighting to regain his balance.

The coat whips up and away, and the gun drops. Mike

struggles, arms teetering. One foot reaches out and comes down on nothing but air.

And then he falls, mouth open, legs churning in mid-air, arms flailing, his body growing smaller and smaller. The wind dies as suddenly as it began, returning to the stillness of early morning. A raven glides past, tilts its wings and wheels off to the west.

When Mike finally hits the river, I close my eyes.

Chapter Fifteen

My legs go numb as the metal beam digs into my thighs. I tell myself over and over again not to look below, but the abyss pulls my gaze down the basalt walls, down to the shadows in the gorge where Mike disappeared. Beauty has never looked so brutal.

A truck roars across the bridge above me, making the concrete shake, and the beam in front of me vibrates in my arms. I shout, but the truck rushes by in a whoosh of air, seventy, eighty miles per hour.

After that, nothing stirs in the silence. Time stretches in front of me, time to agonize over the fact of being here or mull over possibilities, connections, reasons for what happened. I struggle to fill in the puzzle to keep my mind off the distance to the ground. "We took care of the guesthouse," Mike told me. Who was he talking about? And then, "I made a promise." A promise to Jack? It must be Jack.

The steel cuts into my legs, and my arms begin to go to sleep as I clutch the beam. If I ever get out of here, where can I go? Who can I trust? By now Dr. Sykes knows I've disappeared from the clinic, so the police are probably looking for me. What if I tell the police the truth, tell them everything that's happened to me?

I think of Johnny's guesthouse, practically untouched after their search. I hear Maggie's voice saying "The police were great," and Jack saying "We had a few lawyers there." I think of the Daltons' power, their money, their doctors, their tentacled reach into every aspect of New Mexican bureaucracy. I think of Dr. Sykes saying, "When there's been an attempt at suicide . . . the state is allowed to step in." Detective Gallegos would love to send me back to the clinic. No, I can't go to the police.

Tom, I think, and the thought of his face fills me with yearning, followed quickly by resentment. After knowing me for twenty years, why couldn't he see what was happening to me? Why didn't he trust me? He and Johnny used to roll their eyes whenever I lost my temper, and then Tom would talk to me in that careful voice I hated, as if he were the sane one, the responsible, clear-thinking adult, and I was the lunatic. But how could Tom have let them lock me up?

Another car rumbles overhead, too fast, and I think, *you idiots!* Why are you in such a hurry? Why can't you get out of your stupid car and look? The landscape glows as fingers of light creep across the mesa, and the gorge turns to gold as the sun rises. Even at eighty miles an hour anyone can see it's beautiful, damn it.

The raven returns, spreading its broad black wings and tilting its head to study me as it soars by. God, it looks so easy. Arms outstretched, a little lift, and I could fly too, for about six seconds. I keep my eyes glued to the lattice of girders above me until the urge passes. *I do not want to die.*

Is Johnny astounded to see me here, now? My love for him was constantly expressed as worry, and I wonder if it would surprise him to know I never thought of life as a series of dangers until he was born. It makes me cringe to think of the way I used to talk to him, the endless parade of instructions. Don't Go Out, Don't Cross The Street, Don't Run, Don't Touch That, Don't, Don't, Don't, an embarrassing echo of

221

my mother's voice. No wonder he always wanted to be farther away from me than I wanted him to be. Go ahead! I should have told him. Go play with your addict friends in sleazy nightclubs, see if I care.

Someone will walk out on the bridge, I tell myself. Dozens, hundreds of people come here every day. It's the height of the tourist season. *You'll be okay.* My legs and shoulders scream from the tension of hanging for too long above too much emptiness. A series of shivers racks my limbs, and I realize I'm in shock, and my body is telling me this is bad, this is too much, and I can't take anymore. Lightly banging my forehead against the steel to get some feeling back in my neck, I open my mouth and let out a moan.

And then I hear a woman's voice. "Hurry up, honey!" she calls. "Do you have the camera?"

"Hello! Hello!" I call out.

The voice comes nearer. "Oh, my God! Hank, there's a lady down there! Hello? Are you all right? Oh, my God! Hang on! Hang on!"

"I need help," I yell, and burst into tears.

"Don't move!" she says. "My husband has a cell phone! Don't worry! We'll get you up!"

It takes a crew of six men several hours to close the bridge to traffic and organize the rope and tackle and harness to hoist me from my perch. A burst of applause greets me on the bridge, and when I see all the people thronged there I want to sink into a hole and disappear. Two police cruisers are parked behind an ambulance, and cars are backed up on both sides of the bridge, waiting to cross. Tourists and onlookers jostle with TV cameramen, and I duck my head and shake my hair down to hide my face.

My arms and legs quiver uncontrollably when they un-buckle me from the harness, and I fall heavily against a paramedic. The police ask me my name, my reason for climbing under the bridge. I don't talk. I don't say a word.

The paramedics lift me to a gurney and wheel it into the back of an ambulance. One of the medics steps in next to me, and the doors close. The siren cracks the air like a long scream, and we pull away, moving through the blockage of cars with turtle slowness until we reach the highway.

By now the sun has been baking me for three hours against the steel span of the bridge. Desperate for water, I tug the sleeve of the paramedic and mime tilting a drink to my lips. He offers me a bottle, and I drain it.

The paramedic is young, his cheeks furred by tiny blond hairs, his eyes bright with sympathy as he takes my blood pressure and pulse.

"I need help," I say.

He looks startled, then cups his ear and bends over me. "What?"

What am I going to tell him? I stare at his clean polo shirt with his name embroidered on the chest. Alex. He wears black cargo pants and combat boots, and he smells like soap. My clothes are tattered, filthy.

"I need clothes," I yell over the sound of the siren.

Alex nods indulgently. "They'll give you clean clothes at the hospital," he shouts.

I raise my voice again. "I can't go to the hospital. Please. Help me."

His eyes contract with skepticism. "Who are you?"

Unbuckling the strap holding me to the gurney, I sit up and swing my legs off the stretcher. "There are people who want to lock me up. If I go to the hospital they'll find me."

His eyes widen as I babble for the next few miles, begging, pleading with him to trade clothes with me, to let me jump out at a stoplight, to help me get away. The more I talk the more his face hardens into a stubborn look of resistance.

"I have money." I pull out the crumpled hundred dollar bills that Richard gave me and try to push them into his hands.

He shoves them back at me, and looks at me in disgust. "Ma'am, do you have any idea how much this operation is going to cost you? You're looking at a bill for ten grand, minimum. Now please, just be quiet and lie back down."

Through the back window I see the tall cottonwoods lining Kit Carson Park, and the vehicle slows as traffic thickens near the plaza. I don't have much time. The siren echoes off buildings lining the street as the ambulance edges around cars pulled over on the shoulder. We're almost crawling now. Before I lose my nerve, I lunge for the door and yank the handle.

Alex wrestles me away from the door, and I shove him and look around wildly for a weapon. The ambulance jolts over a pothole, and his grip loosens at the unexpected movement. I twist away, grab a fire extinguisher from the wall and swipe at him.

His face is startled, then tense, alert as an animal, and he holds one arm out wide to enclose my movements. With his free hand he pulls a syringe from his pocket, bites off the cap with his teeth and comes toward me. I hurl the extinguisher at him and hit him square in the chest, knocking him to the floor.

"I'm gonna fuckin' *kill* you," he says, leaping up, and jabs the syringe against the side of my neck. Stunned, I sink to my knees. In a hazy flash of peripheral vision I see the red and blue revolving lights of the cop car cruising behind us. Leaning forward, I clutch at the metal leg of the gurney, and miss. My face hits the floor with a crack.

★ ★ ★ ★ ★

It feels like I can't have been out for more than a minute, but when I wake up I'm in a hospital room, wearing a hospital gown, lying in a bed with metal rails. Maggie sits at the foot of the bed, shaking my foot. Her body glows in a tailored white suit, and she looks cool and sophisticated, legs crossed, a white spectator pump dangling from her toe.

As soon as she sees my eyes flutter open she leans forward. "El? Elena, honey? Are you okay? Can you hear me?"

My head feels thick, dizzy, and a wave of nausea spills through me as I turn my face toward the window. Late afternoon light angles through the blinds. At least two or three hours must have passed since Alex stuck the needle in my neck.

Looking back at Maggie, my brain works sluggishly to figure out why she's here. I can't help staring at her suit, the matching shoes, her hair, her face, all so perfect, like an airbrushed commercial for some exciting luxury product I could never afford. "What are you doing here?"

"I thought you might need some clothes." Maggie pulls a large white purse up on the bed and takes out a familiar black linen sheath. She shakes it out, lays it flat on the sheet, then brings out fresh underpants, a camisole, and a pair of black espadrilles.

The sight of my own clothes affects me like nothing else, and I put my hands over my face and cry. I can't stop myself, can't hold it in, can't pretend to be brave, can't put a good face on things for one more second.

"Oh, for heaven's sake," Maggie says, patting me nervously. "Come on, honey, let's get you dressed. You'll feel better."

"You don't know what I've been through," I whisper. The horror of the past few hours comes crashing down on me, the

225

bridge, Mike's body, twirling down and down, the terror of those hours when I was stuck on a twelve inch wide piece of steel, with nothing but air below me.

Maggie goes to the window and peers through a gap in the blinds. "Dr. Sykes just pulled into parking lot. If we want to get out of here without running into him, we better hurry."

"How did Sykes find out I'm here?" I ask. "I didn't tell them my name."

"Apparently somebody at the clinic recognized your face on the news. Dr. Sykes called me about half an hour ago to tell me you'd been found and he was coming to get you. That's how I knew you were here. I've been worried sick about you, El. Come on. He'll be here any second." Impatiently she pulls the sheet off me, then tugs at the bottom of the hospital gown and pulls it up, lifts my arms and yanks the gown over my head. Groggy, I struggle to slide the underpants up my legs, the camisole over my upraised arms, the sheath over my head.

When I stand, dizziness hits me like a sledgehammer. Whatever was in that hypodermic makes my head feel like the inside of a drum, and my vision is fuzzy, out of focus. I press one hand to my forehead and wait for the room to stop spinning.

With anxious, jerky movements Maggie laces the espadrilles to my feet, then pulls me toward the door.

Something about this reminds me of the van, and Mike. It's too easy. Too fast. I twist away, go to the window and look through the blinds. A familiar white van with the clinic logo is parked in the lot below. If Sykes is coming up here, what choice do I have?

"Are the police guarding the room?" I ask.

"There's a chair outside, but if you had a guard he must

have thought you'd be out for a while. I didn't see him when I came in."

"They'll recognize me if I try to walk out."

"Put this on," Maggie says, quickly unpinning the wig from her head.

Without the wig, her hair is plastered to her head, and slivers of scalp show through the dull strands that are more gray than blonde. She looks fifteen years older without that sunny cap of curls.

"What happened to your hair?" I ask, staring.

"Never mind that now," she says, smiling, and pulls the wig over my head, then pokes the loose strands under it with quick, painful jabs. The wig feels tight, hot.

Once we're out in the hall, we walk quickly to the fire exit and clatter down a flight of stairs, emerging into the heat of the parking lot.

Maggie trots ahead of me to a white Jaguar that's parked in a handicapped slot, then slides behind the wheel as I hurry into the passenger's side. The leather interior is still cool from air conditioning, and when I close the door the sound of traffic disappears. I sink into the embrace of the soft white leather, stare out at the people on the street beyond the tinted windows and brace myself for whatever happens next.

She backs out in a hurry, then accelerates over speed bumps in the driveway and lurches into the northbound traffic on Paseo del Pueblo Sur. A horn blares as she cuts off a driver, and I look over my shoulder. There's no sign of pursuit, and I pull off the wig and throw it on the back seat.

"I'd like to go to Tom's," I say.

Her face is intent, both hands gripping the wheel. "He's not there. As soon as Sykes told us you were missing, Tom went out to look for you. Ever since he found out you couldn't have any visitors out there, he's been frantic. He went there practically every day and tried to see you, but they always threw him out. Did you see him? Did he get any messages to you?"

"No." A knot of suspicion in my chest eases suddenly, and I feel a glimmer of hope. "Where is he now?"

"He was sure you'd try to hike out. He's been out there all day, looking for you in the badlands behind the clinic."

"Does he have a cell phone? I'll call him."

"I tried to give him mine, but he wouldn't take it. But he has my cell number. He said he'd check in with me later. We'll have to wait for him to call."

"Then let's wait at your house."

"It's the first place they'll look for you, El. Dr. Sykes knew you were staying with us."

She's probably right. "Then let's go to Tom's."

"Do you have a key?"

"I know where he keeps it," I say. She nods, and I study her profile, wishing I could read her mind.

"Mike's missing, too," she says. "He and Jack had some kind of falling out, and he disappeared a few days ago. Jack's been worried sick about him."

"Mike is dead, Maggie."

The blood leaves her face, and she turns to stare at me. "What happened?"

"He tried to push me off the gorge bridge. He fell. He's still down there."

Her eyes are dark with shock as she turns her gaze back to the road, and she takes a deep breath and passes her hand over her face, then adjusts her grip on the wheel. "We'll talk about it when we get to Tom's. Let me concentrate on getting us out of here, El. They have speed traps all up and down this road."

We head toward upper Ranchitos, our old neighborhood,

where the adobe houses are farther apart and a few cows graze by the Rio Pueblo. A nearly overwhelming fatigue rolls over me as I stare at the lengthening shadows in the fields. I think about Tom searching for me in the badlands behind the clinic, going up and down those steep arroyos, wandering for miles, yelling for me. Good, I think. At least he's trying.

Maggie pulls into the dirt driveway in front of Tom's house, bumps over the cattle guard and comes to a halt. The spare key lies hidden under the loose cinderblock where we always used to keep it, and I unlock the door. As soon as we're inside, Maggie bolts it, pulls her purse off her shoulder and slings it on the kitchen counter.

The phone rings, and I walk toward it.

"Don't answer it," she says. "They'll be looking for you. Tom said he'd call my cell number."

The shrill sound holds us transfixed, and we stare at the telephone until it stops.

"You must be starving," she says, opening cupboard doors. "Tom must have something to eat around here." She pulls out a box, frowns at it. "How about some soup?"

I lower myself to a chair at the table. The last time I ate was sometime yesterday afternoon, but I don't feel hungry. The headache is still there, a dull pounding above my eyes, and there's a metallic taste in my mouth. Maybe I should eat. The kitchen counters are bare except for a set of steel canisters, arranged in descending size. Flour, sugar, coffee, tea. A red and white striped dishtowel hangs over the oven handle.

Tom has hung a mirror above the sink, and his shaving brush and razor sit in a mug on the drainboard. The sight of his razor stabs me with a sudden longing for him, sharp as a splinter. I want to feel his hands around my waist and hug the comforting bulk of him, lay my face against the slope of his chest and forget everything that's happened to me.

Maggie runs water into a pan, sets it on the stove and lights the burner. "Why don't you stretch out on the couch? I bet you're exhausted."

I don't move from the table. "I think we should talk, Maggie." In the mirror I see her reflection as she tears open a packet of Lipton's chicken broth and pours the contents into the pan. She opens a drawer and pulls out a wooden spoon.

Maggie's back is turned toward me, but her hands are clearly visible in the mirror, dipping into her purse, bringing out a prescription bottle. Her fingers tremble as she opens the bottle and pours a cascade of capsules into the pan, then stirs them into the bubbling liquid.

"This'll be ready in a second." Her face is a mask, her voice steady. A minute later she flicks off the gas and pours the broth in a mug.

Fear makes connections snap together in my head like magnets. The way Mike looked at Maggie and Jack, amused, cocky, like he knew something. The way Jack acted strained around him, but never kicked him out. The fact of Mike's presence everywhere, in their house, at their party, even up in the mountains, where they'd never invited him before.

"There was no reporter," I say slowly, figuring it out. "Mike was blackmailing you."

It's a guess, but she turns and gives me a sharp, frightened look, assessing what I know. Her eyes dart toward her purse, then back to me with that same frightened look, not bothering anymore with concern. She holds the mug out toward me. "You need to drink this, El."

I sit rigid in my chair. "I'm not hungry." My hands start to shake, and I hold the table, anchoring myself.

Maggie puts the mug down on the table in front of me, carefully avoiding my gaze. "Please, El. Drink it for me."

"You go ahead. I'll make some later."

She shakes her head as tears pool in her eyes. "You know I can't do that, don't you?"

"What did you put in there, Maggie?"

A tense silence stretches between us. I hear the clock on the wall, the click of seconds passing. The refrigerator comes to life with a hum that sounds ominous in the hushed room, and I push the mug away.

Her whole face seems to melt, and tears roll down her cheeks as she turns back to the counter, opens her purse, pulls out a gun and points it at me. Stricken, I stare at it, mesmerized by its bulk, the way it fits her hand, the unexpected length of the barrel. The dark hole at the end stares back at me. It's like looking at a snake.

My voice comes out in a whisper. "Put it down, Maggie."

The gun quivers in her hand like a living thing, and her voice comes out in a rush. "I don't want to shoot you, El. Please. It would be so much easier for both of us if you drink the soup."

The room seems stifling, and I fight the urge to bolt. I lift the mug carefully, as if it might explode. "Tell me why Johnny died, Maggie. You owe me that much."

All the air goes out of her then, and she sags against the counter and pushes a limp strand of hair away from her face with the back of her hand. When she finally speaks her voice is so low I have to strain to hear her. "You think Johnny's success just happened, don't you?"

A thickness fills my head, followed by a ringing. I put the mug down. "I think he worked hard for it."

She stares at the floor, shaking her head. "Musicians like Johnny—they're a dime a dozen, Elena. Any kid who's won a talent contest in high school could have filled his shoes."

"That's not true," I say, shocked.

She laughs, a dry, mirthless sound, like a cough. "Jack

made Johnny. My God, do you have any idea how much money it takes to launch a singer? To produce a single video? To take an act on the road with an entourage of fifty production assistants? We sank millions into that kid. Jack never let an interview go by without hyping him, telling everyone how talented he was, letting everyone know what a gift his voice was to the world." Her words echo around the kitchen, and she leans toward me, her eyes glistening with tears. "And you know why?"

My mind goes blank, and a queasy feeling spreads through my stomach as I grip the table and stare at her.

Her voice wavers, edgy and intimate at the same time. "Neither did I, at first. Alison kept making up excuses to go to the cities where he was playing, and they'd meet afterward. I was such a fool. I thought Jack was building Johnny's career for her sake, because he wanted Johnny to be his son-in-law. But Jack was just using her."

Maggie stares out the kitchen window, grief etched into every line on her face. "Back in March, Alison came home for a visit, and she ran over to the guesthouse before she even brought her suitcase in from the car. A few seconds later she came flying out of there, and her face was white.

" 'They're kissing,' she said. And then she burst into tears."

For once there seems to be no movement outside, no birdsong, no cars passing by, no grinding gears. The sun has hammered everyone back behind adobe walls.

"I was so stupid, El. I couldn't imagine what she was talking about. I said, 'Who's kissing?' 'Daddy,' she said. 'Daddy's kissing Johnny.' "

My pulse begins to race, thinking of Johnny's sharp, foxy young face, the transparent fringe of fuzz on his upper lip, the wispy extensions of his sideburns. I think of Jack touching him, stroking his hair. I feel myself winding up, vibrating like a crystal about to shatter.

Squeezing the table, I say, "I don't believe you."

Maggie laughs. "Johnny liked men, El. Older men."

"That's a lie."

Her gaze nails me to my chair. "He left you when he was sixteen! He was just starting to admit it to himself."

My brain twitches in my skull, pulsing like an overheated muscle, and I struggle to concentrate, but my mind ricochets off to the past. I think of Johnny's room in our apartment, the posters hanging on the wall. Rock stars, athletes, musicians, all men, handsome men, older men. I think of how Johnny always sounded so relaxed when he talked about girls. Even though he had plenty of female friends, I never saw him hold a girl's hand, or kiss a girl, or even act like he wanted to. Dazed, I sit there, gripping the table as if the room were twirling through space. Jack and Johnny. Johnny and Jack.

Maggie goes on. "When I first met Jack, he told me he loved to watch young men, boys who were just waking up, sexually. 'I can teach them so much,' he used to say. 'They need someone like me. They want someone like me.' I thought it was all so innocent. And my God, it was part of the business, wasn't it? He was a mentor to those kids. He taught them how to strut, how to shine. He had the perfect excuse to watch them."

Anger twists through my gut like a knife as I try to make sense of the words spilling out of her mouth, watching as seams appear in her makeup, where the tracks of her tears have cut through the foundation. Jack. That son of a bitch. Jack seduced my son.

"I couldn't stop him," she says. "And he's still my husband, El. For God's sake, you know how I felt about him, and I still feel that way. We've been married for more than twenty years, and look at what we've accomplished! We have Alison, a beautiful home, this beautiful life together. Besides, it would have wrecked Johnny's career if the truth came out. You know who buys his records? Young teenage girls, that's who. You think they'd go on buying his records if they knew he was gay?"

My breathing quickens, and I can feel myself sliding into a void where nothing is real except the confusion in my chest. Uncertainty drifts around me like a fog. And through the fog I'm beginning to see the bulk of Maggie's truth, advancing like an iceberg to blot out my world.

Her china-blue eyes widen, shimmering with tears. "When I found out what was happening with Johnny, believe me, I tried to scare Jack into giving him up. I yelled, screamed, warned them both—but Jack wouldn't let me kick him out. I had to fire most of the staff, the maids, the cook, the pool boy, anyone who might have seen them fooling around. I went through hell. But I knew it wouldn't last, and I was determined to get through it. I'm not a quitter, El."

I sit there clutching the edge of the table as if the house were breaking apart around us. "Tell me what happened, Maggie."

Standing by the counter, she looks away, distressed, the gun slack at her side. "I walked in on them. They were in bed together. *Our* bed. *My* bed. Jack tried to cover himself with the sheet, but Johnny got tangled in it and then they both started laughing. It felt like they were laughing at me, El. They couldn't stop."

Maggie takes in a long, shaky breath and pulls herself taller. "Mike had given us a gun for Christmas, and it was in the nightstand by the bed." She glances down at the gun in her hand, grasps it more firmly, lifts the barrel toward me.

"I'd never used a gun before, and I wasn't even sure it was loaded, but I pulled it out of the drawer and pointed it at them." Her voice becomes high, strained. "I just wanted them to shut up. I swear, El, that was all I was trying to do, just scare them a little."

My face is numb, and suddenly I can't breathe, can't take in any air at all.

Her voice begins to tremble, her eyes magnified by tears. "Jack was yelling at me, and I was screaming at him. Johnny tried to calm us down, but Jack said . . . Jack said . . . he said I was nothing to him. *Nothing.* He said he wanted a divorce.

"And I could see he pitied me. *Me! Jack* was sorry for *me! I* couldn't bear it, El. I've *worked* and *slaved* for that man, for the business, for *us.* I've bitten my tongue a thousand times, looking the other way while he . . . and this was what he thought of me? I've kept this whole fucking empire running smoothly for him, and he had the *nerve* . . . it's not over. It wasn't over then and it's not over now." Her voice dissolves into a sob.

She gulps air and goes on, tears spilling freely down her cheeks. "At that moment I didn't care what happened to any of us. It was like jumping out of an airplane. Jack must have seen something in my face, something that made him afraid, because he grabbed Johnny and pushed him out of the way, but I was squeezing the gun so hard . . . it went off, El. The gun went off."

I stare at her, unable to move, and a wild feeling rips through me, and a wild sound comes out of my mouth, a low growl, wordless but human. My body is taut, shaking. I can't stop shaking.

Maggie goes on, overflowing with tears, the words tumbling over each other. "We were hysterical—Jack was holding Johnny, and Johnny was bleeding. He was already dead.

That's when Mike came in. He saw me, holding the gun. He saw Johnny."

She takes in a deep, quivering breath and licks her lips. "It all went to hell after that. At first we were going to call the police. Then Mike told us it would destroy Alison if we did. And he was right, El. The tabloids would have had a field day. The publicity, the scandal, having her mother hauled into court and charged with murder—I couldn't do that to her. She's only twenty! She's just starting out in life."

"*Bullshit.*" It comes out as a choked whisper. "You wanted to save yourself." A savage, frightening urgency courses through me, a desire to rip the gun from her hand and shoot her until every bullet is spent.

Maggie deflates under my gaze and moves away, toward the window, plucks back the curtain and scans the driveway, as if she's expecting someone. Then she turns back to me, avoiding my eyes.

The muzzle of the gun droops against her side as she goes on talking. "There was blood all over the bed," she whispers. "Jack was a mess, he was hysterical. Mike wrapped the body in plastic sheeting and drove out to the highway, after it got dark. He left it out there."

"So you got away with murder."

"It looked that way for a while," she says in a small voice. "The police were sure it was a freak shooting, a random thing. But Mike started asking us for more and more money, laying it on thick about family obligations. We bought him a boat, a plane, a hundred acres outside Santa Fe. And then you came to visit."

Her words sift into me like poison, and I nod, learning big things quickly. Her makeup is gone now, eroded by tears, and her face looks slack, exhausted, but determined.

"You told me Johnny was talking to you, and he was

telling you things no one but us knew. Things we certainly didn't want anyone else to know. We were petrified. Mike said we couldn't take any chances—we had to scare you off and get you to go back to Manhattan. So he followed you and Alison to the river, the night of the party. He was the one— well, you know. And when that didn't work, he said we had to do something more drastic."

Maggie waves the gun, irate now. "And you wouldn't give up! You told Jack you wanted to set up a reward to catch the killer. A million dollars. Jesus. What if the pool boy or the cook or the maid came forward and told you about Jack and Johnny? You tore apart the guesthouse, eavesdropped on us in our bedroom. It was a nightmare. And I was terrified Alison would spill the beans about Jack and Johnny—she kept pushing me to tell you. If you hadn't been so goddamned persistent . . . oh, El, this is the only way out for me now, can't you see that? I can't lose everything, not after I've worked so hard to get it. It would destroy me. It would destroy my family. I can't let that happen. Elena, I love you like a sister, but I can't let you do this to me."

There's a sound of a vehicle easing into the driveway, rolling up to the house. Maggie's eyes lock on mine as we hear the car door open and close, and footsteps crunch over gravel.

The knob on the front door rattles.

Maggie walks to the door, holding the gun up to her chest, her voice anxious as she calls out. "Who's there?"

Chapter Sixteen

"It's me."

When Maggie unbolts the door and ushers Jack inside, the sight of him sparks a rush of adrenaline through my veins, a burst of energy that makes me want to lash out, no matter what the cost.

"It's about time," Maggie says. "You got my message?"

"I came as soon as I could. Do you really need that thing?" he asks, nodding toward the gun.

"It's too late, Jack. We don't have a choice. She already knows what happened."

A dull roar fills my head, and I stand abruptly, knocking over my chair.

Maggie swings the gun toward me. "Sit down."

My heart pounds like a big bass drum, so loud I'm sure they can both hear it. "You're going to shoot me?"

"I mean it. Sit."

Slowly I bend down to right the chair and lower myself to sit on it. Every muscle in my body tightens as I watch Jack remove his sunglasses, glance at me, then look away. For once his bright hazel eyes are nervous as they dart from Maggie's face to mine. His confusion makes him jumpy, and he's obviously dismayed by the gun.

"Mike is dead," she says.

Jack stares at her, then leans back against the door as if he's been struck. "You shot him?"

She widens her eyes as if amazed he would accuse her, then tips her head toward me. "El pushed him off the Gorge Bridge."

All the air seems to go out of him, and he walks unsteadily to a chair at the table and sinks down next to me. Elbows on the table, he leans forward, covers his face with his hands and takes a deep, shuddering breath.

"Mike was trying to kill me," I say. "Wasn't that your idea, Jack?"

He looks up at Maggie. "This is getting out of hand."

Again, she gives him that look of disbelief. "Don't be an idiot—we can't stop now. We'll say El was depressed when we left here, and we were afraid she might do something to hurt herself. We'll make it look like suicide."

He stares at her. "You want to kill her? Here? Now? This is your best friend you're talking about."

"This is survival, Jack. I love El, but I love Alison more."

"You love yourself," I say. "That's who you're trying to save."

"It's true," she says, holding Jack's gaze. "I am trying to save myself, to save *us*. Look at what we have, Jack! Are you ready to throw it all away now, after we've come this far?"

Trembling in my chair, I wait for Jack to look at me, and when he finally turns, his face is white as salt. If I have any chance of walking out of here alive, it depends on him. Some vestige of self-preservation screams this inside my head, but rage boils over caution. "You set me up, didn't you? You're on the board at that clinic. How else could Mike have checked into the room underneath mine? You made sure he had access to one of the clinic vans." The words tumble out of my mouth as the depth of his betrayal catches up with me. "You let him *drug me*," I say, spearing him with my gaze.

"Jesus Christ," he whispers. "You think I knew about

this?" He shakes his head. "El, I swear, it was Mike's idea to give you the LSD. Maggie set him up at the clinic to keep an eye on you, but I never thought he'd go this far."

Desperate to get through to him, I reach across the table, clutch his hand and dig my nails into the skin. "I trusted you with my only child. For God's sake, Jack, you were his *godfather*."

He pulls his hand away, eyes glossed with tears. "I'm sorry, El."

"Don't listen to her," Maggie says.

Jack stands, and I rise from the table as Maggie draws nearer. "El, you have to believe me," he says. "This wasn't something we planned. Maggie got carried away, that's all."

"It was murder."

Spots of color darken Maggie's cheeks. "It's too late, Jack. You think she won't go to the police? You think we'll ever have a good night's sleep again, with her out there? She'll ruin us. For God's sake, think what she'll do to Alison. We have to go through with this." She turns toward me, her face hectic with emotion. "I tried to protect you, damn it! I thought you'd be safe in the clinic. I thought you'd give up and go back to Manhattan. But you wouldn't leave it alone. Then Dr. Sykes asked me if Mike really had access to drugs, and why you kept harping on it. You were so goddamn obstinate, he was starting to believe you."

"Good," I say.

Maggie's face takes on a feverish look, her eyes lit with a crazy glow as she turns to Jack. "Don't you see, Jack? She's had a death wish ever since Johnny died. Why else would she keep pushing and pushing like this? This is what she wants. We have to finish it."

"No," Jack says. "No more. I can't do it."

Pleading, she says, "Honey, we've come this far. This is

the only loose end that's left, and then we're done. All we have to do is wait for El to drink the soup."

He looks at her as if he's seeing her for the first time. "I can't do it, Maggie. You were lucky the last time, but this—this is different."

"*Lucky?*" I blurt out, unable to contain myself. "You call it *lucky*, Jack?"

"Shut up!" Maggie says, glaring at me, then turns back to him. "Don't you get it? We don't have a choice. If we don't finish this, it'll only get worse."

His stare intensifies. "It's already worse. Mike's dead. He'd be alive now if it weren't for you."

"I had nothing to do with that!"

"Maggie, it's time to stop," he says.

There's an edge to her laugh. "Do you really think I've put up with your shit for twenty years so I can spend the rest of my life in jail?" she hisses. "Look at yourself. You're forty-two years old. You think he loved you for your body? Your scintillating personality? Wake *up!* It was a career move."

"Johnny wasn't like that," he says. "I loved him."

His words sift into me, leave me feeling hollow and uncertain. *You don't know what my life was like,* Johnny told me, weeks ago, out by the shrine on the highway. *There was love.*

Jack takes a deep breath and squares his shoulders as he faces her, and when he speaks his voice is low and compelling. "Maggie, I still care about you. What you did to Johnny wasn't premeditated—it was an accident. We'll get you the best lawyers. You could get out of this with nothing more than probation."

A sick, painful tightening begins in my chest as I wait, praying Jack knows what he's doing, praying she'll collapse into grief and give him the gun.

Maggie stares at him, a savage look on her face. "Just how stupid do you think I am?"

Jack holds up one hand, palm out. "I'll do everything in my power to make sure you don't go to jail."

"I'm not one of your boys, Jack. You don't tell me what to do."

Jack bristles at this. "You plan on shooting me? You really think you could dig your way out of that?" A look comes over his face, the kind of look you might give a crippled dog, a faint revulsion shrouded in pity. Awareness crackles around Maggie as she takes it in. She's lost him forever, and she knows it.

He takes a step toward her, chin lifted, confidence flowing from his voice. "Come on, Maggie. I'll do my best to clean up this mess, but I'm making a phone call."

Her voice is like steel. "I won't let you do that, Jack."

Sorrowfully he touches her shoulder, then turns and walks toward the phone.

"Stop," she says, and the barrel of the gun swings toward him.

He waves her off as he picks up the receiver.

"I'm warning you, Jack," she says.

Turning to face her, his eyes are perfectly calm. Then he glances down and punches a number.

A soft, percussive *thhhppptt* comes from the gun, no louder than the pop of a cork, and Jack makes a small sound, an exhalation of surprise as he crumples to the floor and falls on his back. His arms and legs sprawl at unnatural angles, and he doesn't move.

All color leaves Maggie's face, and the room is still.

Frozen, shocked, I stare at the bright circle of red blooming on the front of his shirt. A profound silence holds us motionless as Maggie stands there, the air charged with our held breath. The gun drops from her hand and clatters to the floor, and a sob escapes from her throat as she rushes over to Jack, falls to her knees and clutches him to her chest. His arms dangle when she pulls him close. There's no breath in him, no life left in his open eyes, and she unleashes a high-pitched wail that cuts through me. *He's dead,* I think, but I can't believe it. Jack's mouth falls open and his face goes slack as the color drains away. The blood from his chest smears the front of her white suit.

My legs are jelly, but I walk over, pick up the gun and toss it through the open window, out into the tangle of thistles in the side yard. Once the gun is gone my whole body begins to quiver, my knees buckle underneath me, and I sink to the floor on the other side of Maggie, my back against the wall.

The curtains rise and fall over the open window, and a breeze stirs the hot air in the room. The coolness passes over my face like a benediction, and my arms begin to tingle. Johnny is here. I feel him, close as the shadows. Tenderness for him floods through me, a pull as deep as gravity, an exhausted longing to hold him in my arms.

"Why didn't you tell me, Johnny?"

"You know why."

"You were protecting them."

"Bingo."

"But how could you want to save Maggie, after what she did to you?"

"Bringing her down would have crushed Alison. Maggie was right about that. I couldn't do that to her. I'd already hurt her enough."

"So you wanted Maggie to get away with murder?"

"Justice won't bring me back, Mom. Besides, she can't escape herself. She'll find her own way to pay for what she did."

I can feel Johnny taking in the two of them next to me, the

curve of Maggie's shoulder cradling Jack's limp body in her arms, both of them so still they might be carved out of marble.

"Jack said he loved you."

"I know."

"And you loved him?"

"I still do."

"He let Mike take your body and dump it on the highway. I saw the pictures, Johnny. You were spattered with mud, with a hole in your chest. And Jack lied about all of it to keep himself safe. You call that love?"

"You call that safe?" he says, looking at the corpse in Maggie's arms.

Maggie lets out a long, shuddering breath, her head sinks lower over Jack's body, and her back shakes as she weeps silently, steadily.

"Jack was twice your age—a married man, for God's sake. You didn't owe him anything more than your voice."

"You think I don't know that? It was me, all right? I was the one who started it. I wanted Jack more than I'd ever wanted anything in my life."

I feel Johnny looking at me, the way he used to look at me when he'd tell me something private, something secret, and I know he's afraid I won't understand. And he's right to be afraid. I can't. Not this. Not Jack.

"He was older, Johnny. He should have pushed you away."

"He did, Mom. About a year ago, we were alone in the studio. I put my hand on his wrist and looked at him. It was the first time I ever tried to let him know how I felt, and he knew what I was asking. He said one word to me: 'No.' Then he left the room."

"Why couldn't you let him go?"

"I tried. I really tried. We went on working together, pre-

tending it never happened. But it was there. We both felt it. When-ever I walked in a room, Jack turned red. I'd catch him staring at me. He'd catch me staring at him. We went on like that for months."

My body goes cold, listening to this, and a fierce, aching desire floods through me, a desire to save him from every-thing that happened, even now.

"Last December, that was when he finally gave in. We had one winter together. And this is what it cost him."

"It cost you more," I say. "He had forty-two years. You had half that."

"What I had with Jack—you can't measure it in years. You know what it's like. You and Dad had it when you started out. You have it now. It's forever, Mom." His voice fades to a whisper, the faintest thread.

"Don't go," I say, but he's already gone.

A small breeze lifts the curtains. The air begins to sparkle in the space above Jack's lifeless body, and then the sparks disappear. I listen for Johnny, listen so hard I can hear the beat of my pulse, and an unbearable sadness pools in my heart. *Where are you?* I ask the shadows, but there's no re-sponse, and I'm filled with the certainty that he's really gone, now. We won't talk like this again.

Maggie sits slumped against the wall, oblivious to every-thing but Jack's body in her arms. In the silence my mind set-tles on the woman beside me, and I wonder how a lifetime together could end like this. From the crib we shared, to the dusty classrooms of our old Catholic grammar school, to the driveway out in front of this house, where we lay on air mat-tresses with our kids and husbands and watched meteor showers on hot August nights—Maggie's been with me longer than anyone. How many times have I watched her sail into a party on a wave of energy, chest thrust forward like the prow of a ship, exuding life, energy, happiness? Whenever she accompanied me, I felt safe. She was always there, part of my family, part of my heart. I sort through crazy heaps of memory, searching for a sign of the killer who lived inside her.

Finally Maggie releases Jack's body, pushes herself up and stands there unsteadily for a moment, leaning against the wall for support. Instinctively I tense as she towers above me, but Maggie's focus has nothing to do with me.

She's staring at the mug on the table.

Her face is haggard, a portrait of suffering. A sense of calm spreads through me as I watch her, knowing what she wants. Something dark and cold within me waits, willing her to go ahead.

Moving like a sleepwalker, she goes to the table and lifts the mug in both hands. She hesitates a moment, and I hold my breath as she stares at the surface of the liquid. Her hands begin to shake, and she tilts the rim to her mouth and drinks it down in one long, gulping pull. My eyes fill with tears as I watch her, and I'm conscious of a tug of sorrow, of loss. But I don't move. I don't lift a finger to stop her.

When she lowers the mug to the table she wipes her lips with the back of her hand, then gives me a defiant look. "Alison doesn't know anything about this."

"She will."

Her face tightens, and she lifts her chin. "She'll be okay. You'll watch out for her, you and Tom. She had nothing to do with any of it."

Maggie paces the room like a panther in a cage, her motions jerky. Every few seconds she's off in a different direction, raking her fingers through her hair, unbuttoning her jacket, splashing water on her face. Time leaks away, and I follow her with my eyes. The pain of losing her rockets

246

through me. No one knows me as well as she does, and no one can take her place. But I sit there. I don't call for help. I wait.

After twenty or thirty minutes her movements become slower, more haphazard. Finally she sits heavily on the floor, next to me, her back against the wall.

"Jack and I had a good run," she says, wrapping her arms around her knees. "And then there was Alison—I'm grateful for her." She looks at me, and her face softens. "I'm not a bad person, El. Don't let Alison think I'm a bad person."

I don't say a word, and after a moment of silence passes, she says, "You think I'm going to hell, don't you?"

I shake my head. The kind of hell the nuns talked about has nothing to do with what's happening now, and I wouldn't want Maggie to go there even if I could believe in it. But I want her gone. Out of my life, forever.

Her eyelids shutter down as she leans back against the wall. In a murmur so low I can barely hear her, she says, *"Oh my God I am heartily sorry for having offended thee, and I detest all my sins because . . . because . . ."* Her voice drains away to a mumble, then straggles to a halt.

I clear my throat. *"Because I dread the loss of heaven and the pains of hell."*

Her dry, scratchy whisper continues. *"But most of all because I have offended thee my dear God, who . . ."* A long pause. *"Who art all good . . . and deserving of all my love."*

Her eyes are still closed as she clasps my hand in hers, knits our fingers together, then squeezes them lightly. "I'm sorry, El."

Her hand is unexpectedly warm, and I grip it tightly.

"I never meant to kill him." Her voice is slow and thick with sleep. "He was a wonderful kid. I loved him too, you know?"

A great sadness wells up in me, a flood of angry, impotent

sorrow, and I force back the part of myself that still loves her, the part that could forgive her almost anything, the part that wants to call for an ambulance.

"Don't call them until I'm gone," she says. "Promise me, El. I can't face jail."

I nod, my eyes blurred with tears.

Her voice is slurred. "I'm so tired."

"Go to sleep, Maggie."

"God, I wish I had a cigarette," she says. "A Lucky Strike and a glass of champagne."

"Sorry," I say.

"Nobody smokes anymore," she sighs. In the dim light I see her eyes flutter open as she checks her watch, and then she sinks down on the floor with her head on my lap and closes her eyes.

Epilogue

"Pass me the soap," Tom says, and when I hand it to him he starts to lather my back. His bony legs cradle me, and I slump over as he massages the bumps of my spine with the washcloth. The rough cloth is oddly soothing, like being licked by a cat. When he finishes he kisses my neck, wraps his arms around me and pulls me back. Hot water laps at my ear lobes, and I relax against his chest and belly, surrounded by liquid heat.

It's been almost a year since Jack's and Maggie's deaths, and Tom and I have spent most of it gutting the house, putting in new windows, remodeling the bathroom, replacing the kitchen linoleum with tile, installing new counters, cupboards, and appliances, and buying new furniture. The cheat grass is gone from the flowerbeds, the lilacs are no longer strangled by thistles, and this spring we planted twelve fruit trees in a memorial garden for Johnny.

The work has been a kind of penance for me, as well as a necessary destruction, like pecking my way out of an egg. At night my arms ache from tearing out old beams and knocking down walls, and the sheets are always full of sawdust, no matter how carefully we block off the rooms with plastic sheeting. For months we've been edging around piles of lumber and tile and shingles, trying to build something new; something neither of us is certain will work for us, but we're giving it a shot.

The bathroom was the first room we finished, and now it's my favorite place in the house, with its deep, sunken tub inlaid with blue tile, surrounded by pots of geraniums and bougainvillea. We sit in hot water under a round window with a view of Taos Mountain and the sweep of land belonging to the Pueblo. Tom and I often bathe together now that we have a tub big enough for both of us, and some of our best talks take place in here. Heat and steam and water loosen the internal censor in Tom, and calm my need to fill the air with words. In the jungle warmth of the bathtub, we're lazy as hippos, content to bump and grunt and flop on each other.

Tom dries his hands on the towel hanging by the tub and takes a sheet of pale blue overseas stationery from the shelf above his head. "I picked this up at the post office this morning. It's from Alison."

My heart lifts with the hope that this letter will yield an address, or a phone number, or the name of the place she's staying. Until now we've only received two post cards from Alison, one from Tibet, and one from Bali.

After the funeral, Alison and I had one wrenching conversation in the cemetery where Maggie and Jack were buried. Pale but calm, she asked me to tell her the truth about Johnny's death, and I did. It wasn't easy. Sometimes I bitterly regret that conversation, especially since she disappeared shortly afterward. Her lawyers obviously know how to contact her, but she's instructed them to conceal her whereabouts from everyone, and that apparently includes me. It hurts, that absence.

"*Dear Elena and Tom,*" Tom reads. "*My attorney found this CD in a safety deposit box that belonged to my dad. According to the label, Johnny recorded this the night before he was shot. I wanted you to have it, with my love. —Alison*"

"There was a CD with the letter?" I ask.

"Listen." Tom puts the note back on the shelf, picks up a remote from the tiled edge of the window and activates the hidden stereo system. The sound of temple bells fills the room, followed by violins. Twenty of them, at least, a luxurious, silken sound. And then a shimmer of cymbals, leading to a heavy bass rock beat.

I turn my face to lean against the damp warmth of Tom's chest as Johnny's voice fills the room. It's overwhelmingly real, and the shock of hearing him floods me with an old, familiar pain. The words dart in and out of the music, glittering, escaping, cohering in a tapestry of sound until the chorus swells with the force of a battle cry.

I will rise.
I will rise.
I will shine from the sky.
I will wash you with rain.
I will be your new day.
And I'll give you the sun
Hand you the moon
Be the wind on your skin
In our getaway.

We listen, mesmerized as the song gathers momentum and careens into a rollicking, joyous, New Orleans jazz funeral finish. Johnny always loved far-flung sounds, from classical strings to honky-tonk piano, from traffic to the babble of conversation, and he had a knack for weaving sound together in a long, sinuous juxtaposition with his voice. This is what music was meant for, this wildness, this joy, this brilliance.

Finally Tom flicks off the sound system, and we sit there for a moment in silence while he leans back and closes his eyes. There are times when he does this, and I know from the way the color drains from his face that grief has temporarily overwhelmed him again. I know better than to try to comfort him. There are times when I can reach out and times when I have to let him hold it alone.

After a minute or two Tom slides his arm underneath mine, stretches our arms out and balances mine on his, then lowers our arms into the steaming water.

"I'm hungry," he says. "Are there any blueberry muffins left?"

"Sure. Want me to get you one?"

"I'll get it," he says, but doesn't move. It's an old joke, a married joke.

"Don't get up," I say, poking him with my elbow.

"No, no, allow me," he says, lifting me by the armpits.

Laughing, I lean back with my full weight and squash down on top of him. "Oh, I insist."

"Don't be silly," he says, blocking me with his shoulder. "It won't take a moment."

And with one last heave he wins, and I give up and stagger out of the tub. Dripping on the rug, I wrap myself in a towel and walk into the kitchen.

The smells are rich in here: the buttery, yeasty scent of dough rising, along with the remodeling smells of plaster and wood. I can almost smell Johnny, the fresh sweat and sunshine scent of his skin, and when I close my eyes I can still see him at the piano, his blue eyes nailed to the sheet music with a look of thrill and passion. So many memories flow through these rooms, and I wonder if they haunt Johnny as they haunt me.

Once in a while I can feel him near me, but his voice is gone. There are no more conversations, no arguments, nothing but a chill sometimes on the back of my neck, or a ripple of coolness down my arms, and I know he's nearby, watching.

There's no getting over it.

I never stop listening for him.

Whenever I see a boy with blue eyes, and hair as light as milkweed—I have to bend over, sometimes, and wait for the pain to ease before I can move.

The loss is permanent. If I'm lucky, I'll learn to move more easily around this hole, and that's the best I can hope for. Tom and I are like survivors of a fire that's burned everything around us. But at least grief evolves, and it no longer feels like a life-threatening emergency, just a never-ending sense of loss, a scar on my heart.

Next to me on the counter there are three muffins left on a blue plate, and I take one in each hand and balance the third on top. We're hungry. We can finish these off and still have room for more. But for now, this is enough.

About the Author

Lois Gilbert is the author of "River of Summer" and "Without Mercy," as well as dozens of published articles, reviews and essays. Her work has been translated into several languages, and she lectures on creative writing around the world for Norwegian Cruise Line. You can contact her at loisgilbert@msn.com, or visit her Web site at www.loisgilbert.com.